Praise for Maryse Condé

"She describes the ravages of colonialism and the post-colonial chaos in a language which is both precise and overwhelming. In her stories the dead live close to the living in a world where gender, race, and class are constantly turned over in new constellations."
ANN PÅLSSON, Jury, New Academy Prize in Literature

"Condé is a born storyteller."
Publishers Weekly

"Maryse Condé is a great storyteller, she has managed to explore very political issues—gender, race, colonialism, class, postcolonial issues, slavery—and she did that a long time ago, and she did that in a variety of historical and geographical backgrounds. For me, she is a pioneer for us Afro-descendent women writers. She bridges gaps among the whole Black diaspora."
BEATA UMUBYEYI MAIRESSE

"She is part of our Black family ... She has helped us to see ourselves reflected in so many different mirrors that she holds for us ... She is a force of nature, she is an inspiration to women ... She has given us so much."
BISI ADJAPON

"There are lots of things I like about Maryse Condé's writing, but one thing that gets me every time is the lyricism of her prose."
CHIKA UNIGWE

"It's inspiring to see that Condé gives words and meaning to our histories—African histories, Black histories, Black lives."
CLARICE GARGARD

"Maryse Condé has given me the freedom to call myself woman."
EDWIGE-RENÉE DRO

"Maryse Condé is an African literary elder ... she reminds us Anglophone readers that there is a world of Francophone literature out there that we are missing out on. I would like to point out that Maryse Condé built a bridge between Africa and the Caribbean world ... There's this thing she does where she holds the reader's hand, and the reader gets comfortable ... and somewhere along the way you get smacked in the face."
JENNIFER NANSUBUGA MAKUMBI

"Her writing is so rich. It's so vibrant. But, as well, you are learning things all the time. She's just a wonderful storyteller. She's a masterful storyteller. But she also has a sense of realism in her work. It's just wonderful—it's an experience, reading her work."
KADIJA GEORGE

"Maryse Condé shows African lives in a way that's rich, that's glamorous, and in a way that shows the characters to be as flawed as they really are ... It's very rare to come across a writer of fiction who puts so much of their personal story into their work ... Her books challenge one's perceptions of oneself, which I think is one of the greatest things that Miss Maryse Condé does for the Black person. When you read her work you are forced to reexamine the definition of your own Blackness."
LOLA SHONEYIN

"Her work really links the questions that face Black people all over the world ... showing you the conditions that the Black person faces in the world."
MOLARA WOOD

"I love the honesty ... she doesn't go with the flow. It's very easy for someone of her generation to have gone along with the tide of African socialism or Négritude, that sort of thing, but she's

always been honest about any misgivings or disinterest in certain currents of thinking and culture. She's very original in that respect."
NOO SARO-WIWA

"I think she embodies the world. She belongs to the world ... the breadth of her global experience, at a time when we didn't speak about Black women as belonging to the world, is remarkable."
SISONKE MSIMANG

"What I like is that she's honest. I think she has confidence in her readers and lets them think for themselves, and that I appreciate a lot."
VÉRONIQUE TADJO

"Maryse Condé has managed to successfully bridge the gap between Africa and its diaspora. If nothing else, reading her work helps us get into the mindset to know about our brothers and sisters from the diaspora."
ZUKISWA WANNER

"Maryse Condé is a treasure of world literature, writing from the center of the African diaspora with brilliance and a profound understanding of all humanity."
RUSSELL BANKS

"Maryse Condé is the grande dame of Caribbean literature."
NCRV Gids

•

Praise for The Gospel According to the New World

"An ingenious bildungsroman of a messianic figure in contemporary Martinique. ... Condé does a lovely job with bringing her protagonist down to earth, covering the sacred and profane

elements of Pascal's life before his death at 33 in a tragic, unexpected manner. Readers will be transfixed."
Publishers Weekly, starred review

"With *The Gospel According to the New World*, Maryse Condé offers us a poetic and haunting fable-like novel. A newborn left in a garden, miracles and symbols—this is a biblical story that evokes wonder and conjures a welcome optimism. There is no age limit on dreaming."
ELLE

"A moving, gripping humanist novel not devoid of humor. An evenhanded reflection on fraternity and love in the twenty-first century. Maryse Condé is phenomenal."
Aujourd'hui en France

"What a delightful adventure! Maryse Condé has the audacity to reinvent the Gospel, adapting it to her island, today's Guadeloupe. Maryse Condé's usual colorful, rich, sensuous prose sweeps us along. The author mischievously sticks close to the life of Jesus and then breaks away from it with the imagination and verve of a griot: it's a celebration."
La Vie

"An irresistible version of the life of Jesus. What holds this novel together—more than the diversity of the episodes, the beauty of the erotic scenes, and the book's humor—is Maryse Condé's ability to play with our need to believe in a savior and our hope that another world is possible, as well as with the necessity to laugh with that dream. The book's second victory is its portrait of the messiah as a man who goes to college and learns about the complexity of the world by talking to women of all walks of life. The person the author imagines as the next messiah is a humble and loving being."
Le Monde des livres

•

Praise for Waiting for the Waters to Rise

"Condé's text is sprinkled with the names of global literary giants—Aimé Césaire, Jacques Roumain, Ousmane Sembène, Mahmoud Darwish, Derek Walcott—a roll call she certainly deserves to be added to."
New York Times

"Condé puts forth the secrets and histories of a fascinating cast, producing a timeless exploration of the wounds that emerge— and linger—when people lose those who mean the most to them, be it their family, friends, or country. This faithful portrayal of grief and displacement is tough to forget."
Publishers Weekly

"Condé excels in adding depth and texture to lives that are often relegated to the cutting room of disaster footage and humanitarian appeals."
Irish Times

"A love letter to the Caribbean."
The Guardian

"Maryse Condé has lost nothing of her inimitable style, nor of her talent for painting strong and true characters."
Le Monde

"At once touching and devastating, the book explores the effects of loss and grief on a personal, communal, and national level, but does so with a personal voice that feels more like a having a conversation than reading a book—it is a novel that cements Condé as a literary giant who beautifully chronicles the humanity found in some of the most violent places in the world."

"Maryse Condé's novel *Waiting for the Waters to Rise* addresses immigration, nationalism, friendship, colorism, and political power through the intersecting lives of three friends. As the story jumps from locale to locale, it conjures up the sense of statelessness that binds the men together. The prose is fluid, luminous, and evocative of each setting. The subtle cynicism throughout the novel is balanced by the love the men have for each other."
Foreword Reviews, starred review

"While this novel takes its protagonist Babakar through civil wars and other scenes of global strife, it also moves forward and backward in time to illustrate the actions that took place decades and centuries before and contributed to his current state. The result is a moving story of isolation, community, and families both chosen and biological."
Words Without Borders

"When I think of Maryse Condé, I think of stories with a ton of magical flair. *Waiting for the Waters to Rise* is a moving read for the way the language gently draws you in. Condé's language is dreamlike, suffused with poetry. The novel is enough of a page-turner, but what really keeps you transfixed to the page is the writing."
Brittle Paper

"Maryse Condé's *Waiting for the Waters to Rise* begins in her native Guadeloupe but is ultimately a novel that centers on statelessness. The three characters at the novel's heart—Babakar, Movar, and Fouad from Mali, Haiti, and Palestine respectively—are all migrants driven from their homelands. Condé is a master storyteller capable of traversing multiple countries with their own histories of colonialism and political violence so

that we come to know each character more intimately and why the friendship they forge is so vital to their survival."
Brooklyn Rail

"Maryse Condé has that remarkable talent of illuminating characters who are immersed in shadows."
Brune Magazine

"As always, Condé here delivers a sublime novel, mesmerizing, traversed by the destiny of three characters between Africa, the Antilles, and Haiti."
Miss Ébène

"A poignant and discreet story, with endearing characters."
Lire

"A map of anguishes and hopes, written in a sensual and melodic language."
Croire Aujourd'hui

"An enthralling novel, traversed by the destinies of three people, three men linked by an unbeatable friendship, who struggle to break free of their past."
La Gazette

"A dense book, a novel with complex layers, a beautiful lesson of humanity in a hostile world."
L'Avenir

"A novel with multiple twists, but always clear, at the end of which the author leaves us knocked out."
Femme Actuelle

"The author Maryse Condé reveals, once again, her talent as a storyteller à la Selma Lagerlof. She knows how to give body

and soul to those caught in the whirlwinds of a merciless history that often surpasses and sometimes destroys them."
FESTIVAL DU LIVRE

"A translucent novel about the need to make one's destiny intelligible, even while being stateless, an immigrant, exiled, rejected."
Gens de la Caraïbe

"A text of great poetry, and a deep exoticism in which we find traces of Jacques Roumain or Jacques Stéphen Alexis."
Sens Critique

•

Praise for The Wondrous and Tragic Life of Ivan and Ivana

"Condé is at her signature best: offering complex, polyphonic and ultimately shattering stories whose provocations linger long after the final pages. The book is a reflection on the dangers of binary thinking. One is never on steady ground with Condé; she is not an ideologue, and hers is not the kind of liberal, safe, down-the-line morality that leaves the reader unimplicated."
JUSTIN TORRES, *New York Times*

"*The Wondrous and Tragic Life of Ivan and Ivana* is a rollicking, rumbustious and slyly mischievous *Candide* for our times."
MAYA JAGGI, *The Guardian*

"Condé has a gift for storytelling and an unswerving focus on her characters, combined with a mordant sense of humor."
New York Times Book Review

"What an astounding novel. Never have I read anything so wild and loving, so tender and ruthless. Condé is one of our greatest writers, a literary sorcerer, but here she has outdone even herself, summoned a storm from out of the world's troubled heart.

Ivan and Ivana, in their love, in their Attic fates, mirror our species' terrible brokenness and its improbable grace."
JUNOT DÍAZ

"The breadth, depth, and power of Maryse Condé's majestic
work are exceptionally remarkable. *The Wondrous and Tragic
Life of Ivan and Ivana* is a superb addition to this incomparable
oeuvre, and is one of Condé's most timely, virtuoso, and
breathtaking novels. "
EDWIDGE DANTICAT

"Brilliantly imagined, Maryse Condé's new novel presents a dual
bildungsroman of twins born into poverty in the African diaspora and follows their global travels to its shocking ending.
Once again, Condé transmutes contemporary political traumas
into a mesmerizing family fable."
HENRY LOUIS GATES, JR.

"Maryse Condé offers us with *The Wondrous and Tragic Life of
Ivan and Ivana* yet another ambitious, continent-crossing whirl-
wind of a literary journey. The marvelous siblings at the heart
of her tale are inspiring and unsettling in equal measure, richly
drawn incarnations of the contemporary postcolonial individual
in perpetual geographic and cultural movement. It is a remarkable story from start to finish."
KAIAMA L. GLOVER

"Maryse Condé's prodigious fictional universes are founded on
a radical and generative disregard for boundaries based on
geography, religion, history, race, and gender. In *The Wondrous
and Tragic Life of Ivan and Ivana*, the most intimate human
relationships acquire meaning only on the scale of the world-
historical, and as we follow the twins in their fated journey from
the Caribbean to Africa and Europe, we learn about love, happiness, calamity, and, at last, the survival of hope."
ANGELA Y. DAVIS

"It's a polyphonic story. It's a love story, about politics, as always, but about desire, and family ... she shows the dangers of binary thinking."
BEATA UMUBYEYI MAIRESSE

"There is so much tension. And the tension came almost every few pages. Having them as twins, you're seeing both sides of how a life can be and cannot be, especially coming from a colonial Caribbean island, and going to Africa, and then going to Europe. You can see the tragedy that colonialism can bring. So powerful, and so, really, un-put-down-able."
KADIJA GEORGE

"It really challenged my perception of how individuals feel right before they carry out terrorist acts. It was almost as if it was an extreme lack of empathy, rather than extreme emotions, that propelled and enabled Ivan."
KIISA SOYINKA

"A wonderful book. Very layered—layers of history, layers of time, narratives, places—and all sewn together by the story of this one life that Ivan and Ivana live through."
MOLARA WOOD

"Beating in the novel's heart is orality, carrying with it the breath of histories, literatures and languages of Africa and the Caribbean. The truth is not only murky and complex, it is often elusive. All we have is interpretation."
Irish Times

"The turbulent narrative unfolds in a deceptively relaxed manner; incidents happen with the abrupt motivelessness of fairytale, but the novel is all the more powerful for those effects."
Sunday Times

"*The Wondrous and Tragic Life of Ivan and Ivana* is a searing literary portrait of the exploitation of immigrants, the corruption of governments, and the powerful emergence of radicalism,

with astute commentary on how these elements breed trauma, generation after generation."
Foreword Reviews

"Set during the *Charlie Hebdo* attacks, this is a fast-paced saga that reveals a seldom-addressed period of African history. Condé's writing is both lyrical and textured, and showcases her tremendous talents."
Booklist

"Condé's scope is expansive: cosmic, global, and deeply personal. The result is a story from the perspective of the Global South that enthralls as it explores the urgent economic and cultural contradictions of post-colonialism, globalization, class, and alienation."
Arts Fuse

"With this story of a young man from Guadeloupe who finds himself persuaded by the pull of jihad, Condé has written one of her most impressive novels to date, one that seamlessly resonates with the problems of our time."
Le Monde

"Condé's latest novel is a beautiful and dramatic story with its origins in the *Charlie Hebdo* attacks. Masterly."
Afrique Magazine

"Maryse Condé addresses very contemporary issues in her latest novel: racism, jihadi terrorism, political corruption and violence, economic inequality in Guadeloupe and metropolitan France, globalization and immigration."
World Literature Today

"This new novel, written in an almost exuberant style, contains many typical Condé elements, in particular the mix of a small family with global events, and the nuances of existing images."
De Volkskrant

"Told by a charming, lively third-person narrator, the novel evokes its various settings beautifully and takes a penetrating, wide-ranging look at the effects of racism, colonialism, and inequality."
Bookriot

•

Praise for Segu

"Condé's story is rich and colorful and glorious. It sprawls over continents and centuries to find its way into the reader's heart."
MAYA ANGELOU

"Exotic, richly textured and detailed, this narrative, alternating between the lives of various characters, illuminates magnificently a little-known historical period. Virtually every page glitters with nuggets of cultural fascination."
Los Angeles Times

"The most significant novel about black Africa published in many a year. A wondrous novel about a period of African history few other writers have addressed. Much of the novel's radiance comes from the lush description of a traditional life that is both exotic and violent."
New York Times Book Review

"With the dazzling storytelling skills of an African griot, Maryse Condé has written a rich, fast-paced saga of a great kingdom during the tumultuous period of the slave trade and the coming of Islam. *Segu* is history as vivid and immediate as today. It has restored a part of my past that has long been missing."
PAULE MARSHALL, author of *Daughters*

"*Segu* is an overwhelming accomplishment. It injects into the density of history characters who are as alive as you and I. Passionate, lusty, greedy, they are in conflict with themselves as well as with God and Mammon. Maryse Condé has done us all

a tremendous service by rendering a history so compelling and exciting. *Segu* is a literary masterpiece I could not put down."
LOUISE MERIWETHER

"A stunning reaffirmation of Africa and its peoples as set down by others whose works have gone unnoticed. Condé not only backs them up, but provides new insights as well. *Segu* has its own dynamic. It's a starburst."
JOHN A. WILLIAMS

The Gospel According to the New World

MARYSE CONDÉ

The Gospel According to the New World

Translated from the French
by Richard Philcox

WORLD EDITIONS
New York, London, Amsterdam

Published in the USA in 2023 by World Editions LLC, New York
Published in the UK in 2023 by World Editions Ltd., London

World Editions
New York / London / Amsterdam

First published as *L'evangile du nouveau monde*
Copyright © Buchet/Chastel, Libella, Paris, 2021
English translation copyright © Richard Philcox, 2023
Author portrait © P. Matsas Leemage / Hollandse Hoogte

Printed by Zwaan Lenoir, Netherlands
World Editions is committed to a sustainable future. Papers used by World Editions
meet the PEFC standards of certification.

British Library Cataloguing-in-Publication Data.
A catalogue record for this book is available on request from the British Library.

ISBN 978-1-912987-36-8

This book was published with the support of the CNL

This book has been selected to receive financial assistance from English PEN's PEN
Translates programme, supported by Arts Council England. English PEN exists to
promote literature and our understanding of it, to uphold writers' freedoms around
the world, to campaign against the persecution and imprisonment of writers for
stating their views, and to promote the friendly co-operation of writers and the free
exchange of ideas. www.englishpen.org

Company: worldeditions.org
Facebook: @WorldEditionsInternationalPublishing
Instagram: @WorldEdBooks
TikTok: @worldeditions_tok
Twitter: @WorldEdBooks
YouTube: World Editions

To Pascale, no friend could have become
such a perfect secretary

To Serina, Mahily, Fadel and Leina

In homage to José Saramago

Part One

1

It's a land surrounded by water on all sides, commonly known as an island, not as big as Australia, but not small either. It is mostly flat but embossed with thick forests and two volcanoes, one that goes by the name of Piton de la Grande Chaudière, which was active until 1820 when it destroyed the pretty little town that sprawled down its side, after which it became totally dormant. Since the island enjoys an "eternal summer," it is perpetually crowded with tourists, aiming their lethal cameras at anything of beauty. Some people affectionately call it "My Country," but it is not a country, it is an overseas territory, in other words, an overseas department.

The night He was born, Zabulon and Zapata were squabbling with each other high up in the sky, letting fly sparks of light with every move. It was an unusual sight. Anyone who regularly scans the heavens is used to seeing Ursa Minor, Ursa Major, Cassiopeia, the Evening Star, and Orion, but to discover two such constellations emerging from the depths of infinity was something unheard of. It meant that He who was born on that night was preordained for an exceptional destiny. At the time, nobody seemed to think otherwise.

The newborn baby raised his tiny fists to his mouth and curled up between the donkey's hooves for warmth. Maya, who had just given birth in this shed where the Ballandra kept their sacks of fertilizer, their drums of weed killer, and their ploughing instruments, washed herself as best she could with the water from a calabash she had the presence of mind to bring with her. Her plump little cheeks were soaked with tears.

She never suspected for one moment the hurt she would feel when she abandoned her child. Little did she know how the sharp fangs of pain would tear her womb. Yet there was no other solution. She had managed to hide her condition from her parents, especially her mother, who never stopped rambling on about the promise of a radiant future for her daughter; Maya couldn't return home with a bastard between her arms.

When she missed her period, she was dumbfounded. A child! This sticky little thing that pissed and defecated on her, here was the consequence of her torrid and passionate nights.

She had ended up writing to her lover, Corazón, the Spanish word for heart—a name ill-suited for this chiseled giant. As her third letter had remained unanswered, she had gone to the cruise ship offices, owners of *Empress of the Sea*, on whose inaugural cruise through the islands she had met Corazón. When she had asked for information at reception, the high yellow Chabeen perched on her high heels savagely interrupted her: "We don't give out information on our passengers."

Maya had written once more. Once again without an answer. Her heart beat to an intuition. Wasn't she going to be one of the hordes of abandoned women, women without husbands or lovers, who strove to raise their children alone? This was not what Corazón had promised her. On the contrary, he had promised her the world. He had showered her with kisses, called her the love of his life, and swore he had never loved a woman as he loved her.

Corazón and Maya did not belong to the same class; Corazón was a member of the powerful Tejara family who for generations had been slave owners, merchants, landowners, lawyers, doctors, and teachers. Corazón taught history of religion at the University of Asunción where he was born. He bore all the arrogance of a rich kid except this was somewhat subdued by the charm of a gentle smile. Since he was fluent in four languages—English,

Portuguese, Spanish, and French—he had been hired by the cruise line to give a series of lectures to the second- and first-class passengers.

What annoyed Maya was the dream she'd been having night after night. She saw an angel dressed in a blue tunic holding a lily, the species known as a canna lily. The angel announced that Maya would give birth to a son whose mission would be to change the face of the world. Well, call it an angel if you must, but it was one of the strangest creatures she had ever seen. He was wearing thigh-high shiny leather boots and his curly gray hair fell down to his shoulders. The oddest thing was this protuberance concealed behind his back. Was it a hump? One night in exasperation she had chased him away with a broomstick but he had simply returned the following night as if nothing had happened.

The baby had fallen asleep and he gurgled in his sleep from time to time. The donkey never stopped snorting over the baby's head. The Ballandras used to put their cow Placida to bed in this stable but one fine day the poor creature had collapsed on the ground and a thick foam frothed out of its muzzle. Called out in emergency, the vet had diagnosed foot-and-mouth disease.

Turning her back on the baby, Maya slipped outside and walked up the path that wound behind the Ballandras' house leading to the road. She was not unduly worried because she knew that at this time of night, despite the brightly lit surroundings, there was no danger of her being caught by the couple emerging unexpectedly. They were watching television on a recently purchased 50-inch flat-screen like all the other inhabitants of this land where there was not much else in the way of entertainment. The husband, Jean Pierre, was sleeping off numerous glasses of aged rum while Eulalie, his wife, was busy knitting a baby's vest for one of her many charities.

Pushing open the wooden gate that separated the garden from the road, Maya had the impression she was setting off into a zone of solitude and sorrow which would be her lot for the rest of her life.

Setting foot on the macadam, she bumped into Déméter, known throughout the neighborhood for his binge-drinking and bloody brawls. He was accompanied by two of his drunken acolytes who were bawling; they claimed to have seen a five-pointed star hovering over the house. In a great tangle of arms and legs, the three rum guzzlers were floundering in the flood channel where the town's wastewaters churned. This didn't seem to bother them and Déméter began bellowing an old Christmas carol: "I can see, I can see the Shepherd's Star." Maya ignored them completely and continued on her way, her eyes brimming with tears.

If it hadn't been for the unusual behavior that evening of Pompette, Madame Ballandra's dog, a spoilt, arrogant little creature, one wonders what would have happened. Once Maya had gone, Pompette tugged the hem of her mistress's dress and dragged her to the shed. The door was wide open and Madame Ballandra witnessed an unusual sight, of biblical proportions.

A newborn baby was lying on the straw between the hooves of the donkey who was warming it with its breath. The scene in the stable occurred one Easter Sunday evening. Madame Ballandra clasped her hands and murmured: "A miracle! Here is the gift from God I was not expecting, I shall call you Pascal."

The newborn was very handsome, with a dark complexion, straight black hair like the Chinese, and a delicately delineated mouth. She hugged him to her breast and he opened his green-gray eyes, which were the color of the sea that surrounded the land.

Madame Ballandra went out into the garden and walked back to the house. Jean Pierre Ballandra saw his wife returning with a baby in her arms and Pompette jumping around her heels.

"What do I see here?" he exclaimed. "A child, a baby. But I can't see whether it's a girl or a boy."

Such a remark may surprise the reader if they didn't know that Jean Pierre Ballandra had poor eyesight and had already downed a good many glasses of neat rum. He had also worn spectacles since the age of fifteen when a guava branch had pierced his cornea.

"It's a boy," Eulalie told him bluntly, then she took him by the hand and forced him to kneel beside her. They struck up a blessing since they were both firm believers.

2

Jean Pierre and Eulalie Ballandra formed an unusual couple, he with African blood and she, pink-skinned, originating from a rugged isle where the population was said to be descended from Vikings. What occurred in their hearts, nevertheless, was something else. They worshipped each other despite the many years living together. Because of Eulalie, Jean Pierre had never had a woman on the side, a common practice, widely respected by all his fellow countrymen. For years, he had made love to his one and only woman. As for Eulalie, Jean Pierre was her only reason for living. The couple remained childless despite constant visits to the gynecologist. Eulalie's younger years had been scarred by miscarriages until finally her menopause made her mercifully sterile.

Jean Pierre and Eulalie were comfortably well-off. They lived mainly off the income from their nursery, with the banal name of The Garden of Eden. Jean Pierre was a genuine artist. Among other plants, he had produced a variety of Cayenne rose, as a rule a fairly ordinary flower, but the one invented by Jean Pierre had amazing velvety petals and, above all, a delicate, penetrating scent. As a result, it was much in demand by the Social Security and Employment authorities as well as by soup kitchens. Jean Pierre named his Cayenne rose "Elizabeth Taylor" since when he was younger and out of work, he would kill time as best he could at the movies and was especially fond of American films. On seeing his favorite actress in Cleopatra he gave her name to the flower he had created.

The arrival of Pascal in the family was a big event. Early next morning, Eulalie made the rounds of the shops and bought a pram as spacious as a Rolls Royce. She stuffed it with blue velvet cushions for the baby to lie on. Every day at

4:30 p.m. she left the house and made her way to the Place des Martyrs. Situated facing the sea, the square resembled a window cut out from the town's baroque architecture.

Eulalie breathed in the sea air and contemplated the green-gray waters, which frothed as far as the eye could see. Eulalie had always dreaded the sea, that majestic bitch which mounted guard at every corner of the land. But the fact it was the same color as her son's eyes suddenly brought them closer and made them almost friends. She remained a long while staring at it, thanking it for its company, and then headed back to the Place des Martyrs.

The Place des Martyrs was the very heart of Fonds-Zombi and was lined with sandbox trees planted by Victor Hugues when he came to restore slavery following orders from Napoleon Bonaparte. Eulalie walked up and down the crowded paths and made the rounds several times before sitting down near the music kiosk where the town's orchestra played popular melodies three times a week. The women sitting near her never failed to admire her little son, thereby filling her heart with pride and joy.

What a hubbub around the Place des Martyrs! Crowds of teenagers, boys and girls alike, playing truant from school, groups of unemployed men spouting forth pedantically, and nursemaids dressed to the nines keeping watch over the babies dribbling and sucking on their bottles as well as cheeky little brats running in all directions.

Everyone stood up to peer at the pram Eulalie was pushing. People were staring for a number of reasons. Firstly, Pascal was remarkably lovely. Impossible to say what race he was. But I must confess the word race is now obsolete and we should quickly replace it by another. Origin, for instance. Impossible to say what his origin was. Was he White? Was he Black? Was he Asian? Had his ancestors built the industrial cities of Europe? Did he come from the African savannah? Or from a country frozen with ice and covered in snow? He was all of that at the same time. But his beauty was not the only reason for people's curiosity. A persistent rumor was gradually gaining ground. There was something not natural about the event. Here was Eulalie, who for years had worn her knees out on pilgrimages to Lourdes and Lisieux, blessed with a son from our Lord, and on Easter Sunday no less. This was by no means a coincidence but a very special gift. Our Father had perhaps two sons and sent her the younger one. A son of mixed blood, what a great idea!

The rumor gradually took Fonds-Zombi by storm and reached the outer boundaries of the land. It was a hot topic in the humble abodes as well as in the elegant, wealthy homes. When it reached the ears of Eulalie, she gladly welcomed it. Only Jean Pierre remained inflexible, considering it blasphemy.

3

When Pascal was four weeks old, his mother decided to have him christened. One fine Sunday, Bishop Altmayer walked out of his Saint Jean Bosco residence and left the orphans in his care on their own, while the church bells pealed out. Eulalie had dressed her baby in a fine white linen blouse with an embroidered smock plastron. His tiny tootsies wiggled in his gold-and-silver-thread knitted bootees and on his head he wore a bonnet which illuminated his little angel face. The christening had all the pomp of a wedding or banquet and was attended by three hundred guests dressed to the nines, including the children from the catechism class all in white, waving small flags the colors of the Virgin Mary.

Shortly after the dessert of multiflavored ice creams, an unknown visitor turned up. Everyone who saw him was surprised by his appearance. He was dressed in a somewhat outmoded pinstripe suit, and by way of a tie he wore a kind of ruff. On his feet were a pair of shiny turned-down boots like the ones worn by Alexandre Dumas's three musketeers. Even stranger, he seemed to be hiding something odd behind his back, perhaps a hump. The stubble of a graying beard covered his chin.

He made straight for Eulalie who was grinning like a Cheshire cat and holding a glass of champagne. "Hail Eulalie full of grace," he declared. "I am bringing a gift for the child Pascal." Thereupon he held out the package he had been carefully holding. It was an earthen vase containing a flower, a flower that Eulalie, though she was the wife of a nurseryman, had never seen before. It had an amazing color: light brown, the color of a light-skinned Capresse, with curly, velvet-like petals, wrapped around a delicate sulfur-yellow pistil. "What a lovely flower!" Eulalie exclaimed. "What a strange color!"

"This flower's name is Tété Négresse," the new arrival explained. "It is designed to erase the Song of Solomon from our memory. You recall those shocking words: I am Black but I am beautiful. These words must never be pronounced again."

Eulalie did not understand the meaning of his objections. "What are you trying to tell me?" she asked in surprise, but the silence told her that the speaker had already disappeared. She found herself alone, holding her gift and thinking it was all a dream.

Upset, she ran to join Jean Pierre who was laughing and drinking champagne with a group of guests. She told him what had just happened.

"Don't you worry," he said shrugging his shoulders. "It was probably just an admirer who didn't dare express his real feelings. I can make good use of this flower." And he kept his word; soon The Garden of Eden could boast of two marvels: the Cayenne rose and the Tété Négresse.

When Pascal reached the age of four, his mother decided to send him to school. It wasn't because she was tired of showering him with kisses or seeing him caper about and play with Pompette or burst into the nursery. But because education is a precious asset. He who wants to succeed in life must acquire as much as possible. Jean Pierre and Eulalie had suffered too much for having been deprived of it.

At the age of twelve, Jean Pierre was already spraying a landowner's banana plantations with sulfate while Eulalie, at an even younger age, was seated beside her mother selling the fish her father had caught: blue fish, pink catfish, red snapper, yellowtail snapper, grouper, sea bream, and blue-fin tuna.

Pascal was therefore admitted to the school run by the Mara sisters. The Mara sisters were twins whose mother was a well-known figure since she served at the presbytery and every Good Friday took to her bed showing the stigmata of Christ's Passion on both hands and feet. It was no secret that her two daughters were the children of Father Robin, who had managed the parish for many years before conveying his old age to a retirement home for priests located near Saint-Malo. At that time, the priests could get away with such behavior. There were no American or French movies like Spotlight or Grâce à Dieu. Everyone turned a blind eye to transgressions against God's commandments.

The school run by the Mara sisters was an elegant building situated in the middle of a vast, sandy courtyard where the pupils ran around excitedly during recreation. On his first day Pascal wore a blue-and-white suit with matching shoes. The sisters welcomed him effusively, well aware of the splendid catch they had made. However, they soon became disillusioned.

Pascal turned out not to be the kind of pupil they were expecting. He would daydream in class, mixed only with the poorest children, and had nothing better to do than dash into the kitchen where two underpaid servants prepared the school lunches. He would lavish them with caresses and kind words. In return, they showered him with little treats. If Eulalie hadn't been on good terms with the Mara sisters, they would have expelled him.

The day after his fifth birthday Eulalie took Pascal to the shed at the bottom of the garden while Jean Pierre, always lackadaisical, followed them dragging his feet. The shed was extremely clean. The sacks of fertilizer and weed killer were heaped in one corner whereas the floor was covered with white gravel. Eulalie turned to Pascal.

"I have an important confession to make. I love you, that you know, but I didn't carry you in my womb. And you are not a product of his sperm either," she added, pointing to Jean Pierre.

"What are you trying to say?" Pascal exclaimed, dumbfounded.

He found it difficult to comprehend such an unusual story. Although most of the children on the island did not know their father, they knew full well who their mother was. She was the one who worked herself to the bone, slaving away to buy their clothes and send them to school.

"What I want to say is that one Easter Sunday we found you in this shed and adopted you as our son."

"Who are my real parents?" Pascal asked, his voice brimming with tears.

It was then that Eulalie told him about the rumors of where he came from.

It's strange that for many years Pascal attached little importance to this confession and even less to the stream of gossip that reached his ears regarding his origins. He knew he was born in a land of the spoken word where lies are stronger than truth. Then, for no reason at all, he began to lend them an ear, for it is better to be the son of God than the son of beggars. It then became a veritable obsession.

He would stop and gaze at the sky. The heavens had opened up a second time and the mystery of the Incarnation had taken shape. This time the Creator had taken care to make His son of mixed blood so that no race might take advantage over others, as has happened in the past. The weak point was that He didn't explain to His flesh and blood what was expected of him. What was he expected to do with this world streaked with bomb attacks and scarred with violence?

By dint of pondering this enigma, Pascal's character changed. He switched from periods of nervous excitement to episodes of deep silence. He constantly wondered about his origins and was annoyed when Eulalie and Jean Pierre fell silent on the subject as if they had nothing more to tell.

He got on better with his father than with his mother since he disliked the education she was giving him, such as the piano lessons with Monsieur Démon, whom his family had disowned because he had married a mulatto girl. Eulalie reproached Pascal for not reading enough and was angry with him for frequenting the company of lowborn children like himself.

4

When Pascal was seven years old, his mother enrolled him
in catechism class so that he might be taught the lessons by
Father Lebris. As a man of God, Father Lebris could have
debated the growing rumor of Pascal's origins with him.
Unfortunately, he did nothing of the sort; he merely treated
Pascal as a privileged child. On the day of the Ascension, he
placed him at the head of the procession that paraded from
the cathedral up to the church of Massabielle. It was gos-
siped maliciously that Father Lebris was afraid of upsetting
Eulalie, who was rich and kindhearted, never failing to give
to charity and to help the destitute in the parish.

At the age of eighteen, armed with his baccalaureate
obtained with just a pass and no congratulations from the
jury, for to tell the truth Pascal was a mediocre student,
little more than a daydreamer, he decided to look for a job.
His future was all mapped out. His job was waiting for him
at The Garden of Eden. Unfortunately, he disliked potting
plants and flowers, even if they were lovely to look at and
had a pleasant scent. His dream was to open a daycare
center or a kindergarten. He was obsessed by the command
Let the little children come to me, not because the kingdom of
God belongs to them, but because at this tender age they
possess the virtue of tolerance and the wish for a better
world. He didn't dare tell Jean Pierre, fearing he would
object to the expense. On April Fool's Day he joined The
Garden of Eden in the department of succulents: aloe vera,
echeveria, sansevieria, pandanus, Christmas cactus, and
torch ginger.

It was then that Pascal's appearance made a radical transformation. The little boy with the face of an angel and an
enigmatic beauty vanished, replaced by a male women
would have loved to have in their bed. His cotton shirt

opened onto perfect pecs. His stomach was flat and below it stretched his penis which now had difficulty fitting into the small underpants that Eulalie had bought him. Such a transformation was even more remarkable since it was limited to his physical appearance. Pascal remained shy. He maintained his gentle voice, sometimes lisping, and his large eyes brimmed with dreams as if he were perpetually endeavoring to solve the mysterious equation of life.

Shortly afterwards, an event occurred which was to have lasting consequences. Our islands are indecisive and weak-willed, they refuse to see what is staring them in the face. Whereas Jean Pierre was already going on sixty and suffering severe arthritis in his right knee, he was suddenly recognized as an exceptional artist and, as a result, awarded a medal of excellence which he was to receive at Porte Océane, the country's second-largest town.

Hadn't he invented two flowers, two roses, the Cayenne rose and the Tété Négresse, whose beauty remained unsurpassed throughout the world? Although Kenya specialized in the sale of flowers and boasted about having the best of gardens, Jean Pierre managed to receive orders from cities as far away as Tripoli, Ankara, and Istanbul. Oddly enough, Eulalie was not included in this award. Yet it was common knowledge that she was awake at four in the morning in order to arrange the flowers in bouquets, wreaths, and sprays. She selected the most attractive wrappings and tied them expertly with gift ribbon. But she was a woman and consequently could only be an assistant to genius. Without thinking twice about it, Jean Pierre gratefully accepted the honor.

In order to drive to Porte Océane, Jean Pierre rented the latest model of Mercedes. The road between Fonds-Zombi and Porte Océane runs alongside the sea, which stretches for a number of kilometers like a velvet carpet, sparkling here and there. The road then penetrates a series of thick forests.

Seated in front beside his father, Pascal's eyes were glued to the landscape. The closeness of the sea always made him sad of heart since he would have liked to plunge in headfirst every day instead of being reconciled to the occasional swim. In their old age, Jean Pierre and Eulalie seldom went to the beach except on Easter Monday when the family picnicked on the traditional dish of crab and spinach.

Porte Océane sprawled around a sheltered bay where once the slave ships unloaded their shameful cargo. Today, they have been replaced by cruise ships. From ten in the morning, tourists of every origin and nationality—Chinese, Japanese, French, German, and American—invade its streets, squares, and markets. The region's treasures are haggled over in a hubbub of languages and colors.

The palace where Jean Pierre was to receive his medal was called the Rialto, a building dreamed up as a folly in 1943 by the Italian billionaire Massimo Coppini. A close friend of Benito Mussolini, Massimo Coppini had better foresight than the Duce and had fled Italy with his vast fortune before the debacle of the Third Reich. The Rialto housed a series of salons each more luxurious than the next and decorated with paintings by the best artists of the region. Of special note was a canvas by Nelson Amandras from Venezuela and an "Imaginary City" by the Haitian Préfète Duffaut. And yet human beings are never completely cut and dried, as we know, since Massimo Coppini was not just an anti-Semite, but also kindhearted, and manifested proof of his goodness of heart by building a chain of daycare centers called The Drop of Milk where single mothers could stay free of charge with their infants.

Once Jean Pierre, Eulalie, and Pascal had crossed the vast paved courtyard, the pride of the Rialto, they saw with amazement that the entrance was barred. Men dressed in black T-shirts, roughly embroidered with the slogan Equality for All in white letters, were examining intently the guests' invitations. For those who had the misfortune not to have one, they demanded the sum of ten euros on the spot. The sight was too shocking for Pascal to follow his parents inside and to mix with the guests mouthing superficial words.

He caught sight of a puny boy his own age, his chest floating in a faded cotton checkered shirt and his hips squeezed into a pair of jeans of the same miserable appearance. His mop of tangled hair fell down to his shoulders.

"What's going on?" Pascal asked him. "Why are they making them pay for admission? Why are they turning the Rialto into a den of thieves?"

The young man remained unruffled: "Thieves?" he retorted. "They don't deserve to be called 'thieves.' They're workers from the state-run enterprise Le Bon Kaffé."

"Le Bon Kaffé?" Pascal repeated, without understanding a word.

The young man placed his palm on his forehead in disbelief and joked, "Where have you been all this time? Haven't you heard that for weeks these wretches have been roaming up and down the island, except when they're thrown into prison or beaten up by the police, and you're asking who the workers of Le Bon Kaffé are?"

Now that he thought about it, Pascal had seen numerous televised reports of this people's rebellion, but had never paid it much attention. He knew for sure that on this earth some people make do on an empty stomach while others have their fill of the best of foods, that some have no education and yet others have no idea what the future holds in store for them. But he didn't lose sleep over such considerations.

"Calm down," he said. "Come and have a drink on me." However hard the two boys searched the neighboring streets and avenues all the shopkeepers had drawn down their shutters. They ended up finding a bar in a side street that overlooked the sea. If you'd spread your arms and leaped headfirst, you could have plunged and disappeared into the waves.

The puny boy introduced himself: "My name is José Dampierre. My father, Nelson Bouchara, is the richest Lebanese man in this wretched country. He arrived with nothing on his back but his checkered shirt. Now he's rolling in dough. But we have never seen the color of his money. He was merely content to give my mother four boys, the youngest of whom is Alexandre who is mute. Do you hear that? Mute, deaf-mute!"

Pascal handed him his packet of cigarettes.

"Lucky Strikes, Lucky Strikes!" José exclaimed. "In all my life I have never smoked American cigarettes."

5

Pascal and José soon became inseparable. Unable to put up with seeing his mother knee-deep in dirty water scrubbing the floors of the well-to-do while giving birth to one child after another for the richest Lebanese man in the country, José had slammed the door of the family shack at the age of seventeen. He had left Fonds-Zombi and was now living in Bois Jolan at the home of his mother's half-brother who was also his godfather and who had died childless.

Bois Jolan is one of the poorest districts in the country. Nothing is as ugly as its dilapidated and rickety shacks. But it is also the realm of the sea. In a good mood, the sea softly, softly laps the sparkling sand. When it's angry, it hurls its waves against the shore with a furious thundering voice. At night, it quietens down and hums in its inimitable throaty drawl.

When José left Fonds-Zombi he had taken with him his youngest brother, Alexandre, since his mother was unable to pay the meager sum the Mortimer Institute demanded. Alexandre was ten years old, handsome and delicate like a little girl. He couldn't speak, that's for sure, but he knew how to laugh. About what? Probably whimsies and nonsensical things that crossed his mind. All day long, his mouth emitted a dovelike cooing or sharp-pitched but sweet-sounding cries. José adored him and soon Pascal did as well.

Pascal immediately took to life at Bois Jolan, so different from the environment he had grown up in. He liked the fishermen sitting on the sand mending their nets, joking and doubling up with laughter, the housewives braided with cornrows shuffling along in their worn-out shoes, and the smell of brine from the smoked fish so much that he ended up moving in permanently with José. Oddly enough, he never thought of letting José in on the secret of his origins or revealing the supposed identity of his father.

The night when he made up his mind to live with José, he had a dream. A man whose face he couldn't see whispered to him in a strong foreign accent, perhaps Spanish: "Henceforth, I will make you a fisher of men." He woke up shivering in the thick of night. Fisher of men, what did that mean? Men are not gold- or blue-striped fish you admire through the glass of an aquarium. They are not easy to handle, they are rebellious and do exactly as they please.

José and Alexandre did not treat Pascal like a savior but like an older brother especially dear to their heart. Leaving Alexandre asleep on the pile of old clothes which served as bedding, José and Pascal would climb aboard their sailboat every morning and set off into the dawn to fish. It was like the first morning on earth. Everything was shrouded in milky white. Not a sound could be heard, only the whispering of the spirits shaking themselves awake and going about their morning ablutions. Only one thing saddened Pascal: the paltry catch they regularly brought back and which scarcely covered the bottom of the boat.

In order to make amends an idea came to mind, and Pascal seldom stopped asking José, "Why don't we lay our fish traps near the isle of Bornéo, don't you think our catch would be better?"

José would shake his head and answer, "Nothing grows on the isle of Bornéo, there's only sand and the occasional cactus. If we set down our fish traps there we would be burned to cinders in minutes."

One day, quite unexpectedly, José let himself be persuaded. At first sight, his objections seemed justified. The isle of Bornéo, scorched bare by the sun, harbored nothing but stunted cacti growing out of stony ground and a few derelict cabins where fishermen once put their catch to dry or smoke. But the following morning when they came to haul up their nets, their catch exceeded all expectations—

parrot fish, wrasse, red snapper, barracuda, sea bream, grouper, and even small white sharks, all piled into their traps. The boat was so heavy it was difficult to control and they took hours getting back to Bois Jolan.

So much fish! So much fish! In the wink of an eye the news spread throughout the village and there was a rush to the seashore.

In order to understand this outburst of frenzy, you need to realize that before the Japanese and Chinese fleets had accomplished their rack and ruin, fish reigned supreme in Bois Jolan. The elders recalled the good old days when there were no protected species and everything was ripe for eating. Restaurants made their reputation by serving blaffs and brochettes with fish from Bois Jolan, while the smell of court bouillons seasoned or not with hot pepper wafted out of every kitchen. The fishermen weighed on their Roberval scales kilos of green turtle meat and slabs of tuna, whose blood is similar to ours, while skillfully extricating the flesh from the conch shells and remembering to untangle the long tentacles of squid bristling with suction cups.

It was the first of the miraculous catches of fish by Pascal, as they quickly came to be known throughout the country. It was the cause of numerous brawls, conflicts, and quarrels. They could have turned into genuine riots if the mayor of Bois Jolan, Norbert Pacheco, hadn't intervened.

An odd character, this Norbert Pacheco, since he was not only mayor of Bois Jolan but also held an important position on the board of the state-run enterprise Le Bon Kaffé. When the workers had started their marches and demonstrations throughout the island, he had released squadrons of gendarmes to beat them up and throw them into prison.

Le Bon Kaffé provided work for three quarters of the country's able-bodied men and women. In its brochures it boasted of its employee benefits such as modest rents and spacious apartments situated in the concrete tower blocks that mushroomed just about everywhere. It also owned two lycées and a college parents were prepared to do anything to get their children admitted to. The students wore a smart striped uniform and a Panama hat ordered directly from South America.

The reality in fact was quite different and the workers complained they were exploited and grossly underpaid, which explained their discontent.

When the first conflicts occurred at Bois Jolan, Norbert Pacheco resorted to his old habits and dispatched to the beach squadrons of gendarmes who ordered the buyers of fish to get in line and abstain from any comment. Calm had thus been restored at a price.

6

It was after the fourth miraculous catch that Pascal told José of his supposed origins. José interrupted him with a laugh: "I've been hearing that story for some time now. Is it a joke or are you serious?" Pascal was at a loss for an answer and after a silence confessed, "I have no idea. I'd like to have confirmation of what people are saying."

The two friends never broached the subject again.

Months went by, then Pascal received an unexpected visit from Jean Pierre. He was alone as José had accompanied Alexandre to the Mortimer Institute. Father and son hadn't seen each other for over a year. Pascal hadn't been brave enough to face his parents and had only written a letter informing them he was leaving The Garden of Eden for good to move in with José at Bois Jolan. He hadn't dared tell José he wasn't their true son and was constantly looking to define the mission some people were attributing to him. He had merely compiled a number of muddled, convoluted arguments that betrayed the hesitations of his heart and the remorse he was feeling. He argued that he was going to be twenty and was perfectly capable of deciding his future on his own. Moreover, they knew full well that he had never liked the bourgeois milieu they had forced him to accept, particularly its arrogance and selfish indifference towards everything that didn't concern it directly.

Jean Pierre parked his pickup truck in front of José's shack and had difficulty climbing out. Pascal watched him limp towards him with a heavy heart. He would never have thought his father would age in such a short time. He was now bald, potbellied, and most of all had trouble walking, shuffling along and stopping every now and then to get his breath back. The two men embraced.

"What's the matter? Are you ill?" Pascal inquired.

"The doctors say it's arthritis," Jean Pierre replied. "A common occurrence at my age, but it's really painful."

He slumped down onto a chair and groaned: "It's my legs. I'm wondering whether soon I won't be able to walk."

Pascal rolled up his father's gray heavy cotton trousers and discovered two swollen, red-blotched legs covered with a scaly translucent skin pockmarked in black. He massaged them gently. After a while he said, "Stand up and walk." Jean Pierre obeyed and walked a few steps across the room. "What did you do with your hands?" he exclaimed in amazement. "My legs already don't hurt as much."

Father and son looked at each other affectionately, a little bit tearfully, then Jean Pierre pulled himself together.

"I didn't come here to show you my old legs. I'm asking you to come home. Your mother and I think along the same lines. It's not right that given the education we offered you, in the best schools if you recall, you should end up as a wretched fisherman."

Pascal felt offended but Jean Pierre continued without lowering his voice: "But that's not all. Your mother is in very poor health and has terminal-phase cancer. I'm wondering whether she'll live to see the end of the year."

The two men continued chatting for a few more minutes, then Jean Pierre walked back to the parking lot on his new set of legs and sat down behind his steering wheel.

Remaining alone, Pascal felt his eyes brim with tears. So here he was no better than an ungrateful wretch: his mother was seriously ill and he had been unaware of it. He remembered how Eulalie had spoiled him with little treats, showering him with words of affection and encouragement. His mind was made up. When José returned from Fonds-Zombi, Pascal informed him he was leaving Bois Jolan and going back to his parents at The Garden of Eden. José tried to dissuade him but Pascal remained firm.

As usual after dinner the two men headed for a bar they were particularly fond of, the Joyeux Noël. The name of the bar had a hidden joke that only the regulars could understand. The owner's first name was Joyeux, and he was the sixth son of Manuel and Rosa Noël, who had only boys to their name. Calling him Joyeux Noël was a way of beseeching fate that they didn't want another son. The strange strategy succeeded as Rosa's next pregnancy produced a girl, whom the parents christened Bienvenue.

The Joyeux Noël was an open-air bar facing the sea and it was known for its warm and friendly atmosphere. Joyeux Noël was a fat man with a placid face whose lips were perpetually extended in a welcoming smile. An old phonograph belted out the melodies of popular beguines. Every table was occupied by guzzlers downing their glasses of rum. Hardly had José and Pascal taken their seats than José, who was a regular favorite, slipped away to shake hands or grope the waitresses he was all too familiar with. Although he was used to José's little ways, his behavior never failed to annoy Pascal. To give an impression of composure, Pascal poured himself a glass of golden apple juice.

It was then that a man came over to his table. Pascal got the strange impression that he had seen him somewhere before, but the newcomer showed no sign of recognition. His appearance was somewhat unusual. He wore an old-fashioned pinstripe suit and instead of a tie, a white frothy ruff. The most surprising feature of his appearance was that he seemed to be hiding a hump under his twill jacket. In his hands was a packet that had been carefully wrapped.

"May I sit down?" he asked.

A little surprised, Pascal nodded his consent.

Once he was seated, the stranger untied the packet to reveal a light-brown rose which Pascal instantly recognized in astonishment.

"A Tété Négresse!" the stranger said. "You probably think it's your father who invented this rose. Not at all. If I haven't denounced him, it's for your sake. In actual fact, your father simply copied me. I'm the one who created this marvelous rose and gave it to your mother the day you were christened. The rest you know."

Pascal stared at him angrily. He had always believed it was Jean Pierre who had invented the Tété Négresse rose. But at that very moment the phonograph blared even louder and the entire bar burst into song. Pascal was deeply shocked, and exclaimed, "What on earth are you telling me?"

The stranger got up. "Let's get out of here. I've lots of other things to tell you too."

Pascal followed him, and the two men vanished into the night.

When José returned a few minutes later he found the table empty. Where had his companion gone? When he was tired of staring at a half-empty glass and an almost-full bottle of rum, José went out onto the terrace that overlooked the sea. From there, you could see the glow from the lights of Porte Océane and the faint glimmer from the nearby island of Pangolin. The island of Pangolin had an unusual history: first of all, accused by Third World pamphleteers of being a bordello and playground for the West, it had achieved its revolution as had Cuba and several other Latin American countries and was now a chaste republic where tourism was outlawed. It was a scary place and it was rumored that life there had a bitter taste.

What gives life a pleasant taste? In actual fact, José had no time for such considerations. What worried him was Pascal's disappearance. He ran down the steps that led to the toilets, which consisted of two chipped urinals and a stall that didn't lock.

"Have you seen my friend Pascal?" he asked the female toilet attendant, who was wearing glasses perched on her nose and embroidering a baby's vest.

"No, I haven't seen him today," she answered shaking her head.

Increasingly anxious, José ran outside. The heat of the day had broiled and grilled Bois Jolan, but now at last it began to cool down with the evening breeze.

After having made the rounds of the Place des Insurgés, José set off along the street of Pas Perdus and knocked on Carmen's door, a girl he regularly made love to free of charge. He spent the entire night looking for Pascal, helped by his younger brother Alexandre and several neighborhood friends. He telephoned Jean Pierre who, surprised by his call, said he hadn't seen Pascal. José even traveled the twenty kilometers to Fonds-Zombi and searched half a dozen bars. He looked round the Place des Martyrs three times but all in vain. Pascal was nowhere to be seen. The island soon had to accept the fact that Pascal had disappeared.

Those who didn't like him had a ready-made explanation: Pascal had fallen asleep on a public bench and the police had come to arrest him. Since he was unable to produce any ID, they had carted him off and locked him up for the misdemeanor. Pascal's absence lasted almost two months and then one fine day, he reappeared.

7

He reappeared at his parents' home one morning dressed in his favorite blue flannel pajamas, which he was wearing when he had woken up a few hours earlier. He looked around at the familiar bedroom, at his toys and the large photo of Che Guevara whom he thought so handsome and elegant in his beret and combat fatigues.

As usual his parents were tucking into a copious breakfast of sweet melon, hot chocolate, and homemade croissants in the dining room since their grief had not taken away their appetite. Seeing her much-lamented son, Eulalie almost fainted. "It's you! Is it you?" she cried, her hand on her heart to compose its beating. "Where did you go? Where have you been?"

Pascal calmly sat down and poured himself a cup of hot chocolate.

"Why do you always ask me the same things?" he said coldly. "Don't you know that first and foremost I have to understand the world and be familiar with its innermost structure?"

Blown away by this adamant response, Eulalie burst into tears, but instead of comforting his mother, Pascal shrugged and returned to his room.

Subsequently, Pascal provided no information as to what had happened during those two months; even he himself seemed not to know. Although Jean Pierre respected his silence out of discretion and reserve, the same didn't go for Eulalie. Possessive, authoritarian, and intolerant as usual, she bombarded her son with questions: "There must be something at least you remember. How far did you go?" Pascal shook his head and gave a vague reply. "I think the country was desert-like, rippling with barren dunes and shivering at night with an icy wind. I think I slept under a tent."

"Did you see your true father?" Eulalie insisted.

"Alas, no," Pascal replied. "If I did, I have no recollection of it."

What can be said for certain was that on his return Pascal's character had changed. He who was always cheerful, always joking, had turned solemn, sententious, and moralizing. His origins had become more than ever an obsession and an enigma, which he constantly sought to solve. He became pompous as well. Two of his favorite subjects of conversation were slavery and colonization, and countries and societies that have been totally ignored or marginalized; but above all he loved to discuss the place and role of God in the world. He enjoyed talking about the discoveries of new lands, and consequently made a scathing attack on Christopher Columbus, that Mediterranean wop who after brandishing gigantic crosses on the shore to scare the Amerindians, then proceeded to exterminate them to the very last.

His audience would shake their heads in amazement. They hadn't been taught that at school. How could you find your bearings when there were so many versions of History? Perhaps there was one genuine truth that would disprove all the misrepresentations. Or perhaps there wasn't only one truth but merely a set of interpretations.

He bored José, who began to avoid him. As a result, the miraculous catches became less frequent and finally petered out, which had a devastating effect. What use was Pascal after all? It was then by an extraordinary piece of luck that José was awarded a scholarship to study engineering at an American college and he left the country. The day before his departure, determined to ignore the contemptuous looks Eulalie would cast on his faded jeans and his cheap cotton shirt, he came to say goodbye to his friend.

"Everyone says that America is paved with gold," he said. "As soon as I can, I'll bring Alexandre over and the doctors will find his voice wherever it's hiding."

Pascal gripped him fondly by the hand. "Don't you worry about Alexandre. I'll take care of him."

And he kept his word. He even went so far as to recruit Alexandre into The Garden of Eden, but Alexandre was bored to death. He missed the sea, its smell and its sudden whims like those of a pampered madwoman. One morning, Alexandre didn't turn up for work and Pascal understood it was pointless looking for him.

Once José had left for America, Pascal found himself very much alone. He tried to make friends with the workers at The Garden of Eden but they were reluctant to welcome him as one of theirs. For them he was the son of the boss. Such an attitude exasperated Pascal: son of the boss? He was rather the son of nobody. He had never known his father or his mother. Psychiatrists tell us that the fetus is sensitive very early on to its mother's heartbeat and a little later her voice. For Pascal, there was total silence, neither heartbeat nor the echo of a maternal voice.

Feeling helpless and confused, he bought a motorbike he named Pegasus, and went for long drives along the stretch of road that hugged the shore. Sometimes he drove as far as Porte Océane, a town he didn't like very much. Whereas Porte Océane had been modernized and its upstairs-down-stairs wooden houses replaced by concrete cubes topped by a flat terraced roof, Fonds-Zombi remained picturesque. Its wharfs had the salty smell of codfish and the scent of a rum whose barrels were stored in vast warehouses where the sun and the air seldom penetrated.

The main concern during the following months was Eulalie's deteriorating health. She seldom left her bed, and spent hours lying on a chaise longue on the verandah where she leafed absentmindedly through magazines and cheap books.

Our Eulalie had never been in good health. As a small girl, when she didn't have the usual whooping cough, mumps, or chickenpox, she suffered from bronchitis, pneumonia, and pleurisy. At the age of twelve she almost died from a bout of scarlet fever she had caught God knows where since it was virtually unknown on the island. At the age of seventeen, when she met Jean Pierre, she would faint periodically and lose blood from her constant miscarriages. Her condition worried her to such an extent that she finally made up her mind to consult old Dr. Georgelin who had also cared for her mother and grandmother. He made her undergo a battery of highly complicated examinations, then made an appointment for her in his surgery. There he told her in all seriousness, "I think that if you want to stay alive, you'd do better to adopt."

Jean Pierre and Eulalie followed his advice and began a series of visits, first to the Saint Jean Bosco Institution and then to all the other orphanages on the island. They never managed, however, to come to a decision: this child was too white, that one was too black, another one too coolie. In despair they didn't know which way to turn until God gave them this wonderful gift one Easter Sunday by the name of Pascal.

Despite her declining health, Eulalie remained extremely cheerful, her head full of ideas and proposals. One evening at dinner, therefore, she announced in jubilation that Tina was getting married. Who was Tina? The daughter of Marelle, who for thirty years had scrubbed and washed the floors of The Garden of Eden. Tina had been Pascal's childhood play-mate and the Ballandras had watched her grow from a chubby child to an elegant and attractive young woman.

Like her mother before her, Tina worked as a cleaning lady. Consequently, Eulalie was very proud to see her mar-ried at church. It was Milou, in fact, a municipal road worker, who insisted on slipping a ring on her finger as if she were a well-bred little bourgeois girl.

One Saturday then, Jean Pierre, Eulalie, and Pascal set off for the Cathedral of Saint Pierre and Saint Paul. After the religious ceremony, once all the guests had gathered at the

Amphitryon Hotel, they drank to the happiness of the newly-weds. Tina's countless relatives handed round goblets filled with an insipid liquid, which passed as champagne only in name. Eulalie drank a few sips then moaned, "Ugh! How horrible! We should have helped Tina but like her mother, Marelle, she would never ask us for anything."

"Never mind," Pascal replied, exasperated by his mother's persistent remarks. "What counts is that we are all in a joyful mood."

What came next was shaping up to be a catastrophe. Imagine a wedding banquet starting off with slices of unripe avocado mixed with overripe cubes of papaya.

"I can't eat that," Eulalie declared pushing her plate away. "Can't you do something, Pascal, to help them?"

"Such as what?" Pascal asked flabbergasted.

"I don't know," Eulalie continued. "Don't you remember the wedding at Cana?"

Exasperated, Pascal got up and left the room to smoke a cigarette to soothe his nerves. On the terrace he bumped into Tina who was supervising the unloading of a van filled with all kinds of dishes.

"Can I do something to help?" Pascal asked without thinking.

"I can't see how," Tina replied. "Go back inside and we'll serve up the rest."

The remainder of the meal was a delight: a white yam gratin, roasted cockerel accompanied with a ginger sauce, and to finish, a coconut sorbet with frozen meringues. There was even a choice of mulligatawny, an Indian dish made from pork and lentils. But what the guests preferred above all was the exceptional spongy quality of the braided loaves that were served alongside the meal.

Among the different types of bread made by the island's bakers, such as the brioche, rye bread, baguettes, long and whole wheat loaves, the favorite of all is the braided loaf. What is its secret? Nobody will tell. Whatever the case, its dough is white, thick, and wonderfully tasty. It's obtained by braiding the solid strips of bread then placing them in the oven until they are brown and crusty. For some unknown reason the guests who had seen Pascal converse with Tina declared that another miracle had occurred following the earlier miraculous catches at Bois Jolan and called it "the multiplication of the braided loaves." For most of the guests, however, there was no miracle at all.

There had been a strange reversal of opinion since Pascal's unexplained reappearance. Some people had no qualms in saying he was an impostor, a magician who merely practiced tricks he had rehearsed beforehand. Multiplication of the braided loaves, whatever next? In a neighborhood she knew by heart for having scrubbed so many floors, Tina was not lacking in friends who were quite capable of providing the food she needed. Braided loaves were a well-known specialty of a good many bakers.

Pascal could not understand how he had gone from a beloved icon to an object of discord.

8

After a couple threw themselves at his feet on seeing him, almost causing a serious car crash, Pascal decided to take control of his life. Even if he had never seen his father and the latter hadn't explained what was expected of him, he could, nevertheless, guess that his mission was to make the world more brotherly and more tolerant. He decided to create an association in honor of Nietzsche called "The Gay Science," whose role would consist of studying the world's major revolutionary and religious texts.

Alas he only managed to recruit twelve members: two unemployed men who for years had scoured the Paris suburbs only to return home jobless, and familiar with the art of violence; two homeless guys who were probably attracted by the cozy two-room apartment that Pascal gave them rent-free; the remainder of the disciples consisted of the workers up in arms against Le Bon Kaffé, mobilized around a certain Judas Eluthère, head of personnel, himself at odds with the company.

"My name sounds strange, doesn't it?" Judas liked to joke. "It's because my mother lived fifteen years with a man who handed over to her his entire wages and who never spent a night away from home with another woman. The perfect husband, in other words. When he fell from a coconut tree and died from a fractured skull, my mother learned that he had left a widow in tears and a bunch of children in the neighboring village. When had he met this woman? When had he had time to father these children? When I was born a few years later by her second husband, in memory of her past experience, my mother christened me Judas."

Judas Eluthère maintained that Monsieur Norbert Pacheco and his clique received large subsidies from the European Union but in return paid out only meager wages to his workers. The same was true for housing, which was rented out for an exorbitant sum and tailored to customers who didn't even work for Le Bon Kaffé. In his opinion, Monsieur Norbert Pacheco was a dangerous individual who was opposed to the country's welfare and well-being.

This Judas Eluthère soon became the favorite disciple. Pascal was surprised at his feelings towards him. Why did he like him so much? It was true, Judas was an elegant and distinguished person, always dressed in well-fitting linen suits. His frequent laughter rang out melodiously, matching his soothing, captivating gestures. Pascal couldn't help wondering whether it wasn't a homosexual attraction, something he had often experienced. When he was a student, he had sometimes had a weak spot for school friends who were well built and good-looking but it never went any further. When he was in the presence of Judas Eluthère, however, he found his heart beating faster. He would come over with hot flashes. He never tired of conversing with him or hearing him sing "I dream of a world where the earth will be round" with his pretty falsetto voice.

It must be said that Pascal was no virgin. He had slept with a number of women and succumbed to many infatuations. He had often accompanied José on his amorous expeditions, that is until the day he met Maria and his life radically changed.

He hadn't met her in church or at the cathedral but quite by chance, the same way you meet someone who is destined to play a major role in your life. One afternoon in the heat of the day, while he was taking his siesta half-naked, Maria had dashed into the yard of the house at Bois Jolan, running after one of her fowls that had escaped her. She lived two houses down the road and bred so-called Bata cockerels, whose plumage was black and white and who were excellent fighters, raised to win in the cockpit.

Maria first worked as an embroideress, but dressmaking brought in little money. As a result, she turned to another type of commerce which was more lucrative, that of selling her charms. It came easy to her since she was a very pretty woman with amber, velvety skin, golden hair, and luscious lips. In other words, a Chabeen. For Pascal and Maria, it was love at first sight, as the saying goes. Henceforth they spent every weeknight together. In all honesty, we must confess that Maria was a good dozen years older than Pascal; she was thirty-five in fact while he was barely twenty-two. But this age difference didn't show and you'd think the two lovebirds had fallen out of the same nest.

When Pascal returned to live with his parents, Maria had no intention of changing her routine, and one evening she came to spend the night with her beloved. The next morning at breakfast Eulalie made a scene.

"I don't ever want to see that girl again," she shouted.

"What has she done?" Pascal asked in surprise, feigning an innocent, naive look. "Didn't she greet you politely? Didn't she inquire about your health when she saw you lying on a chaise longue instead of watching television in an armchair like everyone else?"

"I know a slut when I see one," Eulalie angrily retorted. "I'm telling you I no longer want to see her in my home."

This quarrel was the last straw. Determined never to come back, Pascal left his parents' house for good and resigned from The Garden of Eden, having saved up enough from his wages.

He decided to buy his own house on the recommendation of Judas Eluthère. It was situated in Marais Salant in a region once covered with a salty soil which fattened up the goats that grazed on it. The butchers claimed that the salt hidden in the folds of this soil gave the meat its unique taste.

If Pascal had been more alert, he would have lent his ear to what Judas was telling him about the tenant of a very charming house located in the neighborhood. For sure, it looked abandoned since the tenant was always absent. She was a certain Fatima Deglas-Moretti who spent six months of the year in Fez, Morocco. The doors and windows were always shut, except when an old couple of servants came to air the place. The ground floor consisted of one vast, dismal room furnished with chairs and benches and Arabic inscriptions on the walls. On Fridays, it became a meeting place for men and women whose heads were wrapped in a thick black veil, which was surprising in a land where a fine head of hair was so important. Was it a temple? Was it a mosque?

Fatima Deglas-Moretti used to go by the name of Maya and had converted to Islam after meeting with Allah. Under what circumstances? If Pascal had been more curious and inquired further, he would have known, and thus would have gotten closer to the truth that had obsessed him since childhood.

Pascal therefore moved in with Maria in Marais Salant. A few days later Maria's sister, Marthe, came to join them. No women could have been more different than these two sisters. Maria spent all her time painting and powdering her face, lining her pretty almond-shaped eyelids in green and coating her lashes in black mascara and coloring her luscious lips in red. Her favorite pastime was trying on dress after dress, shorts after shorts, and swimwear after swimwear. Marthe, on the contrary, neglected her appearance and was always dressed any old how. She was content merely to sweep, vacuum clean, feather dust, scrub the floor, boil the food and serve it up.

This disparity never failed to shock Pascal and one day he drew Maria into a corner and rebuked her. "Can't you do something to help your sister? You let her do all the housework and the cooking."

Maria threw her head back and burst into laughter. "That's what she likes: to feel useful. I would even go so far as to say, to feel indispensable. And she certainly doesn't think that out of the two of us I've got the better deal."

After this conversation, Pascal accepted the fact and no longer intervened between the two sisters.

In actual truth Pascal no longer got on with Maria like he used to. Maria seemed to tire of his constant interrogations about his origins and his wish to find his real parents. At first, he didn't mention it, but the subject increasingly took pride of place in their conversations.

"What are you complaining about?" Maria asked him shrugging her shoulders. "You've got a foster-father and -mother who adore you. That should be enough. What does it matter if they didn't bring you into this world?"

Pascal realized that he was not always as cheerful and carefree as she would have liked him to be. As time went by, he grew dissatisfied with himself and was not at all content with the turn his life was taking.

9

Marthe and Maria had a young brother by the name of Lazare who was eighteen years old. He was so crippled by pain that he had the skinny, sickly look of a disabled boy with thinning hair. He got by thanks to the constant care of Marthe and Maria, as well as Emma, a friend, whom we could hardly suspect of being his mistress since the idea of making love to Lazare would have appeared unseemly.

What exactly did Lazare suffer from? Some people said he had caught dengue fever when he was barely three and that this formidable disease had contaminated his blood. Others suggested he smoked too much eliacin, a plant in the same family as marijuana, in order to calm the pain that paralyzed his arms and legs.

Despite his precarious condition, Lazare was very fond of rum and was a regular at Nostradamus, a bar situated at Marais Salant. Pascal often went with him, leaving Marthe and Maria to watch schmaltzy Brazilian soap operas on the television. The bar was decorated with a huge canvas, the work of the owner's twin brother, Roro Maniga, who had studied in India and had been initiated into the religions of that part of the world. He was well known as a painter and his paintings were extremely popular since they were an explosive mixture of sacrilege and religious beliefs. For example, he had painted a series entitled Virgin and Child, where one canvas represented a Black woman, one an Indian woman, one a Dougla, a Chabeen, a Capresse, a Mulatto woman, and finally an Octoroon, each holding a lovely Black infant.

By dint of enjoying a drink together, Roro had become close friends with Pascal and Lazare. He begged them to intercede with Maria since he had got it into his head to paint "The Tidings Brought to Mary" with Maria as the Virgin Mary. Maria needed a lot of persuading as she was deeply religious, having piously received her first communion and been confirmed.

The record player at the Nostradamus constantly blared out popular songs. Sometimes on leaving the bar Lazare was so drunk he could barely stand and had to be supported by a bunch of men carrying flashlights to light the way.

"One of these days," the badmouths whispered shaking their heads, "he'll fall headlong onto the ground and that will be the end of him." They were mistaken, however, for the very next morning Lazare was up at six pissing on the flowers in the garden.

This carefree existence soon came to an end. While they were still asleep, wrapped in the warmth of a night spent making love, Pascal and Maria were woken by Marthe. "Get up," she ordered in a shaky voice, "something terrible has happened to Lazare." Pascal and Maria dashed downstairs. Lazare was lying sprawled on his bed, eyes closed and mouth open. He was no longer breathing. When Pascal touched him, he gave a start, terrified by the chill of death.

Marthe and Maria were screaming in unison while Pascal attempted in vain to calm them.

"Don't you worry," he murmured with authority, "he is merely sleeping. Soon he'll wake up. He'll wake up, I can assure you." His words came from somewhere deep down, beyond his control. Unfortunately, they didn't seem to ring true, for time went by and Lazare continued to remain motionless, lying like a statue on a tomb.

Shortly before noon, Madame Linceuil showed up. Madame Linceuil was a short little woman with a reddish complexion who taught the children their catechism and knew every prayer for the dead inside out. Her voice was resonant and high-pitched like a professional mourner from Africa.

The wake continued long into the night with Lazare still motionless on his bed and everyone convinced that he had gone to the afterlife for good. Around midnight he suddenly woke and sat up with ease: "What on earth are you doing?" he asked. "I'm hungry, I would like to eat and I need a cup of coffee, and make it strong!" Marthe and Maria threw themselves into each other's arms. "He's hungry," they laughed. "He wants some coffee!" Thereupon they rushed to the kitchen.

This unusual event caused quite a stir. From the north to the south of the island, tongues started to wag. "Lazare resuscitated from the dead by Pascal? Are you kidding me?" some people said, while others were filled with infinite respect. So Pascal was a god of sorts. "Which god?" some people inquired. The proud Christian God whose name has divided the history of humanity into BC and AD? The authoritarian Allah who forbids any depiction of himself? Buddha, who after a short walk in the outside world, discovered human suffering, old age, and death? Papa Legba who stands upright at the crossroads? Sakpata, goddess of smallpox? It was more likely, critics stated, that Lazare had smoked too many eliacin leaves, which had sent him into a coma from which several hours later he awoke.

Bishop Altmeyer, the very same one who had baptized Pascal, climbed up to his pulpit and denounced these blasphemous rumors: "Isn't it common knowledge that Pascal is the adopted son of a well-known couple who own a nursery?"

It became increasingly difficult for Pascal to set foot outdoors, where he was greeted either with admiring smiles or looks of contempt from bunches of hotheads. The rumor of this miraculous event spread even further and finally reached Canada. A television crew consequently came to interview Jean Pierre and Eulalie. Weren't they ideally placed to testify to the origins of their adopted son? Although Jean Pierre, true to character, refused to comply, Eulalie was only too pleased to draw attention to herself. She strutted in front of the cameras, posing and showing off. She delved into her past: "Jean Pierre and I were determined to adopt a child. But we couldn't agree on one point: I wanted a boy and he wanted a girl. He had even chosen a name, Anouchka, the name of the heroine of a tale he had adored when he was a child." At the end of the interview, the journalist declared with a smile, "But a god? ... Isn't that how every mother treats her son?" Neither Eulalie nor Jean Pierre knew what to say. The phrase hit home and became a household word all the way from Fonds-Zombi to Port Océane.

Pascal was not only tortured by this controversy, he was also upset by his feelings for Maria. Love is the child of a bohemian life, it has never known any law, goes the song in Georges Bizet's *Carmen*. Alas, it is so very true. Pascal noticed that these days he felt virtually nothing for Maria. Her body used to drive him crazy but now it left him cold. Everything she did was insufferable, especially her voice, which appeared to shriek when she called him "My King" or "My God" either in play or in all seriousness.

Once upon a time they used to spend a considerable amount of time making love, lying together side by side on a mattress in the garden, both their bodies kissed by the sun. When the kisses became too hot, they took refuge on the terrace and shared a refreshing fruit juice.

Now, as soon as he had downed his coffee, Pascal climbed to the top of the house, to a room he had turned into an office. Grabbing a notepad, he would begin to scribble frantically. Within a few weeks he had filled over a hundred pages. Nevertheless, he was not satisfied with the result. His text mixed hackneyed theories like the class struggle or man's exploitation of his fellow man with more modern meditations on the ravages caused by globalization. He decided not to submit his work to an editor. In his despair, he no longer slept at night, to the point that Maria began to have serious doubts about his feelings for her and inquired about his well-being.

10

There then occurred a tragic and unexpected event: Eulalie died! As the Bambara proverb says, Death does not beat a drum: it takes you by surprise and chooses whom it likes. Eulalie had complained all day long of chest pains and had retired early to her bedroom, unaccompanied by Jean Pierre. As usual he was sipping a neat rum and smoking two cigarettes when Pompette came to tug at his trousers. Irritated by the dog's little game, it took him fifteen minutes to realize that Pompette wanted to show him something and follow her inside. He found Eulalie collapsed on her bed, unconscious, her mouth smeared with blood. Without thinking to call a doctor, he slid down to the floor and wept until morning, at which point he decided to call Pascal.

Eulalie had no family of her own since her father and mother had died a few years earlier. Her only brother, Ingmar, had married a Swedish girl and thought Jean Pierre too black to associate with.

Mysteriously informed of death's onslaught, the neighbors began to flock to The Garden of Eden around eight in the morning. They crowded onto the terrace and along the garden paths. At nine o'clock, a small group of mourners showed up, for Eulalie had been the president of a good many charities and the terrible news had rapidly done the rounds in Fonds-Zombi. The tireless Madame Linceuil arrived on the stroke of ten, beating time as she conducted the choir of weepers:

Closer to Thee my God,
Closer to Thee,
Gladly Will I Toil and Suffer,
Only Let Me Walk with Thee.

Numerous members of the clergy arrived in turn and the living room was filled with people in tears. At the wake that same evening, sympathizers arrived from all over the island, some on foot, others by car or motorbike. Some municipalities had even gone so far as to provide free bus rides for their inhabitants.

Jean Pierre's grief was immense. He kept remembering the happy times when Eulalie was alive. He was barely twenty when he met her at a dance for teenagers organized by one of the parishes in Fonds-Zombi. How lovely she was in all of her sixteen years, holding her blonde hair with one hand and raising her gypsy-style skirt with the other over her shapely legs. The boys were lining up in front of her to request a dance, but she only had eyes for one. Between Eulalie and Jean Pierre it was love at first sight.

But when he came with honorable intentions to ask for her hand from her parents, her family rejected him because of his coal-black color. The couple had therefore run away and set up house on a plot of land that Jean Pierre had bought for next to nothing from a horticulturist who had gone bankrupt. To tell the truth, during those first years, they had only grown flowering shrubs, which needed little care and little water, such as yellow allamandas, white rayo, and yellow and red dwarf poincianas.

Although the bride-to-be was all smiles, the young couple had trouble making ends meet at the end of each month. The stroke of genius occurred a few years later when a herd of goats or oxen, nobody knows for sure, in any case a flock of animals who shouldn't have been where they were, wrecked the greenhouses of The Garden of Eden, which at the time formed a modest nursery. Instead of lamenting the loss, Jean Pierre had the brilliant idea of grafting the damaged shrubs and thus produced the Cayenne rose. From that moment on, the money flowed in and Eulalie's family acknowledged the love they had previously scorned. The wedding took place amid a commotion of joy and good spirits.

Yet Jean Pierre's grief was nothing in comparison to Pascal's, who had arrived on the arm of Maria, since he could hardly stand. He had the feeling he was about to faint. His pain was exacerbated by his remorse. His features were hidden behind a heartrending mask of his own making. He told himself he had not been a good son. He felt he had not been worthy of the love the deceased had shown him.

He remembered above all their last conversation. One Sunday afternoon he had come to visit her while she was resting in her room. The doors and windows were wide open in order to let in the sun's heat since Eulalie always felt the cold. She had dismissed with a wave of the hand his inquiries about her health and looked him straight in the eye.

"You know what would make me happy?" she had asked. As he shook his head, she blurted out, "A child, I'd like you to give me a grandson before I go."

He had replied curtly, "A child? How could that be possible? You loathe and despise the girl I'm living with, and now you want a child from her!"

"It's true she's not the best of women you could have a child with, I must admit," she answered unruffled.

"Not everyone thinks the same as you," he shouted. "Roro Maniga—you know who Roro Maniga is, the famous painter—he wants to do her portrait, he finds her so charming."

Thereupon, without saying another word, he left.

But there was no shortage of pesky individuals who once had backed Pascal but now turned against him. So, the man who had resuscitated Lazare from the dead proved to be incapable of saving his own mother! Did he have a heart? Judas Eluthère had to smash the faces of half a dozen individuals who criticized Pascal's lack of compassion.

A wake is not just an excuse for free food, where some people sit in a corner to down neat rum after neat rum and ackra after ackra. A wake wouldn't be a wake without the traditional thick soup, a delicious mixture of boiled beef, pumpkin, and carrots amply seasoned with garlic and parsley. That evening the thick soup had been cooked by tearful Tina, who was intent on demonstrating her affection to the woman she fondly called her second mother. There was plenty for everyone. Tina didn't realize that she had unwittingly provided grist to the mill of those who claimed that Pascal's miracle during her own wedding, the multiplication of the braided loaves, was nothing more than a cock-and-bull story.

Following the thick soup, it was Madame Linceuil's turn to uplift the mourners in a crescendo of psalms and hymns that lasted till morning when the sky began to be tinged with gold.

11

Eulalie's funeral was to have a lasting effect. It took place at the start of the afternoon, but since the cemetery at Briscaille was a fair distance away it meant that people had to leave early and follow the road to Port Océane until they reached Vauban, where they had to turn left at the crossroads, drive up a hill, and cross a shaky bridge over the Bains Jaunes, thus named because of its sulfur springs, whose virtues were used for treating skin diseases.

A procession of luxury cars lined up at the graveyard, since all those who had the means wanted to express their sympathy. At the head of the procession, in the hearse covered with photos of the deceased, Jean Pierre and Pascal sat on either side of Eulalie's coffin, which was draped in wreaths. One of the photos especially stood out, the one of Eulalie radiant with joy, in the bloom of her youth and beauty, holding her newborn son in her arms.

Despite his grief, Pascal couldn't help wondering whether his presence was not helping to perpetuate a lie. Eulalie was not his real mother. Another woman had taught him to recognize her heartbeat and make out the sound of her voice while he lay hidden in her womb. Where was she? How many doors did he have to open to find her? Would she accept him? The mystery was torture.

The tourist brochures claim that Briscaille Cemetery, dating back to the nineteenth century, is the most beautiful on the island. Its tombs covered in black and white flagstones produce an undeniable effect against the blue of the sky. It is built at the top of a hill and perfectly hugs its slopes.

The Ballandras' family vault had the shape of a Chinese pagoda: the first level was filled with the family's coffins, while the ground level had been fitted out as a music room. On arrival a group of musicians took their seats and picked up their instruments: violin, cello, reed pipe, harmonica, tambourine, and even an ukulele, played by one of Eulalie's former friends. They began with Dvořák's Requiem, which had been one of her favorites. Then Bishop Altmeyer, his eyes brimming with tears, gave a homily which left nobody unmoved. He recalled the deceased's exceptional qualities and the island's enormous loss.

When the ceremony was over the sun took refuge in a corner of the sky, which it inundated with blood-red streaks. A cool wind blew in from the sea and caressed the plants growing alongside the graves. The mourners then crowded along the cemetery's paths and made their way out.

Pascal found himself at the center of a small group of sympathizers who had come to present their condolences. It was then that a young woman, elegantly dressed and wearing a red hat, an unfortunate color given the circumstances, came up to him. She took him by the hand, whispering, "Your mother was an example for every woman. Dear brother, when will you give me the honor of coming to talk it over with me?" Before he even had the chance to answer, Maria intervened and Judas Eluthère intercepted the business card the young woman was handing him.

"Do you know who she is?" he whispered in Pascal's ear, who was surprised by this brutal intervention. "She's Estelle Romarin, the most infamous whore on the island. She's recently returned from Paris where she slept with every influential man for personal gain. She's just been appointed Junior Secretary for the Underprivileged."

Pascal replied absentmindedly and in a gentle tone: "Let he who has never sinned cast the first stone." Used to his mysterious and incomprehensible words, Judas Eluthère made no objection and everyone climbed back into their cars.

The first night after the burial is the most painful as all our thoughts turn to the beloved we have abandoned, all alone, in her final resting place. How will she endure eternity? However much Marthe and Maria handed round coffee and opened packets of red-topped sugar cakes, those back in Marais Salant were weighed down by a heavy heart.

In order to take their mind off things, Pascal, together with Lazare, Judas Eluthère, and a few other friends, set off for the Nostradamus bar. There the atmosphere was festive, since, as the Book of Ecclesiastes says, "There's a time to weep and a time to laugh." Led by a beanpole with white hair draped in a multicolored wrapper, a quartet of dwarves was blowing on recorders while two others were beating out a rhythm on a gwo-ka drum. The crowd of rum-guzzlers were applauding these carnival escapees and bringing the house down. The atmosphere was a far cry from the oppressive ambience back at The Garden of Eden and Briscaille Cemetery.

12

Not long afterwards, while Pascal was endeavoring without much success to recover from Eulalie's death, very early one morning, the postman, a little fat man badly rigged out in his striped uniform, stopped his yellow van in front of Pascal's house and practically pulled him out of bed. He handed him a letter from the Bon Kaffé establishment. When he opened it, Pascal saw it was signed by a certain David Druot along with Judas Eluthère, both staff representatives. They invited him to come to Sagalin, the company's head office, without saying why.

A few moments later, Maria, disheveled and sleepy-eyed, came to join him in his office where despite the early morning hour Pascal was already typing on his computer. He handed her the letter he had just received.

"Don't get mixed up with them," she advised him, after having read it. "You'd do well to stay clear of all that because I had a dream, a very bad dream last night. It told me that something was going to happen to you, I don't know what exactly, but it scared me. You'll notice that the letter is not signed by Monsieur Pacheco, whereas he's the big boss."

Pascal had noticed this omission but had made up his mind not to take account of Maria's opinion, and what's more his situation was getting worse. His life was becoming cramped, inundated with idle gossip as well as words and gestures beyond his control. An ever-increasing number of social circles repeated that they did not believe in his miracles, while others declared on the contrary that he was truly the son of God, without indicating exactly which god they were talking about.

The following Monday, obeying David Druot and Judas Eluthère's invitation, he mounted his motorbike and set off for Sagalin. It was still early when he left. The cattle locked

up for the night in their enclosure were constantly bellowing. You could hear the lowing of the cows, calling to relieve
their udders heavy with milk. Leaving behind the terrible
weather in Marais Salant, it began to turn brighter and
white clouds in the form of rosaces skidded across the sky.
A gentle wind ruffled the jacarandas, which had replaced
the June plum trees along the road, and showered the macadam with their blue flowers.

Pascal, who hadn't eaten a thing since the day before,
stopped in Octavia at a small café that wasn't much to look
at but offered a traditional breakfast for a modest sum. On
seeing him, the owner, a giant with a bald head, dropped to
his knees and exclaimed: "You! You! My house is not worthy
of your presence, but say one word and my soul will be
healed."

Pascal compelled him to get up and almost left, since this
ostentatious welcome was not to his liking. Though he
would have regretted having done so as the breakfast of
smoked herring, avocado, and cassava flour turned out to
be excellent.

When Pascal reached Sagalin, the weather was glorious
and the sky was the color of deep blue like in a child's
drawing. Despite the fact it was prosperous and the seat of
a major company, the village of Sagalin was devoid of
beauty and even rather dirty. Gangs of macaques from the
neighboring forest defecated copiously in the streets
while stray dogs for some unknown reason congregated at
the same spot.

Yet it was there it had all begun. Some fifty years earlier,
a certain Ti-Maurice grew coffee on the acres of fertile soil
bequeathed him by his father. He had set up house with
Mariette, who owned the Bar des Deux Amis and had the
brilliant idea of putting the coffee on the bar's menu under
the name of Aroma Divina. The couple did not balk at hard
work. Up before dawn and retiring late at night, they
planted, weeded, fertilized, watered, and dried the berries

on sheets of corrugated iron before roasting them themselves.

It wasn't long before they were rewarded with success. Sagalin became a compulsory detour on the road to Port Océane and its reputation rapidly spread. It was then that the government, lured by the prospect of making a lot of money, purchased Ti-Maurice's land, developing and nationalizing it. Very rapidly, it became the most prosperous establishment on the island, while Ti-Maurice and his wife, who had collected a considerable sum from the sale, went to enjoy a peaceful retirement in the mother country.

An outer wall, several meters high, painted white and decorated with cups of steaming coffee, curved around the company's head office. Pascal got off his motorbike, almost slipped on some macaque droppings, and pushed the entrance button. After a moment the gate slid open and he found himself in an entrance hall filled with displays of all sorts of brochures. In one corner a woman was sitting behind a rectangular table. Once she had read the letter, she barked a few words with a strong Spanish accent into the telephone close by. Where did she come from? Pascal wondered.

Despite its small dimensions, the island was a mirror image of the wider world. Groups speaking every language on earth, originating from lands as far away as Africa and the Pacific Islands, rubbed shoulders with each other. How could Pascal manage to plant here the tree of harmony and tolerance that his father had entrusted him with? After such a melancholy thought, he plucked up his spirits. Wasn't it perhaps here at Le Bon Kaffé where the change he was so hoping for would start?

After a while a man emerged from an adjacent corridor, and he in turn took the letter.

"Follow me," he smiled, after having read it. "I'm going to take you to Block H where the employee delegates are waiting for you."

Pascal obeyed and the two men went out of the reception lobby into the open.

Pascal had never walked through a coffee plantation before. The young shrubs with large shiny leaves were planted close together, thus maintaining a shadowy half-light. He gazed out of curiosity at these multicolored berries, which when harvested brought in millions of euros, for Sagalin coffee was listed on the stock exchange and could easily match the Arabica, Robusta, and even the Jamaican Blue Mountain species. The wind was blowing, and high up in the sky the sun was playing hide-and-seek.

David Druot and Judas Eluthère were waiting for him in an office where a vast collection of volumes written in every language sat upon an imposing bookcase. A portrait of Monsieur Pacheco and two other dashing fifty-year-olds decorated the walls. David Druot and Judas Eluthère looked alike: same haircut, same elegance, and same refinement.

David Druot got straight to the point.

"During recent months," he said, "eighteen of our employees have committed suicide, while fifty or so others have stopped working without taking the trouble to resign. Each week the remaining workers demonstrate through the streets of every town with disastrous results. Up till now the police have made more than a thousand arrests. Such a situation cannot persist. We have taken advantage of Monsieur Pacheco's absence to appeal to you. We believe you can help us. Monsieur Pacheco is determined to oppose any attempt at reform. At the moment he is on vacation, after which he flies to Japan."

"Japan!" Pascal exclaimed.

"Yes," David Druot replied, "Japan. We recently inaugurated a branch there which has proved very successful. Our engineers have invented a type of coffee bean called Le Petit Kaffé that is hugely popular worldwide. Monsieur Pacheco will be away for the entire year. During that time, we hope to do everything possible to improve the situation and to manage to achieve better relations within the company."

Thereupon Judas Eluthère began to hum jokingly the words to his favorite song: "I dream of a world where the earth will be round ..."

Pascal let himself be persuaded and the three men agreed he would come twice a week to lecture the employees and the classes would endeavor to solve those issues the employees found unacceptable. Following which they sealed their agreement with a cup of Aroma Divina brought in by a winsome secretary.

The ensuing period was rich in activities of all sorts for Pascal. He spent hours preparing his lectures and his heart filled with an emotion he had never felt before. At last, his goal was in sight, he was going to act and offer ways of reforming the world by rejecting any selfish concerns.

We must admit that he was not entirely prepared for the task. Going by word of the constant television and radio reports of angry demonstrators, he believed that Le Bon Kaffé was composed mostly of rebels and malcontents. To his surprise it was nothing of the sort. A large percentage of employees were outright hostile to any change within the company. Very rapidly his lectures turned into free-for-alls where overexcited groups flared up in anger and quarreled with one another, which Pascal quite liked to be honest, since truth and knowledge are born out of contention and dispute.

Wiser, and armed with this new experience, he corrected the pamphlets he had been working on but had never dared publish. His head was teeming with ideas and he was gripped deep down with a burning enthusiasm. The lectures he gave soon reached far beyond the limits of Le Bon Kaffé and became a favorite topic of conversation throughout the island. It appeared that if Pascal was not the son of God, he was very much a troublemaker.

13

Pascal's office, this cramped little room whose only appeal was its view of the foliage in the garden, now became his refuge. He would spend hours on end here, working, searching for ideas, deleting phrases he didn't like, and going downstairs twice a day to the dining room, silent and purposeful, simply to down the succulent meals prepared by Marthe. Sometimes he spent the night on the sofa covered with an orange lap rug.

Leaving the door open due to the heat, he would wake up in the predawn hours and watch the night wage its daily combat as it surrendered to the morning. Gradually the sun rose, brandishing its dazzling disk higher and higher like in *General Sun, My Brother*, the book he had read when he was about twelve. He couldn't remember the name of the author but he had never forgotten this plunge into Haiti's bitter and burning reality.

One evening while he was dozing behind his desk Judas Eluthère walked in with the look of someone who was about to make a major announcement.

"You're still working!" he exclaimed. "Maria is complaining you work too much."

Pascal shrugged impatiently. Judas ignored this and went and sat down on the other side of the desk.

"Rest assured," he said. "I've not come to talk about Maria. What goes on between you two is nobody's business. I've come to tell you of another woman, one who has played a major role in your life."

"A major role in my life?" Pascal repeated in surprise. "I have never known another woman besides Eulalie and a few friends."

"I know, I know," Judas Eluthère replied. "You haven't met her yet. She wanted to come with me tonight but I thought it best to let you know that finally you're going to meet your mother."

"My mother?" Pascal choked. "What on earth are you telling me?"

"Open your ears and listen to me. It's a long story. Your mother's name is Maya Moretti. A few years ago, she converted to Islam and now goes by the name of Fatima."

"You must be kidding me."

"Be patient and listen," Judas recommended.

Thereupon he began the following story:

"Some fifty years ago, Ti-Jean Moretti and his wife Nirva were the happiest couple in the world. They had just given birth to their first little girl, whom they christened Maya. The child was a jewel, pure perfection, a golden buttercup lighting up her surroundings with her grace and beauty wherever she went. But she wasn't only endearing. Whereas the couple could barely read or write—Ti-Jean scrubbed swimming pools for the Immedia company, while Nirva did housework for a living—as soon as Maya went to school she turned out to be top of her class in every subject, from French to Math to Natural Science.

"For her fourteenth birthday Ti-Jean had taken out a loan to buy her a lovely gold rope-chain necklace, while Nirva had given her a plain gold bangle. For her sixteenth birthday, at which time she passed her baccalaureate with flying colors, her parents, neither of whom had as much as their primary-school diploma, both delirious with pride, had saved up to buy her a first-class cabin on the inaugural cruise of Empress of the Sea through the Caribbean. It was a present from the likes of wealthy parents.

"Alas, it did not have the expected effect. Back from her cruise, Maya's mood changed radically and her once agreeable disposition turned somber. She no longer went out, and instead spent hours on end alone in her room.

"It was then that Ti-Jean died. He was strangled by a pool skimmer he was cleaning. People said the horrible accident was due to Maya's change of behavior, but nobody was really satisfied with such an explanation.

"When she was awarded a generous state scholarship to go and study in the mother country, reluctant to leave her old mother all alone, Maya took her with her on board the *Normandie*. The two women moved into a small, plain, but comfortable apartment at Savigny-sur-Orge, a close suburb of Paris. Nirva easily found housework to do, while Maya enrolled at the university to study pediatric psychotherapy. The course was tough going but Maya stuck to it, possessed by an apparent obsession with detecting and treating infant traumas.

"At the age of twenty-two, she met a Moroccan called Ahmed-Ali Roussy, a film director whose talent was much admired. At the Cannes Film Festival his documentary on children from the projects had received critical attention. Between Maya and Ahmed it was love at first sight. It was for his sake that she converted to Islam and changed her name to Fatima. Once again, a smile played on her lips and the couple, bursting with laughter, seemed to be immersed in happiness. Alas, after two years of life together, one evening Ahmed disappeared. She waited for him all night long and in the morning called her friends and acquaintances but there was no news. Utterly distraught, she ended up making a formal complaint to the police, who during the hearing poked fun at her offhandedly. Was it her husband she was looking for or her fiancé? they inquired. What was their relationship?

"Months went by and still there was no news of Ahmed. Maya turned the same thoughts over and over again in her head until in the end she accepted her fate. He had probably left for one of those lawless countries where life hangs from a thread."

"Sounds fascinating," Pascal joked, once Judas had stopped. "But who told you she was my mother?"

"She told me herself. While on the cruise ship *Empress of the Sea* she met a very wealthy young Brazilian by the name of Corazón Tejara. When she wrote to him later to say she was pregnant, he first of all ignored her constant appeals. As a result of his silence, she was forced to abandon her newborn son in the shed at the bottom of the Ballandras' garden. But lo and behold, several months later, Corazón suddenly wrote to her claiming the son she had had to get rid of. That son, Pascal, is you. The day before yesterday she returned from Fez where she spends six months of the year. Let's go and see her, she lives just opposite and she'll explain better than I can all that I've just told you."

The two men climbed down the stairs as Pascal wondered whether it wasn't all a dream. They walked across the garden drowned in night. Not a sound could be heard except for the beating of a gwo-ka drum echoing in the distance, like a heart beating in panic.

On the ground floor of Fatima's house, in the kitchen, wide open despite the late hour, two old servants were downing their glasses of anisette. "Madame is waiting for you in the living room," the man said.

Pascal and Judas dashed up the stairs.

A pretty woman, around fifty years of age, was waiting for them in a pleasantly furnished room decorated with huge paintings. She was wearing an attractive costume somewhere between a djellaba and a dress. Her hair was covered by a heavy black veil.

On seeing them arrive she gave a start and, quickly walking over to Pascal, clasped both hands.

"He's told you everything, hasn't he?" she asked emotionally.

"Yes, he told me some unlikely story. I must admit I have trouble believing it. I'm waiting to hear your version."

"His story is the truth," she assured him.

She repeated how she had abandoned him in Jean Pierre and Eulalie's garden, convinced the newborn was without a father. She had no idea how she had managed to bury this painful secret so deep in her heart. Even more surprising, Corazón, whom she thought to have disappeared, suddenly wrote to her with an even more unbelievable story: he was of divine origin, and in charge of a mission he was eager to share with his son.

"But have you tried to get in touch with this Corazón?" Pascal asked.

She shook her head. "I wanted nothing more to do with him. Afterwards, I met another man; it was for him I converted to Islam and became Fatima Moretti."

Mother and son looked each other straight in the eye.

"The main thing," Fatima suddenly said, "is that Corazón might have been telling the truth. Our son, that's you, perhaps is no ordinary child. From what he told me a prediction had been revealed to him. True or false is anyone's guess."

So, thought Pascal, the rumors and gossip circulating with regards to his origin might be legitimate.

Fatima squeezed his hand and whispered, "Have you suffered because you have never met your true parents? Have you suffered because you thought you had been abandoned?"

"No," Pascal lied, "because my foster parents have been wonderful to me."

Fatima leaned closer, her face flushed with the violent feelings that haunted her. "Deep down, way down, what do you feel?" she insisted.

If Judas Eluthère hadn't been present, the conversation would have gone on far into the night, but here Pascal put an end to it.

"I'll come back to see you, and ask all the questions that cross my mind."

Pascal and Judas climbed down the stairs. Once in the garden they went their separate ways.

"Let's forget about all that for the moment. Give me time to think things over."

Pascal could not sleep at night. He did not know what to think. After having looked for his mother all these years, she was in fact right next door. He had the feeling he had made a major step forward and finally could look life straight in the eye.

14

The very next morning Pascal went to visit Fatima. From that day on, their relationship took an unexpected turn: they became inseparable, as thick as thieves as the saying goes, or quite simply like mother and son. On those mornings when he didn't leave for Le Bon Kaffé at Sagalin, Pascal went to see Fatima. She would be waiting for him with her head wrapped in her inevitable black veil yet otherwise dressed in a glamorous pair of red linen shorts.

For over an hour they would ramble across fields, trampling on brambles, Guinea grass, and iron weed, and climb hills at breakneck speed. They only stopped to catch their breath once they reached the Millevaches plateau. By then, the sun had begun to scorch the trees as well as the gigantic torch cacti that grew just about everywhere in those parts.

They would then go for a swim in Josephine's Bath Tub, as the little creek protected by a coral reef was called. The waters were so clear you could see the tiny fish wiggling on the seabed of sand that was as white as snow. At that point Fatima had no option but to remove her black veil and replace it with a rather plain bathing cap. Pascal gazed in amazement at her momentarily revealed squirrel-gray mop of hair. It aged her and immediately made him realize the number of years that separated them.

In the afternoon, they would get down to work. Oddly enough, they barely mentioned Corazón Tejara, as if the one time they had spoken of him already was enough. Pascal was no ordinary mortal and had a mission to accomplish. Corazón embodied a renewed energy that would redress the errors committed throughout the world. Fatima would mark with red the pages Pascal gave her, as if it were a school exercise book. From time to time, she would shake her head.

"You're too intolerant," she protested. "Partisan, I would say. Even colonization, which has done us so much harm, has its gems and pearls, some of which we have put to good use."

"Colonization?" Pascal protested.

"Have you read the 'Anthropophagic Manifesto'?" Fatima asked him.

"The 'Anthropophagic Manifesto'? What kind of a joke is that?"

Fatima explained in all seriousness, "It's not a joke. It was written by a Brazilian by the name of Oswald de Andrade. He endeavored to prove that the Tupi Amerindians who devoured the Christian missionaries were not the savages we thought they were, but demonstrated their superior intelligence by ingesting the qualities of those who were attempting to convert them."

Pascal then got the idea of taking Fatima along to his classes so that she could elaborate her ideas. The students, therefore, would no longer accuse him of being too rigid in his opinions and would stop calling him pigheaded. When he told her of his idea, she eagerly accepted.

One Saturday morning they both left for Sagalin. Fatima was wearing an elegant shirtdress and her hair was covered with a black silk scarf embroidered with silvery motifs. What Pascal hadn't predicted was the effect she would produce. The small Room 104 where he gave his lectures was packed. The rebel-mongers filled the first rows and attacked Fatima with an extreme violence, accusing her above all of converting to Islam, a religion responsible for so many bombings and the massacre of so many innocent people throughout the world.

"That's not how I see Islam," Fatima protested. "When I was younger, I fell in love with a Muslim who took me to spend a few months in his village. We lived near a mosque. To hear five times a day that magnificent raucous voice calling the believers to prostrate before God was heartrending.

I wanted to run into the street and answer to a higher authority."

"So schmaltzy!" they all cried. It's an understatement to say the class was rowdy. Pascal remained on the defensive and did not say a word. He wanted neither to support Fatima nor reveal his disagreements with her. All things said, he enjoyed such a brutal confrontation and persisted in believing something good would come out of it, since the clash of ideas is always beneficial.

On a personal level, there were other things to worry about. As the days went by, he found it increasingly difficult to put up with Maria. He who had once been an assiduous and tireless lover, always prepared to make love over and over again, now found himself devoid of desire at the sight of Maria's nudity. In bed, he turned his back on her and pretended to be asleep, claiming he was too tired to respond to her caresses.

Maria sensed the change that had come over him. She would go into fits of anger: "You can't even get a hard-on," she would shout. Or: "Are you in love with another girl?"

Pascal shrugged her off: "You're talking nonsense!" he said, taking offence.

"You're in love with a young girl," Maria exclaimed, paying little attention to his objection. "That's how men your age like them, when they still have the taste of milk in their mouths."

Such words crucified Pascal, who was constantly trying to find an elegant way of putting an end to their liaison.

By way of a distraction, Pascal would tell her the most preposterous stories that came to mind.

"You know what happened to me when I was a child and I still haven't forgotten, even today? One year, two boys from my school, two strapping guys with eyes screwed up with spite, would regularly beat me black and blue calling me 'Nobody's Boy.' *Nobody's Boy* is the title of a book by Hector Malot, which we'd studied in class and which was very popular with the students. I would come home in tears, sickened by this nickname, and throw myself into Eulalie's arms. 'I'm not a nobody, am I, Maman?' "

In his distress, Pascal took refuge; first of all, in alcohol. He who practically never drank—outside of an occasional neat rum to please Jean Pierre—began to get systematically drunk with Lazare. Almost every evening he could be found at Nostradamus enjoying endless bouts of alcohol. The owner had ingeniously invented a new attraction by the name of "Music of the World" where singers ran off a list of popular melodies, some coming from Cuba, others from Japan and Iran and even Australia. It was also a way for Pascal to return home as late as possible and thereby avoid another tête-à-tête with Maria.

The other subterfuge was to take refuge with his mother. Late into the night, he would discuss with her the role he was expected to play in the world.

"What do you think I should do?" he asked Fatima.

"I don't know exactly. Corazón would no doubt explain it better than I can," she replied with an inspired look. "Many are those who believe that our world, so incomprehensible, so violent, needs someone who can make it tolerant and reasonable again. Such an individual would base his actions on the experiments that others before him have attempted and not been able to achieve. Perhaps such a man is you."

One evening when he had stayed with Fatima until four in the morning, he found Maria waiting for him, dressed as if to go out.

"What are you doing here?" he asked.

"I was wrong. It's not a young girl you've fallen in love with but an old hag!"

"An old hag?" Pascal repeated dumbfounded. "It's nothing of the sort. I can explain everything."

But Maria was no longer listening and ran to her car. The glow from her headlights vanished before Pascal could gather his wits.

He went up to the first floor and shook Lazare awake. Sitting up in bed, rubbing his eyes from sleep, Lazare declared: "You say she left? Well, she's talked about doing it for a long time, but we never took her seriously. She was right: if you were no longer in love with her, you should have told her."

Pascal felt on the verge of relief. He had probably lacked courage, but who could throw the first stone? Few men are capable of looking a woman straight in the eye and telling her they no longer love her and that the relationship must end. In his distress, Pascal's only solution was to persevere with his nightly visits to Fatima who comforted him as best she could while talking of his mission.

One evening she greeted him as usual but her outpouring of affection was tinged with excitement. She handed him a briefcase filled with handwritten and typewritten documents.

"In my life," she declared, "I have loved two men: Corazón Tejara and Ahmed Ali-Roussy. Both of them abandoned me because their ambitions were greater than their love for me. They thought love for a woman to be despicable. But could we change the world without the help of women? Read these documents and come back when you have finished. Then tell me what you think."

Clutching the briefcase to his chest Pascal obediently went home. He clambered up to his office and began to read.

15

Throughout the eighteenth century, the little island of Asunción, situated to the south of Brazil, was a favorite of the captains of slave ships. They liked its deep-water creeks sheltered from the wind. They spent weeks there reviving the slaves who had suffered during the crossing from Africa, selling them later in Bahia as black gold.

The natives of Asunción had a pleasant disposition. They sold wild guinea fowl and succulent berries that grew between the rocks. Asunción had nothing in common with Brazil. It had been discovered by another navigator, this time a Spanish sailor. There had never been any thought of war or annexation between the two territories.

At the end of the nineteenth century, when slavery was finally abolished in Brazil, Asunción was left entirely without resources. Leaving behind the arid limestone plateaus which covered the small island, the population migrated en masse, mostly to the region of Recife. They worked in honorable professions such as as lawyers, doctors, and notaries, and married preferably light-skinned women. Common parlance took account of their characteristics and very soon, "honest as a Tejara from Asunción" became a household phrase.

Corazón Tejara was born on May 29, 1949, in Bahia, taking the life of his mother who died a few hours after giving birth. His father, Henrique, a physician by profession, chose the name Corazón in order to show how much he had loved his late wife. He raised his son with religious devotion, aided in this by his brother Espíritu.

Little Corazón was a brilliant scholar and became professor of history of religion. As for his character, he was both captivating and carefree. Women were attracted to him, and there was no counting the number of women he had bedded; one year it was twin sisters, the following year two first cousins, and later a mother and a daughter.

While he was a student at the University of Coimbra in Portugal a series of major events occurred that would change the course of his life. Unfortunately, there is no trace of what actually happened. Then one fine day, to everyone's surprise, he left his prestigious job as professor, exchanged his elegant linen and cotton clothes for a Mahatma Gandhi–type loincloth, and founded an ashram he called The Hidden God as a tribute to the philosopher Blaise Pascal. There, one could meditate on the state of the world and consider ways of building a better future.

The ashram's reputation gradually spread throughout the world; people came from the farthest corners of the planet to immerse themselves in its doctrine of peace and harmony. As for Corazón, he let his fawn-colored hair grow and curl down to his shoulders. Walking with a stick, he looked like a genuine hermit.

Pascal interrupted his reading and pushed aside the open documents. In compliance with Fatima's recommendation, he had read all night long and through part of the morning. One by one, the stars had been snuffed out by a great wind that had blown in from God knows where. Daylight had broken and the air was still cool. He could hear the roosters in the neighboring farmyards crow their first cock-a-doodle-dos while the street sweepers climbed down from their municipal garbage trucks to start washing the roads and pavements.

He had made up his mind. He was going to leave; he was going to discover Asunción and finally meet this father they had been talking about for years. Such a voyage would have nothing in common with his disappearance a few years back, of which he had no memory. This time he would keep his eyes wide open so as to learn who he was, where he came from, and above all, what was expected of him. He would fully grasp certain truths. He would visit the ashram his father had created.

Reading the documents his mother had given him was not enough. He needed to quench his thirst from a more torrid source, from life itself. Yet his decision had been made for more shameful reasons, which he kept secret. He had never traveled. He had never left this wretched island. Oh, to leave! To breathe a different air! Discover new faces! Visit other places and travel other paths! Suddenly, he felt he had been living like a prisoner all these years.

He decided to inform Fatima, Jean Pierre, and Judas Eluthère, the three people who meant the most to him, of his project. Fatima greeted him as usual showering him with kisses on his face and neck, something which oddly enough repelled him, as if their relationship didn't permit it.

She motioned to him to sit down next to her on the white sofa inlaid with purple pineapple motifs, and listened to him religiously. When he had finished, she declared, "I was expecting your reaction. You know what I think of Corazón Tejara. I shall never forgive him for having abandoned me, even though later on he insisted on writing to me. I was barely seventeen when he seduced me; I wrote letter after letter informing him of my condition. He pretended he had never received them. Is that how an individual who claims to be of a higher authority is meant to behave? If a man is incapable of managing his own life, how can he possibly claim to be equipped to change the face of the earth? I won't say anything more for fear of influencing you. If you want to go to Asunción, it is entirely up to you."

Jean Pierre, reserved as usual, refrained from passing comment. He merely asked Pascal if he had a passport since he never went anywhere. On hearing these words, Pascal realized that his father, too, regretted that he himself had never left the island. When you thought about it, there was something pathetic about this in comparison to his classmates who spent the summer months in the mother country and returned with eyes brimming with echoes of the films they had seen and mouths humming the words to songs they had heard. It was because Jean Pierre and Eulalie belonged to a generation who had no idea what the word "leisure" meant. The only time they took a break was when they visited Eulalie's family on their native island of Sargasse, who claimed they descended from the Vikings. Eulalie was very proud of her Swedish patronymic Bergman, like the world-famous movie maker.

Pascal loved his grandparents' old wooden house, porous to every noise. When the shadows reigned supreme, there was a burst of sounds: the croaking of frogs, the rustling of crickets, the whir of hummingbirds, and above all, the doleful cries of the spirits as they went about their business. Everything fell silent at dawn, awaiting in terror the start of another torrid day.

Finally Pascal went to look for Judas Eluthère, who rarely saw Fatima now. Pascal asked him to invite "the twelve disciples," as they were jokingly called. Where would they meet? At his place? That seemed out of the question ever since Maria and Marthe had left. In order to compensate for the loss of Marthe in particular, Pascal took his meals in a small restaurant called Le Mont Ventoux, managed by a young couple straight out of their native Provence. He ordered cod fritters, a court bouillon of red snapper and white yam, and, a specialty of the owners' native region, a sort of pizza stuffed with olives called a graton.

Pascal sensed that this meal before his departure for Asunción would be of capital importance. He predicted it would go down in history and be embellished with foreign terms such as *la última cena* that would go on to inspire some of our greatest painters. Consequently, he rummaged through the large wardrobe Eulalie had left him and found a set of hand-embroidered table linen with cross-stitched motifs that a friend had brought back from Madagascar. As soon as he spread out the tablecloth, the room took on a festive look.

The disciples arrived on the stroke of eight. Marcel Marcelin and José Donovo, the two homeless men who now lived in a cozy apartment paid for by Pascal, limped in last. The day before, Marcel had hurt himself raking the garden and he was in considerable pain.

Nothing extraordinary occurred during the meal and nothing memorable was pronounced. At most, a declaration from Pascal while he shared out the gratons: "Eat this in remembrance of me."

And yet he was filled with a strange emotion. Halfway through dessert he turned to Marcel Marcelin and said, "Let me take a look at your wound." Marcel obeyed and revealed his bruised legs wrapped with a huge dressing. Pascal, moved beyond words, went to fetch a bottle of antiseptic disinfectant and washed the terrible wound. He could not fathom why he felt the need to serve, to be humble among the humble. "All of you show me your feet," he commanded. At first the disciples, taken by surprise, refused, then they obeyed as if surrendering to a higher authority. They uncovered their feet, all bunions and corns and cracked nails, feet that suffered from being constantly imprisoned in their shoes. Pascal washed them all. When he had finished, he clasped his hands together and raised his eyes to Heaven. His mission was about to begin. He felt entirely free to lead his new existence.

The day before he left, he was beset with doubts once again. What was the point of going to Asunción? What would become of those he left behind? He could not help thinking of his foster father, mute and steeped in silence. When all was said and done, Pascal knew very little about him. Ever since he had laid his hands on his father's legs at José's, Jean Pierre had been feeling better. But was this the moment to abandon him? The years had aged him. Ever since Eulalie had died, he seemed he wanted nothing better than to go and join her.

At the end of the day, Pascal mounted his motorbike and drove straight ahead as if guided by an invisible hand. After having crossed Marais Salant, he arrived at the inlet at Viard, where slender coconut palms and toxic manchineels grew. Yachts anchored here to let off their well-to-do families, back from the isle of Petite Terre. Pascal lay down on the sand and the burgeoning shadows leaned over him, and took him up in their arms like an infant who can't understand why he is suffering.

16

The company who managed Frantz Fanon Airport claimed to have cultural ambitions and was called Aux Armes, Citoyens! after a well-known television program in the mother country. An exhibition by the name of *The Likely Lads* had been on display for weeks in the departure hall. The paintings depicted musicians from the 1920s who were almost as popular in their own right as the songs in vogue at the time.

The centerpiece depicted the famous Maurice Sylla putting his lips to his country flute, an instrument that reigned supreme on the island thanks to its subtlety and grace. The legend goes that a woman was in the depths of despair because she had lost her only child, who had been carried off by a sudden illness. One morning, on waking, she heard the inimitable sounds of a country flute and that's how she knew her child had been returned to her. Maurice Sylla was a handsome man of mixed blood, his thick black hair tied behind in a ponytail. In the image he was surrounded by a guitar player, a pianist, and a cellist.

For the moment none of the passengers were looking at the canvases, but were instead staring at Pascal who once again realized with annoyance how quickly people recognized him. Why did he arouse so much excitement? Why did the unlikely adventure of a new messiah destined to harmonize the world get so much coverage? Why did some people take sides with him while others held him to public obloquy? People were nurtured by a void and a malaise that no elections by universal suffrage could satisfy: they felt that neither the elected nor their ministers represented them.

Confronted with this wave of curiosity, Pascal never knew what attitude to adopt. He would indulge in such futile actions as smoking a Lucky Strike cigarette, munching gum, or sucking mint-flavored sweets. In spite of these attempts to weather it, he got the impression he looked ridiculous.

At the other end of the hall, a group accompanied a young girl, probably giving her words of encouragement. She was pretty in her bottle-green dress and her hair tied in a chignon. She seemed to make up her mind and sidled over to him in a way that betrayed her embarrassment. Holding out a notebook with a pink cover, she asked him: "Can I please have an autograph?"

"An autograph?" Pascal replied. "I'm nobody of interest. What use would it be?"

"What use?" the young girl exclaimed, surprised.

Feeling even more ridiculous, Pascal signed reluctantly and the young girl went and rejoined her friends.

The wait was soon over. Without informing him, the airline had upgraded Pascal and he found himself seated in first class among a set of elegant and self-satisfied passengers who, reassuringly, ignored him superbly. They probably wanted to prove that they held in contempt the gossip of the proletariat.

These passengers brought back memories of his childhood. Every day, once their work was done, friends of Jean Pierre and Eulalie used to come over for rum punch and sometimes even their evening meal. Pascal recalled their complacency, their cheap jokes, their tall stories, and he wondered whether his hatred for this class hadn't contributed to shaping his character, in particular that aspect of being perpetually dissatisfied.

He would have liked to visit Montreal, Paris, and especially New York. For some it was the door to the American dream, for others it was a noisy, chaotic metropolis that destroyed both body and soul. But the plane was traveling another route. He ended up falling asleep and only woke up when they landed.

On arrival at Castera, the capital of Asunción, although it was late afternoon, it was still very hot. Two men were waiting for him in the arrival hall; one was short and skinny with a magnificent moustache, the other seemed strangely familiar. It was not so much his pinstripe suit buttoned up to the collar nor his turned-down patent leather boots, like those of the three musketeers, that struck him. It wasn't his bearing either, for it looked as though he was hiding something behind his back. Perhaps a hump? What was it that made him both strange and familiar?

"Do I know you?" he asked with a smile. "Haven't we already met somewhere?"

The man did not answer the question and merely smiled vaguely: "I'm Espíritu Tejara, your father's brother. This is Victor, our chauffeur. You're in safe hands with him."

Thereupon he grabbed Pascal's suitcase and the three men went out. On reaching the street, Pascal thought he remembered and turned to Espíritu. "Didn't we meet at the Joyeux Noël bar?" Once again Espíritu evaded the question, and they climbed into the car.

Castera was a surprisingly attractive little town. Pascal had not expected to be so charmed by these old Spanish houses with their colorful facades in yellow, blue, and pink, like a child's drawing, some built around baroque fountains, others half-hidden under leafy trees. He envied the kids who were shouting and playing ball. He had never been like that, he thought. He had always been prim and proper, too well dressed, like a child prodigy, holding Eulalie's hand—herself clad like a ship setting out to sea—or else gripping the hand of a more simply dressed servant.

Espíritu suddenly turned to him. "I have something rather unpleasant to tell you. You will not see your father unfortunately. He had to leave in a hurry for India."

"India?" Pascal repeated in amazement, wondering to himself, Father, why have you forsaken me?

The car careered down a slope, went up a hill, made several turns, then stopped in front of the ashram The Hidden God, which comprised a long, low building that housed the lecture rooms and classes to the left, and, to the right, the lodgings—genuine monks' cells furnished with a bed, a table, and two chairs. Espíritu and Victor rapidly took their leave. "I imagine," Espíritu said, "you must be exhausted and would like to sleep."

How true! Pascal threw himself onto his bed and immediately fell into a dreamless sleep until he was woken up by the sun streaming into the room, as he had forgotten to close the shutters. Despite the early morning hour, it was already very hot and you could sense that the day would be suffocating. Pascal quickly got dressed and was about to go out to have breakfast in the restaurant he had seen the day before on the ground floor when there was a knock on the door. It was Espíritu pushing a trolley.

"I hope I'm not disturbing you," he apologized. Thereupon he laid out the coffee table and the two men sat down opposite each other for a frugal breakfast.

"I've come to explain," Espíritu declared, "that your father left for India on purpose."

"On purpose?" Pascal repeated, increasingly disconcerted.

"Yes," Espíritu continued. "It's because he does not want to tell you exactly who he is and, consequently, who you are. I'm telling you the truth, because I've grown very fond of you."

"I don't understand what you mean," Pascal said, staring wide-eyed.

"For instance," Espíritu retorted, "death."

"Death," Pascal repeated. "Now I'm even more confused."

Espíritu waved his hand and repeated, "Yes, death is at the center of our lives. As the saying goes: nobody gets out alive. And yet we each transform death into what suits us. For Christians it's the door to eternal life, for Muslims it leads to the Garden of Allah, and for Hindus it's the gate to Nirvana."

Thereupon Espíritu burst out laughing. "Don't take me for a pedant, drink up your coffee. You probably don't know it, but it was me who raised your father. When he was small,

I put him on my back and off we went on our travels. You can't imagine the countries we visited: South Africa, Australia, Sri Lanka, and more."

During this conversation, Pascal gradually recuperated his senses. In actual fact, he resigned himself to making the most of an unexpected situation. His father was absent, tough luck for him.

The following morning, he attended a class on the history of religion. The room was packed. There were Argentinians, Colombians, Americans, and Chileans; as if all these people, so different from each other, had gathered together in their search for a better world.

The following days, Pascal became friends with a group of Indians from Jaipur whose leader, called Revindra, wore a loincloth like Mahatma Gandhi. Objecting to the notion of *Homo hierarchicus*, they were all in favor of making the untouchables full-fledged citizens. They organized a colloquium entitled "The Equality between Men: The Unattainable Myth." Listening to the speakers one after the other, Pascal realized for the first time that they were speaking the truth. Equality between men is a myth. No need to go as far as India to track down untouchables though, he thought.

17

Among the group of Indians, there was a certain Sarojini. Sarojini had all the grace and beauty of an *apsara* and in the pools of her large black eyes swirled the pain and revolt of a humiliated youth. "My father and mother," she liked to recollect in her contralto voice, "were in charge of emptying and washing the chamber pots of entire families, since at that time in Jaipur there were no such things as running water or water closets. My father would then collect the excrements in a bag and empty them out as fertilizer over a field on which we grew asparagus. Throughout his life, an atrocious smell, a veritable stink, clung to him and I could never bring myself to kiss him."

Pascal soon fell passionately in love with Sarojini.

Ever since Maria had left, he had lived in extreme solitude. Everything had happened so quickly. Marthe and Lazare had left the morning following his quarrel with Maria. When Pascal had knocked on the door of the house where they had taken refuge, Maria had refused to come and meet him in the living room and he had been unable to explain matters. Later he heard that she had set up house with a Frenchman who raised chickens and sold them in the market.

Although she intimidated him, he opened his heart to Sarojini. To his surprise, she let herself be fondled then kissed and soon the couple fell into a routine. Sarojini was very athletic, much like Fatima. Wearing a straw hat, but, unlike Fatima, hiding her legs in a pair of white cotton stretch pants, she would sprint over the limestone rocks worn away by time and send them rolling. She then took Pascal to the Blue Lagoon, an American floating-village resort. There she would swim the butterfly stroke, much to the admiration of the students come to practice with their teacher. When she came out of the water, they applauded her. Some even asked her for a selfie. How far she had come as the daughter of untouchables!

During his daily visits Pascal never tired of the Blue Lagoon's beauty. To the right, the sea; the sea forever starting over and over, rippling as far as the horizon, like molten metal in places. And to the left, the long stretches of white sand and the red and green leafy sea grape trees.

One lunchtime, while they were drinking a refreshing fruit juice cocktail, Sarojini suddenly put down her glass and looked Pascal straight in the eye: "You know what people are saying? They say you are the natural child of Corazón Tejara."

"Natural child?" Pascal joked. "What does that mean? Aren't all children natural?"

As he remarked that his joke had fallen flat and that Sarojini continued to look at him in all seriousness, he shrugged his shoulders and confessed. "Yes, Corazón Tejara is my father, but he was never there to take care of me. I came here to meet him but he has left. You are perhaps luckier than I am, for I have never seen him. Have you met him?"

"I met him in India," Sarojini said. "Corazón Tejara is a god. He founded an association to bring together all the untouchables, whom he calls the Children of God. He lends us his support in all our struggles. After Mahatma Gandhi he is without a doubt the most admired personality in India."

Pascal was at a loss for words. What had he achieved? What had he to offer? He still hadn't done anything to make the world more at peace or hospitable to its inhabitants.

Despite the fact that there was an excellent restaurant at the ashram, Sarojini insisted on inviting Pascal to the little house she shared with two other Indian women, Gayatri and Ananda. Since she was vegetarian, she took pleasure in having him relish the taste of fish, seafood, and shellfish. Strangely enough, Gayatri and Ananda took an immediate dislike to Pascal. Taking refuge behind their poor knowledge of French and English, they barely spoke to him at all.

One day he ended up complaining to Sarojini, who simply replied rather brusquely, "It's because they have other things on their mind. Do you remember why we are so far from home, why we have come to this ashram: because we are waging a struggle." On hearing these inimical words, Pascal felt hurt. It's true he was lighthearted and obviously did not take the work at the ashram as seriously as Sarojini.

In fact, there was no time wasted. Every afternoon was devoted to classes, lectures, and conferences. Every topic was given top priority: the reception of migrants in Europe, the sequels of apartheid in South Africa, the fires in the Amazon rainforest, and the mass shootings in the USA.

Pascal accompanied Sarojini obediently but reluctantly to every event, convinced she would do better to focus on improving her behavior since she was not as agreeable a partner as Maria.

She could remain hours on end without saying a word, ruminating thoughts which she kept to herself. At other times, on the contrary, she was voluble. She would pour out her feelings to her heart's content, shedding tears when she remembered something painful, detailing every endeavor she had undertaken to get where she was today, i.e., head nurse at the main hospital in Jaipur. Such verbosity was a surprise to Pascal, who was a man of few words and little inclined to take pity on himself. Such outpourings allowed him to discover the sensual delight of talking about oneself.

Sarojini's great passion was dancing. Every evening she would tie a bracelet of bells around her ankles and go and join the dancers at the ashram. Then they would go and have dinner in a nearby tavern where the waiters served them carafes filled with the national drink, cachaca.

They had to wait for nightfall until they were both finally alone. They would then go to Pascal's place and throw themselves into each other's arms. Love took on the form of a long-repressed savage cry. Unfortunately, once again, Pascal was not entirely satisfied, since Sarojini refused to spend the whole night with him. She would wash herself in the tiny bathroom and leave in the dark while he remained prostrate and disillusioned.

This relationship lasted several weeks, then the love that had timidly wormed its way into Pascal's heart took root and dominated him entirely. He could no longer imagine life without Sarojini. One day he was unable to restrain himself any longer and, after a concert at the ashram, he asked Sarojini to marry him and return home with him.

She looked up in amazement.

"You want me to marry you? You did say the word 'marry'?"

"I want nothing more," Pascal replied, his heart beating like a stripling who declares his passion to his beloved for the first time. "My country is small. Some will tell you nothing much happens there, but I will make you love it as much as I love you."

"It is only fair to tell you that I live with someone else and he is waiting for me in Jaipur," she said.

Pascal got the impression that someone had hit him over the head and that he was suddenly blinded by a thousand stars. "And I must confess," she continued, "he's not an Indian, but an Englishman, a 'White man,' as we say back home."

"And so what?" Pascal replied in amazement.

Thereupon she got up, rapidly collected her belongings spread over the table, and angrily uttered, "Don't tell me it's of no importance. Don't give me one of those rosy speeches we hear at the ashram. Don't tell me you think it's normal for an Untouchable to live with an Englishman. If you do, then you're pretending to ignore the humiliations and suffering being heaped on your unfortunate untouchables."

Before he had time to react, she walked out of the bar and into the night. After such a quarrel, there was no question of her spending the night with him again. Pascal was mad with grief but didn't know what caused him the most pain. He had confessed his love and it had gone unheard. He went home sadly. All night long he soaked his pillow with tears while his blood aroused his body in burning waves.

The first thing he did the following morning was to dash to her house. Gayatri and Ananda, seated in front of their morning coffee, claimed they did not know where Sarojini was. All day long, Sarojini remained invisible. Pascal dined alone on a tuna sandwich and slices of avocado. Filled with a disastrous premonition, he went back to the ashram for the last time, but could not find the girl he was looking for. Sadly, he went back home and climbed into bed.

18

Very early the following morning there was a knock on the door. It was Espíritu.

"She's gone," he declared. "I've just dropped her off at the airport."

"Gone? Who's gone?" Pascal asked, dumbfounded.

"Sarojini, of course!"

"Sarojini! Didn't she at least leave a letter or a message?"

"No, nothing at all," Espíritu replied. "But, you know, women are fickle creatures, that one in particular. She has a very bad reputation; I should have warned you. For over ten years she's been shacked up with an English guy. It's an open secret. When they meet at receptions, they pretend not to know each other."

Pascal put his head between his hands. Espíritu sat down familiarly on the bed. "On the other hand I've got excellent news for you. Your father, Corazón Tejara, will be at the ashram tomorrow. He managed to leave India earlier than planned."

Pascal's heart was torn between pain and anger. Both devastated and furious, he thought, He won't find me. I shall be far, far away before he gets back. Who does Corazón Tejara take me for? For a plaything? For a toy you can have fun with and pass around from hand to hand until it's of no further use and then throw away?

Pascal quickly ate his breakfast with Espíritu and, when the latter left, he walked across the square in front of the ashram and went to find the taxi driver he vaguely knew. The driver needed some persuading, but then agreed to drive him to Recife the next day for a small fortune.

He had a whole day to kill. Whenever he didn't know what to do with himself, Pascal went to look at the sea, but he avoided The Blue Lagoon, which was always filled with a crowd of students from the neighboring colleges or with residents from the ashram. Its vast expanse of deep blue soothed his anxiety. So, this stay at Castera had ended in a double failure. Not only had he not seen his father but he had been unable to seduce the woman he had hungered for. Sarojini had left for Jaipur and most likely he would never see her again.

The following morning at dawn he left Castera. Previously, a rickety wooden bridge had linked Asunción to the land of Brazil. A complicated system of green and red flags indicated when it was safe for motorists to cross. Then, at the start of the century, an American company had built a suspension bridge along the lines of the Golden Gate Bridge in San Francisco, a bridge so perfect the locals took photos of themselves leaning on the railings of the pedestrian walkway. Exhausted, Pascal fell asleep on exiting the bridge and slept while they drove along the wide highway lined with red cedar and mahogany trees reaching for the sky.

This time, his sleep was not dreamless. He saw Espíritu, a pair of white wings spread out behind his back, looking like one of the archangels, Gabriel or Michael, in all but the sardonic expression on his face. He saw Sarojini running away but he never managed to catch up to her. He also dreamed of his unknown father, to whom he attributed a handsome bearing in keeping with everything he had heard about him: a well-groomed beard, his hair parted down one side, and a fine suit of clothes.

Suddenly he woke up. It was probably because the car had unexpectedly stopped. The highway was clogged with vehicles at a standstill, all their headlights full on. Night had fallen and the low purple sky was streaked with white clouds blown along by a scorching wind.

Pascal had the impression he had become a little boy again, a time when his nights were constantly peopled with nightmares and he would wake up trembling and soaked through in his bedroom despite the huge Sacred Heart of Jesus on the wall. He would then utter cries of terror that reached the ears of Eulalie who, serene and soothing in her white dressing gown, would come and comfort him and dry his eyes.

"What's going on?" he asked the driver.

"Apparently there's been a bomb attack in Recife," the driver answered. "They're stopping all the cars coming in and going out."

"A bomb attack?" Pascal cried. "I had no idea they happened here in Brazil as well."

"They happen everywhere," the driver retorted. "The world's gone crazy."

They came to a virtual standstill for almost two hours in a traffic jam of cars and motorbikes. Finally, four policemen drew level with them and brutally shone torches in their faces.

"IDs. Vehicle registration papers," they barked. Pascal and the driver complied. The policemen bombarded Pascal with questions since he was a foreigner and consequently a potential suspect. When he explained in detail why he was in the country, they let him go.

They reached Recife around four in the morning. Pascal had chosen the Sanseverina Hotel because it was close to the airport; he didn't expect it to be lit up like day in the middle of the night. In the lounge, an elegant crowd was laughing and chatting excitedly. Waiters in impeccable uniforms were serving whisky and cachaca and everyone was clinking glasses and drinking merrily.

Without knowing exactly how, Pascal managed to find himself in with a group of men and women, some of whom were very pretty, especially one redhead with large, elongated green eyes, who went by the name of Oriane.

"Recife is one of the loveliest towns in Brazil," one of the men declared. "You're leaving tomorrow? Then you won't see anything."

"It's because I was at Castera," Pascal answered apologetically, and since the others didn't react, he thought it necessary to explain: "I was at The Hidden God ashram."

Everyone burst out laughing. "Don't tell us," one of the men said, "that you're one of Corazón Tejara's disciples!"

Pascal nodded. "I came a long way to meet him."

The group laughed even louder. "Don't you know he's crazy?" one of them said. "He talks about improving the world. Inequality is engraved at the core of the universe. Some people are beautiful, some are ugly, some are tall, some are short, others are fat and others are thin. How can he solve such disparities?"

"Have you heard he's created a political party?" another person asked.

"A political party!" a third person exclaimed. "That's impossible. What will he call it?"

"The Religious Lunatics," someone suggested.

Once again there was a general outburst of laughter. But we know full well how disjointed conversations are, and soon they broached another topic.

After a while, Oriane grabbed him by the wrist. "Come with me," she smiled. "I want you to look at the paintings in the other room." Was it an invitation? Pascal hesitated then followed her and it turned out to be one of the most delicious nights he had ever spent. Yet when he returned to his room in the early hours of the morning he felt terrible. He took no pride at having seduced Oriane so easily. On the contrary. He felt ashamed recollecting the cries they had both uttered. He knew only too well he was not the first of Oriane's partners, and certainly not the last. She would soon forget him and he'd be nothing more than the vague souvenir of a passing moment.

In his despondency he began to regret not having met his father. If he hadn't been stupidly flushed by a whimsy of self-conceit, perhaps he would have discovered who Corazón Tejara was. Was he a benefactor or the half-crazed messiah they said he was? If he hadn't left, he would have found out for himself.

When he went back to his room, he opened wide the window and gazed at the night that had flooded the town. Faced with this curtain of black silk he swore that henceforth he would not be The Man Without Qualities but An Inconsequential Man. He didn't know that such promises are impossible to keep, for life plays tricks on you which you can't outsmart.

19

The plane landed at Frantz Fanon Airport at six in the morning and Pascal breathed in the inimitable smell of his island: the smell of salt, the sharp tang of the sea, the brackish smell of the mud churning around the crater of the volcano, and the smell of ripening fruit displayed on this gigantic tropical tray. This time it was a group of lycée students off to the mother country under the supervision of their French teacher who came to ask him for an autograph. He willingly complied before taking a taxi to drive him back to Marais Salant.

On arrival, he thought the house looked filthy, empty, and abandoned. Distraught, he climbed up to his office, which would perhaps be more welcoming, and without further ado began to write about his latest experiences. To his surprise, his head was teeming with ideas. At the outset, he thought this sojourn had been a complete failure. He soon discovered it was quite the opposite.

First of all, India. Thanks to his stay at the ashram, his perception of the country had changed. He had thought India was a land swarming with men and women sentenced to a life of famine. On the contrary, he had been dazzled by its extraordinarily rich culture. He had also realized the diversity of the world and the complexity of its problems. For example, so many years after the end of apartheid, why did South Africa remain a divided land still in search of stability? As for his violent passion for Sarojini, he told himself it allowed him to assess his human nature.

In short, his pen was racing across the paper when there was a knock on the door. It was Maria—the last person he expected to see at such a moment.

"You! What do you want from me?" he asked brutally.

She showered him with kisses and murmured, "I've come to apologize; I had no idea Fatima was your mother."

"Who told you?" he asked.

"Judas Eluthère," she replied.

It turned out that Pascal was only too happy to see Maria again, for her adoring looks were a comfort against the painful rejection he had recently suffered. He could still be desirable. He was not lacking in charm.

The same afternoon, Maria moved in with him at Marais Salant and they resumed their life together. To tell the truth, in the days that followed, Pascal got the impression he was not being entirely honest and was ashamed of those impulses he was unable to control. He decided to go and spend a few days on the island of Sargasse in the house that once belonged to the Bergman grandparents. They had both died a few years previously, but the house was still standing and was maintained as best as possible by Eulalie's brother. One morning then he and Maria climbed aboard the ferry, making their way among the sailors who were noisily piling crates of salt fish and smoked herring at the front of the boat.

Soon, lapping gently against the wharf, the sea began to surge and heave, and a great many passengers fell ill and vomited in little paper bags handed out by the crew. The crossing lasted forty-five minutes. At the jetty in Sargasse, the market women screwing up their faces against the sun and wearing large straw hats were selling the island's specialties: crab pâtés and cakes made of honey or stuffed with crystallized fruit.

Pascal regretted he hadn't come to Sargasse more often. It was a breath of fresh air such as he hadn't felt since he was a child. The Bergman grandparents had barely been able to speak French; the grandmother was always full of delightful and unexpected expressions such as "the body is not feeling well today" and "the body is in a scrunch this morning." She used to tell tales to little Pascal, which he had difficulty understanding. She would let him swim naked in the sea. It was at Sargasse he had his first erotic experience at the sight of Manon, a young girl who deposited two bottles of fresh milk, tinted slightly blue, every morning on the kitchen worktop from her father's cows. Gazing at her breasts, her buttocks, and her legs Pascal had a hard-on, though at that time he did not yet know what a hard-on meant.

On Sundays, Grandfather and Grandmother invited their friends for lunch, a dozen descendants of Vikings like themselves, who would bounce Pascal on their knees despite his color. At lunchtime they served white sausage, Grandmother's specialty; she would replace the pig's blood and the stale bread with a spicy conch purée. Some thought such a mixture inedible, others delicious, but everyone stuffed themselves full.

Of an evening, Grandfather Bergman took little Pascal's left hand and Grandmother Bergman grabbed his right and the three of them would set off for a two-kilometer ramble. Since the grandfather did not like wearing shoes—not flip-flops, sneakers, or button boots—his large white feet would pad along the paved road, his toes inflamed with corns. They would reach a bar called Les Diablotins overlooking the sea, which you could hear raging below as it thrashed over the reefs. Grandfather Bergman then perched the child on his knees and allowed him to put his finger in his glass of rum and sometimes suck it. Pascal would fall into a delicious sleep. Yes, it was a rare time of perfect bliss.

Up till then, Pascal had been especially susceptible to Maria's charms: the rounded curves of her breasts, the high lift of her buttocks, and the medial line down her back. At Sargasse, since his desire for her had lessened and he often had to force himself to take her in his arms, he took an interest in her spiritual side.

One day she asked him, "You went to look for your father. What did he tell you?"

Pascal frowned. "You'll be surprised to know that I never met him. The trip was a complete waste of time."

She didn't say another word, preferring to keep her thoughts to herself and remaining discreet with regards to her emotions and those of others.

At the age of four she had lost her father. He had left her mother with four rabbit hutches where a variety of red-eyed iceberg rabbits scampered around, so called because of their very white fur. At the age of five, she accompanied her mother to the market where she had a stall. She had very little schooling. Yet together with her sister Marthe, she had educated her young brother Lazare, who had passed his vocational training certificate and at one time had taught mathematics at a private school.

Pascal was heartbroken to have to set off again for Marais Salant. Two days after they got back, Marthe and Lazare turned up without a word of explanation, but, judging by the number of suitcases and wicker baskets, Pascal understood they had come back to move in with their sister as if nothing had happened. He could no longer put up with this lack of consideration for others and simply kicked them out, sending off Maria too for good measure. Deep down, he told himself he could no longer tolerate the lies he had lived. If he was to go on thinking he could change the world, he should get used to looking the truth straight in the eye.

Once again, he found himself alone and glad to be so. In the morning he would carefully prepare his class for Le Bon Kaffé and, since two of his disciples had decided to write about him, how they met, and what they had learned from his teaching, he spent the afternoons correcting their text.

He devoted some days to writing a book he called *Just a Word or Two*, which would be his major work wherein he intended to prove that this globalization, which we're sick and tired of hearing about, was in fact a modern form of slavery. The rich nations of the West forced the poor countries of the South, where labor was plentiful and cheap, to manufacture the goods they needed at minimum cost.

He was also anxious to see his mother who had returned home. Unfortunately, he did not find her in the mood he had hoped for. She was living with a writer whose book *I Submit* was on the point of becoming an international bestseller. She had only one idea in mind: couldn't this writer too give lectures at Le Bon Kaffé? Pascal promised to talk it over with Judas Eluthère—reluctantly, for the writer looked conceited and pleased with himself. As for the purpose of his visit to Castera, Fatima merely asked him nonchalantly, "So you didn't even see your father? I'm not surprised. I told you so, didn't I?" That was her sole remark.

Once he had appointed a manager to run The Garden of Eden, Jean Pierre rented out the huge place he had lived with Eulalie for fifty years and came to settle in Marais Salant. He too asked Pascal offhandedly, "So you didn't see your father?" Pascal thought he discerned a note of satisfaction in his voice as if he was only too happy not to have to share his paternity.

20

Pascal could not forget Sarojini. She was increasingly on his mind. Untouchable Sarojini. He thought about her not because of her physique or because, with hindsight, his pride was flattered that he had held her in his arms and possessed such a partner, but because of her complex and changeable character, which had given him so much trouble. He imagined her and her shiny black hair striding along the hospital corridors or shopping in the market. In his wildest dreams, he could see himself turning up in Jaipur, dispensing of her English lover, and bringing her home to his island.

Thanks to Sarojini, he realized what counted was not simply a woman's physique—her breasts, her buttocks, and her lips, a constant source of elixir—but the way she helps you understand the complexities of this world. Finally, he couldn't stand it any longer. He decided to write to her at the address at The Hidden God hoping the ashram would forward his letter. But after many long weeks he still hadn't received an answer. Never mind, he would wait as long as it required.

He made a regular habit of walking along the seashore every evening. Dusk fell, fleeting like the love he had experienced with Sarojini. At this time of day, the sea was considered too cold for a swim, so there were just a few teenagers kicking a ball, secretly hoping one day to become another Lilian Thuram or, who knows, King Pelé. Pascal dropped down on the sand, and gradually darkness sewed him in like a jersey which has become too tight. He decided to return home now that the sea breeze was becoming cooler, making him shiver.

When he was not walking along the seashore, he would delve into the heart of the crowded districts of Fonds-

Zombi. Bordering the little streets that wound haphazardly through La Treille and Saint Ferréol, the shacks were left wide open once the heat of the day had died down. Children were running and quarreling along the pavements. At every crossroad, women were seated on small benches selling codfish fritters, topi tamboos, and fruit-flavored sorbets. Sometimes he would go into a small bar by the name of Le Calalou Fumé but whenever he entered the conversations would stop and all heads would turn in his direction.

Pascal was now used to being recognized everywhere he went. What did they expect from him? He didn't know exactly. He had no idea that this popular fervor, as heady as a perfume, could suddenly disappear or change nature. He had little inkling that these expressions and smiles now so gentle could become as scathing and razor-sharp as a hurl of stones. In short, he hadn't taken into account the meaning of the hackneyed saying, "One is reminded of the fine line between triumph and disaster."

A few weeks after his return to Marais Salant, a strange event occurred. One Sunday, on coming back from mass, the Martins, the charming neighbors who were devout Catholics and lived next door to the left, stopped off at Pascal's house with one of those sheepish looks that indicate something unpleasant is about to be said.

"Have you noticed," they whispered, "there's a homeless man living in a shed at the bottom of your garden?" Pascal was very surprised and hadn't noticed anything out of place. The homeless were badly treated on the island. When they roamed along the beach, they were accused of being a blight on the tourist industry and the police would sweep them up and manhandle them at the police station where they sometimes spent several days.

"It's because," the Martins continued, more and more embarrassed, "he pisses and defecates shamelessly all over the place. Our little girl who's just turned four might see him and it would be outrageous."

Pascal dashed down to the bottom of the garden and indeed saw a rough shelter made of cardboard and plywood planks that had been erected behind the mahogany trees. For the moment the place was deserted but when he tried to push open the door he was assailed by a terrible stench. He left, but concerned he returned a few hours later: a lamp had been lit inside and was casting a yellowish light.

When he knocked, a man appeared. He got the feeling he had already seen him somewhere. It wasn't just his pinstripe twill suit he thought he recognized nor his high turned-down boots like those of the three musketeers, but mainly his posture. It was as if he was hiding something behind his back. A hump, perhaps?

"Haven't we already met?" Pascal inquired, intrigued. The man shrugged his shoulders distractedly. Burning with curiosity, Pascal took a closer look and after a while it suddenly dawned on him: "You look a lot like Espíritu Tejara, my father's brother." The man threw back his head and burst out laughing, which could have meant a number of things.

"Aren't all men brothers?" he said. Thereupon he suddenly stopped laughing and took on a solemn air. "Can't you see this dark shadow? This shadow all around you that's weighing you down?"

"What shadow?" Pascal asked, irritated.

Once again, the man did not answer and went inside his makeshift shed. Braving the stench, Pascal followed him.

"I've come to warn you," Espíritu or his spitting image said, "that you are heading for trouble. Get ready to be treated like a pariah, but don't be surprised, it is our lot and our role as Tejaras."

Pascal decided not to take notice of his incomprehensible words, and declared, "I could call the cops; they would take you by force to the nearest police station. But it's not in my nature. I prefer to ask you politely to leave. Whoever you are, you have nothing to do here."

The man smirked. "I only came to help you."

"To do what?" Pascal asked.

The man rummaged in his pockets and pulled out a small red case mounted on a leather strip. "Whenever you need my help, press on this and I'll come to your rescue."

Pascal took the object, looked at it curiously, and stuffed it in his pocket.

Early next morning, Pascal once more dashed down to the bottom of the garden, but found the makeshift shed empty apart for a bucket full of a yellowish liquid that turned out to be urine. He trudged back to the house, wondering whether he hadn't been the victim of a cautionary nightmare. Why had Espíritu come to Marais Salant? What was he trying to tell him? Why did he talk of a threatening danger? What was this shadow weighing him down? What did it all mean? By dint of filling his head with all sorts of questions throughout the day, he didn't sleep a wink that night. The following morning, however much he downed all sorts of herb teas, he was left with a high fever and a thumping heart.

21

Despite the troubling visit by Espíritu or his spitting image, Pascal had little inkling of the thunderbolt that was about to turn his life upside down. The man had been right: a shadow was oppressing him and it suddenly burst like a flash of lightning. One morning he received a letter from Monsieur Pacheco, back from Japan, bluntly informing him that his classes at the company were cancelled and he was dismissed from his job.

Seething with anger, he went straight to Judas Eluthère's place. Judas Eluthère had revealed his true colors and announced his coming out by setting up house with Kassem Kémal, a Lebanese lawyer he had met in the mother country. Pascal was not surprised. He too had almost fallen for the charms of this young man, who was so handsome, so elegant, and so sophisticated. Judas and Kassem, both vegetarians, were sharing a dinner of codfish chiquetaille and plantains when Pascal called.

After having read the letter, Judas thundered, "This is illegal, it's a breach of contract. During the meeting we had on the subject, he promised us he would do nothing of the sort. We'll show him he can't get away with it. Just you wait and see!"

Thereupon he invited Pascal to sit down and have dinner with them.

They were eating dessert, a cake layered with bitter orange marmalade, when a visitor walked in. Dominique Origny was a nondescript, balding little man but a star on national television. He had made a name for himself a few years earlier on account of his TV programs featuring famous international personalities such as John Kennedy, Robert Kennedy, Indira Gandhi, Nelson Mandela, Mikhail Gorbachev, Oprah Winfrey, etc. For the time being he was known for his program *Face to Face*, which consisted of inviting two people to openly debate their different viewpoints. He was full of anecdotes about the celebrities he met on a daily basis and his appearance made a lively end to the dinner.

At one point he turned to Pascal and asked, "Would you be willing to appear on *Face to Face?*"

"Me!?" Pascal exclaimed.

"Yes, you. You would make an excellent debater," Dominique claimed, "face to face with Monsieur Pacheco whose ideas, Judas tells me, you don't agree with at all."

Pascal refused to commit himself. "Let me first of all meet him," he said.

"He's a great charmer," Kassem warned him.

"Charmer or not," Judas Eluthère exclaimed loudly, "I'll give him a piece of my mind."

Apparently Judas's rage had no tangible result, since days passed and Pascal heard nothing more about his position. At the end of the month, he sadly mounted his motorbike and rode to Sagalin where he was to give his last lecture and finally meet Norbert Pacheco, who had invited him to lunch.

To his surprise his students were waiting for him. Crowded into the main courtyard, they welcomed him with a volley of cheers. The classroom was crammed full. Even those who had never come to his lectures before arrived now in such numbers that they had to sit on the floor. And even those who had always challenged his ideas seemed sorry to see him go.

Once the class was over, he shook numerous hands, and with beating heart Pascal went to join Monsieur Pacheco for lunch. His office was on the top floor, richly furnished and decorated with photos of men Pascal didn't recognize. He thought one of them might be the Pandit Nehru, but there again he might have been mistaken.

No question about it, Monsieur Pacheco was a very handsome man, elegantly dressed and wearing button boots by a famous bootmaker. Yet you could conjecture the formidable predator that lay hidden deep inside him. It was rumored he had seduced several of his female employees and even fathered a child with two of them. He was accompanied by two men, both dressed as elegantly as himself.

"Here's my enemy!" he smiled, taking Pascal familiarly by the arm.

On hearing his words, his two acolytes burst into fawning laughter.

"No way an enemy!" Pascal protested. "I'm not your enemy. Let's just say we don't share the same ideas."

"There's no good restaurant in Sagalin," Monsieur Pacheco continued. "If you like, we can drive as far as Saint-Marcelin. There I'll take you to a small bistro, which is nothing to look at, but where the cuisine is some of the best I have ever tasted."

The four men went out to the parking lot, which was guarded by an old man who stood to attention, made a brief military salute, and greeted Monsieur Pacheco with a servile "Good day, Boss!"

They drove off to the village of Saint-Marcelin. Did it deserve the term "village"? It consisted of a dozen shacks lined up along the seashore, where the sea lay quiet and blue and good as gold. Monsieur Pacheco set off towards one of the more modest dwellings made of wattle and daub and summarily painted gray and green. The owner, an Indian with curly hair, rushed towards the arrivals and embraced Monsieur Pacheco as if he wanted to make a point to everyone that he was one of his best customers.

"Today I can offer you a tuna tart served with a breadnut gratin. I'm sure you'll love it!" he proclaimed.

The men sat down and drank their rum punches.

Monsieur Pacheco turned to Pascal. "Don't think I canceled your lectures as a kind of harassment. Quite simply, I think our employees need time to reflect on your ideas. Apparently you've just come back from Brazil. Such a magnificent country, isn't it?"

"I wasn't there as a tourist," Pascal replied. "To be exact I was at Castera, at The Hidden God ashram, with people who want to change the world and make it better."

"And what solutions did you come up with?" Monsieur Pacheco asked, jokingly.

"We haven't found the answer yet. For the time being we are at the stage of thinking it over," Pascal replied, susceptible to his mockery.

Monsieur Pacheco ran his fingers through his hair, which floated down to his shoulders.

"We at Le Bon Kaffé have found a solution. We believe that in order to improve men's lives you need to give them excellent wages and good housing—something we do with our employees. We also believe that their children require a good education in the best of schools so that the social ladder functions correctly."

"That's probably why your employees are demonstrating en masse across the island," Pascal said sarcastically.

One of the men held out his hand. "Don't argue," the man said brusquely. "We're here to exchange ideas."

The meal ended without further incident, all four of them talking about this and that. Just another useless conversation, Pascal said to himself, disappointed.

22

Now that he was deprived of his classes at Le Bon Kaffé, Pascal felt his life sinking into boredom. He was not getting anywhere with the writing of *Just a Word or Two*. Most of the time he stayed idle. While correcting his disciples' texts, he realized that what they pompously called his teaching amounted to next to nothing. A series of clichés, the same old ideas, in short nothing but precepts passed on by others before him.

In order to take his mind off things, he went back to Fonds-Zombi to listen to the writer who lived with his mother. This literary evening ended up demoralizing him. Sitting in front of a public of affluent, well-dressed, well-heeled, well-groomed readers, the writer was frenetically signing his books, which were selling like hotcakes out of a bookshop in the capital.

Once this ceremony was over, Pascal went home, had dinner, and went to bed. He had finally accepted Dominique Origny's offer, after Dominique had insisted that the *Face to Face* encounter with Monsieur Pacheco would be the ideal opportunity to express his dreams for a peaceful society on a sound footing.

A few days later, he received an invitation to attend a country flute concert for the fortieth anniversary of Le Bon Kaffé followed by a lecture entitled "How to build a company best adapted for the modern world." Despite this tempting program, he decided not to go. It would only contradict the *Face to Face* opportunity he had just accepted. He therefore stayed home and, in order to pass the time, watched an old film by Alfred Hitchcock on the television: either *Marnie* or *The Birds*, he couldn't say which. In any case, the heroine was blonde, young, and pretty. He ended up falling asleep in front of the TV set.

When he woke up with a bitter taste in his mouth around two in the morning the television programs had been turned upside down. An hysterical newsreader was announcing that an attack had been carried out at Sagalin, at Le Bon Kaffé. Suddenly wide awake, Pascal was wondering how on earth there could be an attack in a place where all local leaders did was to take orders hat in hand from the mother country. An attack! They must be kidding!

Not knowing quite what to do, he climbed onto his motorbike and headed for Sagalin. He wasn't the only one to have this idea. The road was choked with charabanc coaches, their passengers weeping and chanting hymns.

The hospital at Sagalin was an old wooden building with no modern services. A considerable crowd had gathered in the garden; it drew aside on seeing Pascal, who was surprised by the sudden onslaught of hostile looks. Did they think he was mixed up in this tragic business? He who hated violence and wouldn't harm a fly.

He learned that Monsieur Pacheco had been killed by two bullets to the head and that there were a dozen dead and many more wounded. Monsieur Pacheco, such a handsome, well-dressed man, and who had made such an impression on him. The strange thing about death is that although it is journey's end and unavoidable, it never fails to surprise whenever it occurs.

The black sky was streaked with red as if the blood of the victims had climbed all the way up to better shout their revenge. While wandering among the crowd, Pascal bumped into Judas Eluthère, his arm in a sling and accompanied by a dozen policemen. His eyes were brimming with tears and he looked haggard. He explained to Pascal what had happened: despite violent back pain, his friend Kassem Kémal had insisted on accompanying him to the ceremony. As he was very fond of the country flute, Kassem had stayed behind with the musicians in the room where the commando of killers had entered. As a result, he had received a bullet to his chest and had died immediately. Pascal uttered words of condolence—which always ring superficial and formal in such cases—and returned sadly to Marais Salant.

The next day at eight in the morning the police arrived on the premises, at the very moment when the parents were dragging along their children who in turn were wailing at the prospect of another day at school. That morning all the teachers had just one thing on their minds: Who was responsible for the attack? Where did they come from? Where were they hiding? Everyone hoped they would be caught very soon.

There were ten police officers. Ten policemen, Pascal said to himself, could mean two things: either the police force were excessive in number, or else they had attached undue importance to his person. He had them come up to his office. The oldest or the most senior began first to ask basic questions such as age, place of birth, and personal address, but soon his face changed to an aggressive scowl. "You mean to say you don't know what Hitchcock film you were watching: you have no idea whether it was *Marnie* or *The Birds?*"

"It's because I'm not a movie buff. When I was ten or twelve years old, I saw a film by François Truffaut called *The 400 Blows*, it was nothing like my childhood. Consequently, I have never forgotten it and it's the only film I can remember."

"Could someone at least bear witness to the fact you were watching television?" the policeman insisted.

"Nobody," retorted Pascal. "I told you I was alone at home."

When he had finished, the officer gave him his statement to sign and grinned sardonically: "Follow us, please."

"Follow you? Why do you want me to follow you?" Pascal protested. "I've nothing more to say to you."

The officer smirked. "You never know. Perhaps you have forgotten something that you'll remember."

"You're on the wrong track," Pascal declared. "The fact that I have accepted an offer to appear next week on *Face to*

Face with Norbert Pacheco clearly indicates the way I intend to resolve my difference of opinion with him. That is, provided there is a difference."

It was obvious the police had an idea up their sleeve: the staff had asked Pascal to teach classes at Sagalin, Norbert Pacheco had brutally canceled them on his return from Japan, and consequently, Pascal had taken his revenge.

Not familiar with police procedures, Pascal wondered if he was now being taken in for questioning. They climbed down the stairs and exited the building. A large crowd had gathered out front. Once again Pascal was amazed at the sudden change of the public's behavior towards him. Only yesterday, prior to the attack, people had showered him with smiles and asked him for autographs. Now he was being assailed with hateful looks.

In 1920 the prison at Fonds-Zombi had been the scene of a major revolt. Dozens of prison guards had been killed and a hundred or so prisoners did a bunk. As a result, it was rebuilt with thicker walls featuring narrow wire-meshed cell windows, and a watchtower on every exercise yard. It rose up like a formidable blockhouse in the center of the town. Today, given the increase in violence caused by drug addiction, it had once again become too small and so the prisoners slept three or four to a cell. In addition, the prison guards were understaffed.

Two policemen led Pascal to the first floor. The cell was cramped, dirty, and ill-lit. A young man was asleep on a filthy mattress placed on the floor. The police kicked him awake: "This is Damien Darmianus, an old friend of ours. He's leaving at four and then you'll have the cell to yourself."

Damien Darmianus stared wide-eyed at Pascal as if he was seeing a god. "It's you?" he exclaimed in disbelief. "Is it really you?"

"Just me," Pascal replied.

Damien Darmianus couldn't have been older than twenty. He had served a short sentence, once again, for selling drugs outside the lycée. He worked for serious drug traffickers who received the substance packed in the hold of ships on course from South America.

"I could never go to school, however much I wanted to," he told Pascal. "I had to help my mother, who hired out her services to the rich while I looked after my brothers and sisters. If I could, I'd like to be a writer."

"Writer!" Pascal exclaimed, surprised. "Writing is a dead loss. You can't earn a living from writing."

"It's because one day," Damien went on to explain, not listening, "I was tidying up the room of one of the boys for whom my mother worked and came across a book by François Mauriac with an odd title, The Little Misery. What did it mean? It's the story of a handicapped boy who committed suicide together with his father. I have never again come across anything so moving."

Unfortunately, this interesting conversation was interrupted when the police came to fetch Damien at 3 p.m. Pascal found himself alone and, not knowing what to do, lay down on the filthy mattress. He fell asleep, worn out and plagued with anguish.

He had been asleep for several hours when two women appeared. One of them was short and obese and was pushing the dinner trolley. The other ... my goodness, how beautiful she was! Despite her heavy cloth khaki uniform, she had a gorgeous figure. "I couldn't believe my colleagues," she exclaimed, "when they told me you had been arrested during the attack. Let me introduce myself: Sergeant Albertine Lachalle. We're bringing you your dinner. Tonight, you're having pork chitterlings and green bananas."

My God, Pascal repeated, she's so beautiful, so lovely! What he couldn't guess was that this ravishing woman, who had made his heart beat faster in an instant, was a dozen years older than him. She was almost thirty-six, though she didn't look her age. Pascal was no womanizer; he didn't fall passionately in love with the first bit of skirt that came his way. But here he was now attracted to two women: Sarojini, whom he would never manage to forget, like rediscovering the long-lost smell and taste of strange scents and flavors, and this Albertine, with whom little did he know what the future held in store for them.

He gulped down the stew, which was delicious, then, tortured by an unquenchable desire, he lay back down. Shortly before ten, the lights went out and this was followed by a strident alarm bell. A few hours later the door opened and Albertine made her entrance. She sat down beside him and declared, "I can sense that despite our difference in age, our love will stoke the fires of passion and eventually devour us."

23

Pascal knew nothing about Albertine. The straitlaced prudes of the Fonds-Zombi middle classes had nothing good to say about her. "She has six children from six different men. She's a slut! Three years ago, her latest lover, a gendarme who went back to the mother country, managed to get her enrolled in the police. Can you imagine a depraved woman like her in charge of punishing those who break the law! It's enough to make you die laughing," was what the goody-goodies whispered.

For Pascal, life was now split in two, so much so that he wondered whether he was one and the same person. Hadn't he become two individuals involved in two radically opposed experiences? His nights, a land of carnal delight, belonged to Albertine. She came to join him shortly after lights out; he could hear her tiny steps along the prison's flagstones then the jingle of keys turning the lock and finally she came in. She took off her uniform and, dressed only in her nakedness, curled up against him. They made love all night long, insatiable, tireless, pausing merely to catch their breath or to whisper snatches of memories, as poignant as dreams.

"Our love," Albertine declared, "is unlike any other. It's true I've been with many men before you, some of whom have given me children. I've a whole litter of offspring of every color, and yet I feel like a virgin again when I'm in your arms."

Unfortunately, she had to leave at dawn to prepare the trays for breakfast.

Starting at seven, Pascal became another man. A guard led him to the bathrooms at the end of the corridor. The day had begun. Pascal didn't receive a single visit. Was it because of the enormity of his crime that he deserved such treatment? He tried to interrogate the prison guards but there was no reply. Moreover, he was haunted by the image of Judas Eluthère, whose U-turn he could not understand.

It had all begun the morning after he arrived at the prison. He was sitting with the other prisoners in the small recreation room when he learned that the triumvirate who managed Le Bon Kaffé had been replaced by José Louis, Frédérique Dondenac, and, surprise, surprise, Judas Eluthère himself, who to everyone's amazement had graduated from Sciences Po in Paris and was thus perfectly capable of assuming his new role.

Judas Eluthère, the very soul of the demonstrations against Le Bon Kaffé, was now a member of the new management! He was now guaranteed a comfortable salary, the huge company mansion at Bois Jolan, and the annual vacation in the mother country.

The day Norbert Pacheco's funeral was televised Pascal was amazed to see Judas among the delegation of mourners. When interviewed, Judas said how grieved he was and that he had always felt a deep admiration for the deceased, even though he may not have agreed with all of his ideas. Deep admiration! Pascal thought, dumbfounded. Had he forgotten everything he used to say about him? Why was he, Pascal, thrown into prison like an unsavory individual while Judas Eluthère hadn't once been bothered by the police? What was going on? What did it all mean?

Pascal remained in jail for a week. Then, on the Saturday, two guards came to inform him he was free. All charges had been dropped against him. A homeless person who had taken shelter on the terrace of his house in Marais Salant had even come and sworn on his honor that on the night of the attack Pascal had been watching television and had only left the house very late on, as had most of the island's inhabitants. Who could this homeless person be? Pascal wondered.

He went down to an office where the prison guards handed him back the articles they had confiscated a few days earlier: a pack of Lucky Strike cigarettes, a box of matches, a bag of mints, and the mysterious red box that Espíritu or his spitting image had given him.

The guards pushed him out as if they were suddenly anxious to get rid of him. He crossed the yard where a dozen young prisoners in striped shorts were running in circles, and walked out onto the pavement.

It was early, very early. The sky was blue, as blue as the eyes of a European baby. A group of women were returning from the nearby church where they had attended dawn mass. The garbage collectors were emptying the trash cans into orange-painted garbage trucks. Pascal's heart was split between the joy of feeling free at last and his sorrow at having to leave Albertine so suddenly, without being able to kiss her goodbye and explain what had happened.

He hailed a taxi at the corner of the street and drove off to Marais Salant. Throughout the journey, the driver glared at him unceasingly through the rearview mirror and almost caused an accident.

Back home, Pascal pushed open the front gate and couldn't believe his eyes. Piles of vegetable peelings, remains of leftover meals, and rubbish of all sorts were heaped up on the lawn and terrace as if someone had emptied out the entire contents of several trash cans. The house was filthy. Wrapped in a sheet, Jean Pierre was sprawled on a bed on the first floor.

"Why is the house in such a state?" Pascal inquired, still unable to believe his eyes. Jean Pierre brushed Pascal's forehead with a rapid kiss and casually replied, "It's your neighbors."

"My neighbors?" Pascal repeated.

"Yes," said Jean Pierre. "They want you to go and live elsewhere. They say you're the disgrace of the neighborhood. They're on my back every day."

Pascal ran to his mother's. He hadn't seen her since his imprisonment. She showered him with kisses and asked,

"Your time in prison wasn't too painful, was it? I was about to circulate a petition demanding your immediate release. I didn't expect to see you so soon. When I came to see you in prison, they told me you were banned from the visitor's parlor because of the enormity of your crime. But I knew they could never bring charges against you."

Pascal hadn't come to talk about himself nor of his time in prison, for he had no intention of revealing his passionate affair with Albertine. Returning to his now singular obsession, he asked, "What do you make of Judas Eluthère? Aren't you surprised by his behavior?"

"Why do you say that? Judas Eluthère was wounded during the attack and he almost lost an arm," she said.

"Was that why he was rewarded and appointed company director?" Pascal joked.

Fatima appeared shocked on hearing his words and assured him, "It was the company employees themselves who requested his promotion. He always made good wherever he went."

Pascal realized he would have a lot of trouble convincing her of his suspicions, and turned his back.

"Are you off already?" she asked in surprise.

Feeling abandoned, Pascal returned home.

Early afternoon, he could stand it no longer and decided to call Judas Eluthère. A woman's voice, probably a secretary, answered saying he was in a meeting and could not be disturbed. Despite this chilly reception, he left his name. He then called his disciples to let them know he was back and invited them to come and see him. Marcel Marcelin and José Donovo were overjoyed and dashed to Marais Salant.

He asked them the same question: "What do you make of Judas Eluthère's behavior?"

But they also didn't seem shocked. Marcel Marcelin said, "I haven't seen Judas Eluthère since the attack. I think he merely prefers to keep quiet and not add to the chaos the company is having to deal with. Moreover, it's thanks to him that the wages have been increased and the intruders evicted from the company lodgings that they were illegally occupying."

Marcel Marcelin and José Donovo refused to stay for dinner and Pascal and Jean Pierre ate with little appetite a fricassee of octopus and red beans that they had ordered from Mont Ventoux. After which they went to bed.

The next morning when he opened the double doors Pascal was amazed to discover that the front of the house had been stained red with the word ASSASSIN. Crosses had been painted under the insult and one of them bore the words: You deserve the same.

Pascal remained stunned and felt like a navigator who suddenly sees the waves surge up and converge on his frail craft. Unfortunately, he was still not out of the woods: the following morning when he opened the doors a nauseating stench forced him to retreat inside the house. This time it was as if the entire contents of a latrine and its chamber pots had been emptied out. The day after that, it was even worse. A pig with its throat slit had been hung up by its trotters outside the front door and was filling a tub with its blood. It was like a cruel parody of the fate reserved for pigs on Christmas day when voluntary butchers set to work making strings of black pudding. This time, Pascal feared for his life.

Then he remembered the red box that Espíritu or his spitting image had given him and his mysterious words: "If you need help, press this button and call me." He dashed up to his office, looked for the strange object, and pressed it with all his might.

Shortly before midnight, Pascal was gloomily breathing in the stench from the garden when he saw a taxi draw up and a man step out. Who was it? Espíritu or his spitting image? It was indeed Espíritu, who gave him an affectionate punch while exclaiming, "Why did you send for me?" Pascal explained in detail what had just happened: the attack, the jail time, and the ensuing threats and insults.

Espíritu didn't seem particularly moved by his story. "You know, in our countries, people are quick to forget. You only have to keep quiet for a few months and they'll forget all about it. But if you want me to help you, I'm at your disposal."

In the ensuing silence Espíritu took Pascal by the hand. "You haven't asked me for news of your father. Isn't he important to you?"

"It's rather me who isn't important to him," Pascal said sadly.

"You haven't understood a thing," Espíritu cried. "Your father doesn't want to influence your free will. There are three questions a man worthy of such a name must ask: Where do I come from? Why am I on this earth? Where am I going?"

"Perhaps you're right," Pascal acknowledged unenthusiastically.

Part Two

24

In 1610 a slave ship by the name of *J'espère en Dieu* anchored off the island in order to unload a cargo of Mondongues, captured on the outskirts of the town of Abomey in West Africa: fifteen men and as many women and children, much appreciated by the plantation owners for their slender arms and bodies. At that time the mere mention of the name Mondongue aroused terror in the hearts of men since they were known for being cruel and bloodthirsty. The reason being that their founding gods, the twins Mahou and Mahia, were crazy for human blood. Consequently, they were forever at war with their neighbors in order to procure it. They would pierce a hole in their victims' backs and let the blood trickle out until they died a few days later of a hemorrhage.

The Mondongues refused to be enslaved in the plantations around Fonds-Zombi or to pay their respects to the realm of sugar cane. They spurned the white sandy beaches for the harsh slopes of the volcano to the north. There they founded a domain, which they called Caracalla, meaning "Land of the Gods" in their own language. Much later it became the refuge of the Maroons, who, too, were smitten with liberty and built a solid wall around Caracalla that they covered with inscriptions and drawings in order to ward off assailants.

Today, all that is ancient history. Some Mondongues converted to Catholicism. One, an apostolic nuncio, even ended up in the Vatican with the Pope. Other Mondongues became Muslims or Buddhists. Some of them never gave up honoring their traditional gods, feeding them chickens' blood now they no longer practiced human sacrifices.

The Mondongues were not wanting in detractors. Firstly, because of their physique. They had jet-black skin, their red-highlighted hair rounded their head like a bombshell and their pink gums were planted with white teeth like splinters of bone. "Ugly as a Mondongue" became a household term—but ever since a young Mondongue girl was elected a finalist in the Miss Universe pageant in 2019, people hesitated to use the expression.

But it's only true to say that the Mondongue detractors had more serious reasons. From their very beginning the Mondongues had been unable to produce a Robert Badinter, who abolished the death penalty, and they practiced capital punishment with impunity. Those whom they called major criminals were brought before a firing squad who quickly perforated their chests. Previously these executions were an excuse for popular entertainment and rejoicing. But times had changed. Today the Mondongues have adopted the American system of the electric chair, which we can all agree is more discreet.

The Mondongues now form a peaceful community and these days live mainly by making brightly colored wooden toys, which they dispatch worldwide. Now that wood is considered to be healthy and eco-friendly, they have accumulated a fortune. Their main client is Australia and they have a permanent representative in Perth.

In Caracalla, the sky is hidden by the panoply of trees, a feature which contributes to a refreshing, salutary penumbra for body and soul. The colony is governed by a quartet of members elected for four years by universal suffrage: a director of social affairs, a director of public affairs, a director of cultural affairs, and a director of finance. All four are placed under the supervision of the supreme guide, Mawubi or "Our Father," who is only seen at the ceremonies celebrating the National Holiday.

The colony of Caracalla is divided into seven sectors, six of which governed by a provost who supervises a territory that spreads down to the jagged cliffs facing the sea. The seventh sector is named Cayenne because it houses the prison and the lodgings for the prisoners' families.

Maru, the director of cultural affairs, gazed at Espíritu and Pascal seated on the other side of his desk. "We won't pay him," he declared. "No wages. You know what we think about money: it's the cause of most crimes. But we'll give him a comfortable hut and a woman, a subaltern who will cook his three meals a day and do the housework. He can do what he likes with her." He said that with a saucy expression, which contrasted with his severe, heavy-featured face. Intrigued, Pascal wanted to ask him certain questions, but Maru continued. "Do you agree?" he insisted. Espíritu and Pascal looked at each other, then nodded. Deal well and truly settled.

Maru drew out a bundle of documents from the drawer of his desk and laid it in front of Pascal. "Here is your temporary integration contract," he said. "Initial every page and sign the last one." Once this was done, he stuffed it back into the drawer and declared joyfully, "I think our agreement deserves a celebration. Come and have a drink."

Espíritu apologized. Always in a hurry, he had a plane to catch at Porte Océane in two hours. The three men left the building, on which THE DIVISION OF CULTURAL AFFAIRS was written in capital letters, crossed the parking lot, and split up. Once they had bid farewell to Espíritu, the two remaining men made their way to a drinking establishment.

Since the Mondongues had forbidden alcohol, they preferred the term "drinking establishment" to "bar" or "refreshment stall." They had replaced rum and its punches, once so popular on the island, with all sorts of juices, teas, and infusions. They served excellent turmeric herb teas and delicious bougainvillea and Cayenne-rose infusions.

Pascal rediscovered the blissful sensation he had forgotten of being anonymous. When they entered the drinking establishment no heads turned. When Maru introduced him to a few customers seated at their table, it was obvious it was the first time they had heard the name Pascal Ballandra.

Maru and Pascal each made their choice from the list of drinks, Maru ordering a golden apple juice while Pascal made do with a guava juice, a taste he was already familiar with. When they had downed their drinks, Manu took Pascal to his lodging at 102 rue Nelson Mandela, Sector 4.

Since Caracalla was an egalitarian community, everything was conceived to avoid the trap of well-off neighborhoods contrasting their wealth against the poorer districts. As a result, private property was forbidden and the Mondongue government rented out the property it owned. The lodgings were all the same: a series of huts painted green and consisting of two spacious rooms with an attic reached by a spiral staircase. Those with large families were free to rent two or three huts as they liked. When they arrived at 102 rue Nelson Mandela, Maru gave Pascal the traditional Mondongue handshake. "Tomorrow you'll have dinner at my place," he said. "I'd like you to meet my wife."

Ever since he had left Marais Salant, Pascal had a deep feeling of deliverance: nobody expected him to undertake actions for reasons he knew nothing about; above all, nobody was there to despise or hate him for acts he had never committed.

He began to put away his personal items. After an hour he heard a knock on the door and went to open it. A young girl of sixteen or seventeen, somewhat well-rounded as is often the case at that age, appeared, as if straight out of a novel by Margaret Atwood, wearing a heavy scarlet skirt down to her sandals and a same-color tunic printed with the word subaltern.

"Master, I'm Amanda," she declared. "I'm your subaltern and have been designated to serve and please you."

"If you want to please me," Pascal retorted, "stop calling me Master. I'm nobody's master, not even my own. It might be better if you called me Father since I'm considerably older than you."

The girl burst out laughing, revealing a set of very white and tiny teeth. "But seriously, if you don't want me to call you Master, what do you want me to call you?"

Pascal shook his head: "Call me Pascal, it's much simpler."

She nodded and continued. "What would you like for dinner?"

Pascal, who had never bothered much about cooking, was at a loss for an answer. "Make whatever you like," he ordered.

"Would a fillet of sea bream and a yam gratin be to your liking?" she insisted.

"I told you, make what you like," he repeated.

Two hours later, she served him a meal which he thought excellent.

The national television channels were banned from Caracalla since they were considered vulgar entertainment and liable to addle people's brains. Consequently, of an evening, plays and concerts took place on the main square named after Derek Walcott. Pascal went on his own. He was enchanted by the performance of a female griot singer from Guinea who was accompanied by a trio performing in front of what were admittedly few spectators.

When he returned home Amanda was asleep on a chair, woken at hearing the sound of the door.

"Why did you wait up for me?" he exclaimed. "Off to bed with you!"

Amanda stared at him in amazement, shock even.

"You want me to go to bed? You no longer need my services?"

What was she talking about? Pascal wondered, preparing to go to bed. Whatever was she thinking I needed after midnight? He fell asleep with an odd feeling.

At barely seven the next morning there was a knock on the door. It was a personal trainer, for the Mondongues believed in the saying "a healthy mind in a healthy body," or *mens sana in corpore sano*. The coach was a short little man, as ugly as a Mondongue—only too true this time—whose hair stuck up like loose oakum fibers. For two hours the two men practiced all kinds of activities such as stretching, planking, push-ups, weight lifting, and parallel bars. Then, as if that was not enough, the instructor dragged Pascal up and down rue Nelson Mandela. Finally, he informed Pascal with a smile: "Same time tomorrow."

25

After these sports activities, Pascal went to the lycée Sékou Touré where he taught philosophy to a class of twelfth-graders. The school complex, called La Vie Heureuse, was spread out over several kilometers. Everything was doubled: two lycées, two middle schools, two elementary schools, two kindergartens, and two daycare centers, since the Mondongues did not believe in coeducation and as such the girls were carefully separated from the boys. This deeply shocked Pascal, who had always considered coeducation as a major step forward, demonstrating that both sexes were equal and should be taught identically.

When he entered the teachers' room around ten, a young man who seemed to be waiting for him stood up immediately on seeing him arrive. Wearing a baseball cap, he looked the perfect Yankee. He introduced himself: "My name is Joseph Serano. You arrived in Caracalla yesterday like me but I hope you haven't come from as far away as I have."

"Where have you come from?" Pascal asked, shaking an outstretched hand.

"From Menlo Park," Joseph replied. "It's a small town next to the University of Stanford, where I graduated and taught."

"You came from Stanford?" Pascal inquired in stupefied admiration.

Joseph handed Pascal a pack of cigarettes and smiled. "It's a long story. Several years ago, my father, a Mondongue, fell in love with a young blonde American come to teach English at La Vie Heureuse and he wanted to marry her. A wedding between a Mondongue and a White American girl was not to everyone's liking. Since he still hadn't managed to obtain permission to marry her after five years, he emigrated to the US where he was able to wed his sweetheart. Despite these setbacks, he and my mother raised me with the nostalgia of Caracalla. And here I am, come to see if they were telling the truth."

Joseph Serano was in fact hiding the real reasons he had come to Caracalla. He had lived a pampered childhood spoilt by his mother's family who thought it only natural they were bringing up a little mixed-race boy. At that early age, there was no question of color. It was one July 4 when he was eight years old, while setting off fireworks with some kids the same age, that the police swooped down on him. It was his first experience of police violence. The officers had dragged him to the police station where he emerged minus at least two incisors and with the taste of blood in his mouth. From then on things went from bad to worse. At university, his half-brother, Malcolm, had been arrested and sentenced to a heavy prison term, for it was said he had attempted to pass off counterfeit banknotes in a supermarket.

After that a president of color had been elected, but he hadn't been able to do much to change the lives of Black folk. He had been succeeded by a democratically elected White president who opened the box where racism had been hiding. It was as if we had gone back in time to a period when Billie Holiday mistook the lynched bodies of men hanging in the trees for strange fruit. It was then that Joseph had decided to go and see whether life had as bitter a taste elsewhere.

Pascal and Joseph soon became inseparable. In the morning they practiced boxing together and delivered uppercuts worthy of professionals. At noon they lunched at the Vie Heureuse cafeteria where, oddly enough, nobody ever came to sit at their table. Of an evening they dined at Pascal's, since Joseph, for some unknown reason, had dismissed his subaltern. Amanda cooked delicious meals every day, as succulent as Marthe's at Marais Salant.

Sometimes they were joined by Amanda's brother, Najib. He was a taciturn boy in charge of garbage collection in one sector of the town; perhaps his unwholesome job was the reason for his morose character. Once a month, Pascal and Joseph were invited to dinner at Maru's, whom, together with his wife, Jézabel, they were both very fond of.

Maru was a genuine Mondongue. Unlike Joseph, he had never left his native Caracalla, where he had met Jézabel, the daughter of a gym instructor. The couple's misfortune was that they were childless and consequently lived surrounded by a swarm of nephews, nieces, godchildren, and adopted kids.

The trio, Pascal, Joseph, and Maru, got along famously together. The only time Joseph annoyed Maru was when he took the liberty of criticizing Caracalla and scoffed at the prohibition of alcohol.

"They're hypocrites," he asserted. "Everyone knows that in the evening the men get blind drunk same as everywhere else. Moreover, they're male chauvinists who don't believe in coeducation. That's proof enough that they don't accept gender equality." Pascal didn't intervene in the discussion, he had no definite opinion on the subject. He let Maru defend those he blindly admired.

At Caracalla, Pascal resumed the rich scholarly life he had briefly known at Marais Salant. He had given up writing about The Hidden God since, in his opinion, he had been obsessed at the time with his love for Sarojini. All that was worth saying on the subject would have been a pamphlet describing how to lose a woman dear to your heart. At Caracalla, he had started writing his autobiography, in which he searched for his true origin and endeavored to define the nature of the mission to which he had been assigned. He often thought about those he had left behind: Fatima, Maria, Marthe, and Lazare, his old father, Jean Pierre, whom perhaps he would never see again, and above all, Albertine, to whom he had been unable to explain the reason for his departure.

He by no means neglected his physical exercise. In addition to the sessions with his personal trainer, he enrolled in an association that organized forest hikes. Once a week they disappeared into the mountains, sometimes reaching the summit of the volcano, whose last eruption in 1913 had destroyed hundreds of acres of agricultural land. Pascal loved these hikes in the penumbra and cool of the upper slopes. To sum it up, his life was relatively happy.

Suddenly, everything changed. It would soon be Christmas, a very Catholic holiday. Amid the general indifference in Caracalla, Pascal remembered the fervor of the Christmas carols and the midnight mass when he was a child living with Eulalie and Jean Pierre. Now, foie gras was considered to be the very symbol of an animal's subjection to man and champagne was forbidden. Even so, a few shops dared display blocks of foie gras, but Christmas had lost its sparkle: no Christmas Eve dinner, no sizzling black pudding, and above all, no alcohol. Pascal was quite unprepared for the maelstrom that was about to turn his life upside down.

One evening while he was waiting with Joseph for a concert of their favorite reggae music on Derek Walcott Square, a commando of men dressed in white togas tied at the waist with wide navy-blue belts erupted onto the stage.

One of them stepped forward and shouted into a megaphone: "Go home. There will be no concert tonight. Maru, the director of cultural affairs, has been dismissed from his post." Questions came thick and fast: "Dismissed from his post?" "Why?" "What crime has he committed?"

"What crime?" one member of the commando replied. "He has personally pocketed the payments for orders from eight Latin American countries who had bought toys for their children."

Stupefied, Pascal and Joseph dashed to Maru's where they bumped into the new tenants who had moved in with their recently arrived furniture. They were unable to answer the questions Pascal and Joseph plied them with. A few days prior, the municipality had simply informed them that the house was at their disposal and that the previous tenant had been thrown into prison. What offence had he committed? They had no idea.

Pascal and Joseph found themselves out in the cold, damp night as a keen wind began to blow. Although Pascal remained silent, shattered by these sudden events, Joseph hollered, "Imprisoned! I bet he didn't get a fair trial. That's the way the Mondongues do it. If need be, I'll get lawyers to come from America to plead his case." He rapidly thought up a plan. "Starting tomorrow I'll circulate a petition asking for Maru to be tried. You'll see, they won't get away with it. Maru will get a fair trial."

A week went by and nothing happened. Pascal and Joseph had collected only a handful of signatures, as if nobody could care less about Maru's fate. They were unable to interrogate the people in charge of Sector 7, the division of cultural affairs once managed by Maru, and it was impossible to obtain an appointment with his successor to discuss Maru's misdeeds. One evening on Derek Walcott Square, totally powerless, they attended the instatement of the new director, who apparently had occupied an important post in one of the National Theaters over in the mother country.

Life then resumed, at least on the face of it. For Pascal, however, nothing was the same. He couldn't help thinking of Maru: was he really a thief as they said he was? He found it hard to believe that Maru, who seemed so respectful of the institutions at Caracalla, who believed the community was a model of excellence and virtue, was now considered a traitor.

26

Everything now went from bad to worse. Pascal had barely recovered from these events when he was dealt a second blow, more brutal than the first. The rumor began to circulate that Joseph had asserted to his class that Communism was the last illusion and that Stalin had massacred as many men as Hitler. On hearing such monstrous claims, his students denounced him. By way of reprisal his classes were suspended and a public retraction on his part was demanded. "Never!" he bristled, rejecting with a wave of the hand the timid objections by Pascal. "Perhaps you should have used the conditional," Pascal insisted. "Perhaps you should have said that Communism was a dream gone wrong and not a lost illusion."

"I shall do nothing of the sort," Joseph brutally asserted.

As a result of this categorical refusal, what was going to happen happened. His classes were canceled, and from one day to the next he was struck off the payroll of La Vie Heureuse. Soon he was deprived of both his salary and his lodging. One morning, while he was still asleep, a group of soldiers came to drag him out of bed and he was obliged to take refuge at Pascal's, his only friend. Such a situation couldn't last and after a few days he decided on the only solution possible: to leave.

He frenziedly negotiated his return to Stanford, where fortunately he still had friends and the majority of teachers admired him. When he received his letter of agreement, he said to Pascal, "You don't know America, do you? I'll invite you whenever you like."

The day before he left, Amanda surpassed herself and cooked Cuban lobsters in a black mushroom sauce.

Pascal could no longer sleep. What should he make of Joseph's eviction alongside Maru's imprisonment? Was this justice, or a form of despotism? Didn't a teacher have the right to express his opinions? What crime was there in searching for the truth?

The next day he accompanied his friend to Porte Océane for his flight. The landscape on this part of the island was magnificent. To the left, the crumpled blue texture of the sea, sprinkled with patches of light, and to the right, the wall of jagged mountains reaching up to the sky. But neither Pascal nor Joseph had eyes for Nature's spectacle since they were both lost in the somber thought of their imminent separation.

Pascal had never liked Porte Océane; whereas Fonds-Zombi had an old-fashioned, aristocratic charm about it with its wharfs and streets lined with almond trees, whose leaves sometimes turned green, sometimes red, and its public squares sprinkled with fountains flowing with crystal-clear water, Porte Océane claimed to be the temple of modernity. The streets intersected at right angles and the houses looked like concrete cubes, displaying cramped little balconies where potted plants wilted.

Pascal and Joseph sat down in one of the airport bars and ordered rum punches. Pascal hadn't drunk rum for over a year and this sensation of warmth trickling down his throat felt so good and pleasant that he ordered a second then a third. Gradually he felt less gloomy and came back to life. Suddenly he understood the meaning of the popular song about the beverage: "I'm neither king nor queen, but I make the earth tremble." Had he not been focusing on the benefits of rum, he would have realized that nobody was looking at or paying attention to him. Espíritu was right, memory is quick to forget. Joseph had barely disappeared behind the airport doors than Pascal was overcome again with grief. He had no idea how he managed to get home to Caracalla without causing an accident.

Amanda was looking out for him on the veranda. "Has he left?" she asked. Pascal nodded. Her figure had filled out lately and she had become dumpy. An idea crossed Pascal's mind: Could she be pregnant? He quickly waved the thought aside. When she had finished serving dinner, she promptly went up to her room where she slept alone. When not busy in the kitchen, she embroidered children's clothes with cross-stitches, which she sold to a shop in town. The only man she frequented apart from Pascal and Joseph was her brother.

Pascal had been living in Caracalla now for over a year and relations between himself and Amanda had meanwhile been clarified. Gone was the unwitting blindness he had suffered at the beginning. He finally understood that if he took Amanda as his mistress, nobody would be offended. Subaltern: a term reserved for young girls who had been unsuccessful at school or who did not have the good fortune to belong to a privileged environment. All that had created in Pascal's heart a niggling affection and a guilty feeling; he blamed himself for not having taken Amanda by the hand in order to help her carve out a place for herself in life.

Her father, a garbage collector like his son after him, had died when she was just a few months old. She had been raised by her mother, who left on her own, sold charcoal in the market. Why charcoal? Because the densely wooded mountains surrounding Caracalla housed a treasure, the logwood tree, whose wood gave off an incandescent flame.

At the age of twelve, Amanda had been oriented to a school of domestic science where they taught cooking, sewing, and embroidery. Very quickly she had excelled at cooking, and at the sumptuous graduation ceremony she was awarded the title of subaltern, which meant she could be hired by the most meticulous families. Unfortunately, she had never found a permanent job and was merely cooking banquets from time to time at the point she was assigned to Pascal.

Pascal had attempted to get her interested in reading but without success. She found Émile Zola's books too long,

Jean-Paul Sartre's and Simone de Beauvoir's too intellectual, Aragon's too political, and Stendhal's so Italian you got confused as to who was who between Fabrice del Dongo, the Sanseverina, and Count and Countess Mosca. When she decreed that *Madame Bovary* was boring and that not much happened in the book, Pascal put an end to his endeavors.

To say that after Joseph's departure life became miserable is an understatement. Pascal had the impression of falling into a black hole; he was no longer interested in anything. He went to bed and got up in the morning mechanically. At school he churned out his lectures to his students who, it was obvious, were less and less attentive. As for his meals, he ate practically nothing and wondered why Amanda went to so much trouble.

One morning, he barely noticed that she had come down from her attic holding her cardboard suitcase and dressed in her scarlet uniform for going out.

"Dear Brother," she declared (that was the term they had both agreed on), "I have come to say I am leaving."

"You're leaving? To go where?" Pascal asked.

"I'm tired. I need a rest."

"Rest!" Pascal exclaimed. "But you can rest here as much as you like."

She shook her head.

"No, I prefer to go back to my mother's."

"Will you come back?" Pascal asked, gripped with a sudden intuition.

"Frankly, I don't know."

When she reached the door, she quickly turned back, clasped his head between her hands, and planted a long kiss on his lips before leaving for good.

That day, Pascal reeled off his lecture even more mechanically than usual and lunched on a sandwich at the Vie Heureuse cafeteria. Here, again, he realized that if nobody had ever come to sit with Joseph and himself, it was because they were too different. The people from Caracalla sensed that the two of them were somehow out of place and didn't correspond to what was expected of them.

That day he went to bed early and his sleep was troubled by the same dreams: What had become of Joseph? What was he doing at Stanford? All he had so far received since his departure was a hastily scribbled letter providing no real information about his life.

It must have been around five in the morning when the telephone rang. The Bon Pasteur Hospital informed him that his subaltern, Mademoiselle Amanda Normand, had just been admitted for a severe hemorrhage. "A severe hemorrhage?" Pascal inquired, half-asleep.

"Yes," answered the voice at the other end, "she perforated her uterus trying to get rid of her baby."

Pascal was brutally brought back to earth. So, he was right. Amanda had been pregnant.

27

The Bon Pasteur Hospital was the pride of Caracalla. It was an ultramodern building, which had received a donation from an American couple who admired the Mondongues and bequeathed them a considerable fortune as a legacy. The garden housed some very rare species. Despite the early hour, the hospital was crowded with worried relatives.

Pascal dashed up to the second floor. He found Amanda lying on a bed in a small room, her eyes closed and a waxen mask covering her face. She was surrounded by her mother, Eudoxia, an old, obese woman who was crying her heart out, and a few relatives. Najib, her brother, looking drawn and haggard, was chain-smoking. Tobacco, of course, was banned in *Caracalla* but they made a nice-tasting cigarette substitute from an assortment of powders.

Najib shouted at Pascal: "Pregnant! She was pregnant. She slit her womb open to get rid of the fetus."

"Who got her pregnant?" Pascal asked.

"We don't know yet," Najib replied.

Yet his eyes betrayed a hateful accusation.

Thereupon an intern entered and uttered a stream of reassuring words: "Mademoiselle Normand has lost a lot of blood, it's a fact. But she is young and robust. She had not slit open her womb as we had feared and that's the main thing. She will soon be going home." Even so, Pascal got the impression that this was just the beginning and a monstrous epilogue was brewing.

The next morning Amanda went home as the intern had predicted. The day after, she was dead.

The circumstances of her death were both striking and painful. When Eudoxia brought up Amanda's morning turmeric herb tea, intended to set her back on her feet, she found the bed empty and the room deserted. Panic-stricken, she rushed downstairs and ran across the garden to alert her neighbor, when she stumbled upon the body of her daughter, lying among the potted plants. Her corpse was already stiff. She had succumbed to the ingestion of a well-known virulent poison called Marie-Cécile which grows on the upper slopes of the mountain. The police were unable to decide whether she had deliberately drunk this decoction or whether someone had forced her.

At Caracalla, like everywhere else, the poor are not treated seriously. Very quickly her death was classified as a cold case and after a few days the body was handed back to her family.

Barely thirty people gathered for the wake. A group of relatives, putting on sorrowful looks, comforted the mother, who hadn't stopped crying now for days on end. Najib, too, seemed at the point of giving up the ghost.

The funeral took place early afternoon. One of the Mondongues' principles is that we are all equal in death. The coffin was taken by identical hearses and state undertakers to the cemetery, named The Last Dwelling, where identical black-and-white square tombs overlooked the sea.

Previously Caracalla included a second cemetery located amid the dense mountain vegetation, this one known as The Star-Spangled Domain. In order to be buried there you had to have been a credit to the community, either by living a generally exemplary life or having written a major work or painted or composed a masterpiece.

Under the reign of Mawubi xiv all that changed. Mawubi xiv still went by the name of "The Libertarian." It was he who decided that all Mondongues were equal and that no special status should be assigned to an artist, as is usually the case. Believing that artists are in no way responsible for the gift they have inherited, they must accept it as inevitable, despite the fact that from time to time they unwittingly give it free expression. This quarrel on the subject of artistic creation lasted for years. Finally, Mawubi xiv was deemed correct and The Star-Spangled Domain was closed. Henceforth, the only visitors to the cemetery were groups of students led by their teacher lecturing them about Caracalla's past.

Once Amanda's funeral was over, Pascal sat down on a tomb and put his head between his hands. For the first time, he thought about leaving Caracalla. All his friends here, one after the other, had come to harm: Maru had been thrown into prison, Joseph had had to flee, and Amanda had committed suicide. Who was left? What was he doing in this dreaded place? What could he hope for? It now appeared that this community he once thought so virtuous—banning money, alcohol, and private property—was not a source of happiness for its inhabitants.

Someone had seduced Amanda, thus condemning her to death. Someone had reported Joseph's ideas to his superiors, forcing him into exile.

When the breeze turned cooler Pascal got up and walked home. At this hour, before the evening rush to the concerts on the public squares, the streets were deserted. From 7 p.m. the first rows would begin to fill up since nobody wanted to be left standing on the sidelines. American films with their scenes of sex and violence were outlawed. A board of twenty or so handpicked members of the community selected what was appropriate for the population. They mainly came up with romantic comedies, melodramas, and mushy action films, which in the end nobody was really interested in.

In the days that followed, Pascal lost all notion of time. He was puzzled by the sunlight on the gardens, trees, and house facades, and couldn't understand when night fell why it donned its mantle of mourning while the moon played hide-and-seek among the clouds.

One morning while he was getting ready to go to school, he received a visit by Najib, dressed in his ungainly garbage collector's uniform: a fluorescent tunic and trousers and a woolen bonnet clamped over his hair.

"I owe you an apology," he declared when the door closed behind them. "I was convinced you were responsible for the death of my sister or that it was one of your friends, for example, the one who fled to America. I can't recall his name. In actual fact there was another man. While I was going through Amanda's belongings, I came across a passionate correspondence she had with him and which she hadn't had time to delete from her computer. And it was there I learned she had an appointment with Madame Dormius, the midwife, or back-street abortionist if you prefer. Everything is perfectly clear now.

"But who is this other man?" Pascal exclaimed, aghast.

"The provost of Sector 4, for whom she often did the cooking," Najib replied. "A few months back he got married with great pomp to the daughter of a dignitary such as himself. As you can imagine, there was no place for the little bastard my sister was carrying. But he won't get away with it. I'm going to find him and make him pay, for Amanda's sake."

Pascal had heard similar words from Joseph after Maru's downfall and knew full well it was nothing but bravado and bluster.

28

The following week, during the ten o'clock recreation at the lycée, when the students, especially the boys, have time to tuck into the assortment of pâtés and pink-topped sugar cakes on sale by the market women stationed around the school, a blue van stopped in front of the gate and eight policemen climbed out.

Once they had negotiated with the old gray-haired guardian, crowned with a permanent straw hat, for the whereabouts of the person they were looking for, they strode across the yard in quick time. At the sight of them, all the sounds, all the voices, the bursts of laughter and horsing around came to a stop and everyone froze.

As if they already knew him, the policemen headed straight for Pascal, who was sprawling on a bench having finished reading Rousseau's *Social Contract*, which he was to discuss with his students an hour later. "Monsieur Pascal Ballandra?" one of them asked. On receiving an affirmative answer, he opened his briefcase and pulled out a blue type-written sheet. "We have come to hand you a summons," he said. "You are requested to be present tomorrow at 10 a.m. at the office of the provost of the fourth sector."

"What is this about?" Pascal asked in amazement.

The policeman smiled. "We know nothing about it. All we know is that it is a matter that concerns you." Thereupon he withdrew with his colleagues the same way they had come.

"A matter concerning me," Pascal said to himself, terri-fied. Police are the same the world over. These ones with their stiff, awkward posture, their ill-fitting uniform and their kepi planted lopsided on their heads looked exactly the same as those who had arrested him at Marais Salant. A matter concerning him! It could only be about the death of

Amanda, his subaltern. When the bell rang at the end of recreation, Pascal had no inclination to discuss Rousseau's *Social Contract* and instead gave his students a written test.

As the time gradually drew nearer, he worked himself up into a state of fear. What did they want? What was the provost of the fourth sector going to ask him? Amanda had been his subaltern, that was a fact, but he had never asked her to do anything else besides the housework and the cooking.

With beating heart, he ran to Najib's. A man with his mouth full of nails had barely opened the door when Pascal realized what was going on. It was a repetition of what had happened to Maru the previous year: a family of new tenants. A woman came out: no, she had never heard of Najib Normand. The day before, they had been informed that they had finally been allocated the community accommodation they had spent years waiting for. They couldn't believe their ears.

Puzzled and bewildered, Pascal left and closed the gate behind him. He was walking up and down in front of the house, his legs shaking, when a stranger came up to him and whispered, "Are you looking for Najib Normand? He was arrested yesterday."

"Arrested?" Pascal repeated in dismay.

The stranger nodded. "Yes, arrested and thrown into prison."

"But what has he done?" Pascal exclaimed.

"That, I couldn't say. All I know is that it's something awful. As for his old mother, she was admitted to a hospice. I advise you not to meddle in the affair as it doesn't look good."

With that, he let go of Pascal's arm and walked away.

Pascal stood there wondering whether he hadn't been dreaming. All that was left for him to do was to climb back into his car and leave as quickly as possible. During the drive home, he was convinced the police were on his trail, from the one helping children to cross the street to the officer assisting an old lady to the one directing the traffic. They were all traps. Fakes, who had been assigned to spy on him.

Once he got home, he spent the afternoon shaking like a leaf and jumping at the slightest noise. What did they want from him? This question haunted him. In the early evening, incapable of remaining alone, he walked to Cheikh Anta Diop Square where they were giving a concert of country music. As a rule, he did not like this type of music, but it made him think of his friend Joseph. Should he escape as well? He who thought Caracalla would be his new home instead found himself terror-stricken. He needed to go home, to go to bed and sleep.

At five in the morning, he was already up, turning over and over in his head the same questions. He went downstairs to have breakfast in the tiny yard behind the house. Amanda had used it to pile items for cleaning: a garbage bin, brooms, brushes, and floor cloths. There was an unpleasant, acrid smell in the air. He had barely sat down than he had the impression a blue cloud was walking towards him. Three policemen. These people never ask for permission to come in. Pascal recognized them as the same ones who had brought the summons the day before. "Take your time," the oldest one declared with a sugary smile, "we came to fetch you as it's very difficult to park at the fourth-sector headquarters."

Pascal no longer felt hungry, and followed them outside. On the pavement, they bumped into three other policemen, dressed identically in blue. "Take your own car," one of them advised. "Follow us and we'll guide you to the parking lot."

Pascal was convinced his time was up. His entire body was frozen as a block of ice. There was no doubt in his mind that they were going to find him guilty for the murder of Amanda.

The fourth-sector headquarters was something between a town hall and a cultural center. In the VIP lounge a photo of the provost had pride of place, depicting a young man with regular features, an arrogant appearance, a crew cut, and a manicured moustache. Perhaps he was Amanda's murderer; whatever the case, he had something to do with the dramatic events which were now occurring.

Pascal and the police officers climbed the stairs until they reached a small office where a secretary reigned half-asleep. "Let's wait here," one of the policemen said. "Hopefully, the provost won't keep us waiting long."

"Where are the toilets?" Pascal stammered, wriggling like a small boy. They pointed to the end of the corridor where he saw a staircase to his left. Without knowing exactly what he was doing he charged down and found himself in the garden. His car was parked close by in the Salvador Allende garage. He dashed inside and started the engine, letting himself be guided by a force beyond his control.

Normally, it's difficult to leave the colony. He had realized that a few months ago when he accompanied Joseph to Port Océane. The entrance was protected by armed guards who demanded your identity, the reasons for your leaving, and the approximate time of your return. At this early hour, the guards, having nothing to do, were asleep. One of them was sleeping with his mouth open, displaying a set of crooked yellow teeth, while the other was snoring like a sea lion.

He drove like crazy for about ten kilometers, following the ring road, then turned left onto the main road. Suddenly his strength gave out and he parked at the side of the road, collapsing onto the steering wheel.

How long did he remain unconscious? An hour or perhaps two? He was incapable of saying. His head was filled with the same cruel looping images as in a nightmare: Here was Amanda when he first met her, a somewhat chubby young girl, a broad smile framing her white teeth. There was Amanda when he bid her farewell, a mask of yellow wax over her cheeks. And, finally, Amanda during her funeral wake dressed in the only acceptable poplin dress her mother could find.

A series of sudden taps on the car window brought him back to his senses.

29

Pascal saw a man of a certain age tapping on the car window. His face looked familiar. He had a strange bearing as if he had something hidden behind his back. Perhaps a hump. No, it was not Espíritu. What would he be doing here on the side of the road? Why would he be dressed like a miserable wretch? Pascal quickly lowered the window and the man scolded him: "It's not wise to sleep in your car. You risk being attacked by poachers. There are a lot around here because of the logwood." Pascal motioned to him to come and sit beside him. "Climb in," he said. "Can I drop you somewhere?" The old man accepted the offer without hesitation. "Take me to my place, it's not very far, just a few kilometers."

After a few minutes' silence, the man asked, "You've come from Caracalla, haven't you?"

Pascal nodded.

"You've seen," he continued, "what men do when they want to fashion the world to their liking? They think that all they have to do is impose a series of taboos, unlike God, who always respects an individual's free will. The greatest gift God has given us is the gift of liberty."

Pascal thought he'd heard this somewhere before but he made no comment.

The old man introduced himself: "My name is Nestor. It's a common name, but that's the one my father gave me. He left me several acres of forest and, in order to earn a living, I make charcoal from logwood assisted by my son, who is also called Nestor. But my true calling is breeding birds. I've got a hundred or so flying around the house. Sometimes they darken the sun. In the morning they chirp and twitter for me to come and feed them. I've got all sorts of birds: hummingbirds, turtledoves, thrushes, blackbirds, and the ones I'm especially fond of, macaws from tropical America."

Pascal listened to his voice as sweet as a song. As lovely as a birdsong, you might say.

They drove for about a dozen kilometers and on reaching a signpost roughly drawn with the words *Harmonie, Population 118* the old man motioned to Pascal to stop. They then set off along a path, treading through razor-blade clumps of Guinea grass and iron weed.

Nestor's hut appeared around a bend, concealed behind a curtain of dwarf ebony trees. It was not painted but built with a brown hardwood timber from Guyana and was shaped like a bell or a squashed cage under its heavy sloping roof. Dozens of birds flitted around it, some perched on the yellow allamandas and the rayo in the garden while others were pecking away on the ground.

As soon as they saw Nestor, they began to chirp louder and flew to meet him, some even went so far as to perch on his head and shoulders. "It's because they're hungry," Nestor laughed, waving them off. "It's feeding time. They used to eat worms, insects, cockroaches, and all sorts of nasty bugs but I gradually made them understand that you have to respect all living creatures and my birds have become vegetarians." He said this with a great burst of laughter and kicked the door, which creaked open.

The hut consisted of two large rooms. One was furnished with wickerwork armchairs, dining chairs, and a long table. The other was cluttered with mattresses. What made it even stranger was that the walls were hollowed out with niches fronted by tiny cloth flaps.

"This is my hospital, my clinic. Nobody realizes how much birds, who symbolize freedom, are in fact endangered species."

"Are you a magician?" Pascal asked.

Nestor burst out laughing.

"Me?" he exclaimed. "A magician? No, this is where I live humbly with my son. I'm made of the same flesh and blood as you. Come, follow me instead of asking questions without rhyme or reason. I was telling you that nobody can imagine how endangered birds are. Children hunt them with stones or trap them with glue. During open season, men shoot them down with their guns. They kill them, even going so far as to make delicious meals out of them. It's awful!"

Pascal sat down on one of the armchairs, surprised by the huge weight that once again fell on his shoulders. "I had two thrushes," the old man continued, "who couldn't walk. Fortunately, I managed to mend them."

Pascal placed his head between his hands. On one side, he was relieved to have escaped from Caracalla, yet on the other, he had the disagreeable sensation of having abandoned Najib and, above all, of having been unfaithful to the memory of Amanda.

Nestor disappeared for a moment into the cubbyhole that served as a kitchen and reappeared with a cake made with an ocher-colored flour and covered with brown sugar. When the two men had finished eating, Nestor got up and rubbed Pascal's hands and forearms, making the blood circulate in his limbs and giving off an agreeable warm feeling.

"That's where you catch chills and all sorts of illnesses. Wouldn't you like to lie down? You look as though you need to recuperate."

When Pascal woke up, night had fallen. The large mocking eye of the moon peeped through the window and he could hear a murmur of voices coming from the next room. He was surprised to feel suddenly so strong, so alert, and pushed open the door.

A dozen men and women were seated on the floor around a young boy who was playing a harmonica. He was the spitting image of Nestor, minus the squirrel-gray hair and moustache.

"How are you feeling?" Nestor inquired. "This is Nestor Jr., my son. Unfortunately, his mother left us a few years back. She'd had her fill of this wretched life, of the smell of bird droppings and feathers, which she breathed in from morning to night. I hope that wherever she is, she has found happiness."

All heads turned toward Pascal who, overcoming his shyness, awkwardly introduced himself. "I love music," he smiled. "But I must confess I don't play any instrument."

"Apparently you've come from Caracalla?" one of the men asked. "I tried to get admitted to the colony but, alas, was not accepted."

Pascal stayed a week at Nestor's place. In the afternoons he would ramble on his own in the forest, constantly turning over in his head the events he had lived through at Caracalla. What should he conclude? He had learned that it wasn't enough for society to ban certain toxic elements, such as those of alcohol, money, and tobacco; it was men's hearts that needed changing, but he hadn't learned how to do this. All around him the tree trunks stood smooth and straight as the fingers of a hand and their dense foliage blocked the sun's rays. Patches of light, however, managed in certain spots to dapple their bark and form sparkling pools on the humid, brown soil.

After these forest wanderings, Pascal would go and join the two Nestors for a vegetarian dinner of herbs, seeds, and roots, for which they alone knew the secret. After which they would go and end the evening at one of their friends' places for a concert of country flute, harmonica, or accordion. Pascal loved these sonorities, which harmonized with the night and seemed to emerge from the innermost recesses of his soul.

People treated him with a mixture of respect and familiarity. He knew that behind his back they had nicknamed him "Cardamom" after the name of the spice they added to their food. It amused him a lot but at the same time he wondered what was missing from his own life that would give it a better taste.

It was the day after a memorable evening, during which a musician had played melodies from Nigeria, that Pascal bade farewell to his friends and set off for Marais Salant.

30

When he finally arrived, exhausted, at his destination after a journey of almost ten hours, he had no idea of the commotion his presence would cause. Hadn't Espíritu reassured him: "People have short memories. If you keep quiet, after a few weeks nobody will remember who you are."

At first this had seemed true, since nobody had recognized him as he accompanied Joseph to Porte Océane on his way to Stanford. One thought haunted him: how could he explain his silence of more than a year to those he had left behind such as Maria, Marthe, his mother Fatima, not to mention Albertine, who had given so much of herself to him? Would his old father, Jean Pierre, still be alive?

The so-called Great Northern Road, well maintained and with not a pothole or rut in sight, stretches out between the groves of smooth-leafed banana trees that topple over at the slightest gust of wind. You often drive over rickety bridges spanning rivers with delightful names like Ravine Madame, Ravine des Pères, or Ravine du Pendu, and Pascal could well imagine Water Mama sitting on a rock, combing her long mulatto hair and singing softly so as to lure men to their death.

When he finally reached his house, he saw that a colony of Rastas had pitched blue and white tents in the garden. The numerous Rastas on the island confined themselves to the southeast, an inhospitable region where the police seldom came looking for them. Their prize plant, the Ganja, had taken over the garden and had replaced the beds of hibiscus and bougainvillea. A group of women were breastfeeding their babies on the veranda, which had been closed off on three sides by plywood planks to form a makeshift shelter where a huge portrait of Haile Selassie, once known as Ras Tafari, took pride of place.

Pascal caught sight of a young man who was staring at him wide-eyed and seemed to be the head of the colony. He was handsome, so handsome, with his jet-black skin and a head of hair crowned with tiny locks. Hands crossed against his chest, he kept murmuring, "You? Is it really you?" Pascal ignored his words and replied curtly, "I realize I was wrong to leave the house empty for so long that you thought it had been abandoned. But now that I'm back, I'm asking you to leave quietly as soon as possible."

"Don't you worry," the young man asserted, nodding his head. "We don't want to make a fuss; we'll leave as soon as we've found another place. But people were saying you'd gone up to join your father in Heaven."

Pascal was annoyed at hearing these words. "A load of crap!" he exclaimed. "But perhaps you know the whereabouts of the old man who was living here. He is my true father."

The young man looked deeply saddened. "He was your father? In that case I have some sad news to give you: he died a few months ago."

Pascal was heartbroken. Jean Pierre had died and his son had not been there to close his eyes, an eventuality Pascal had feared would happen.

"Rest assured," the young man quietly continued, "there were crowds of people at his funeral, for he was a man whom the entire island loved and admired. My wives, Maggy and Domitiana, grew very fond of him. They cooked his meals and took great care of him. He departed content to join his wife who had died a few years previously."

Pascal couldn't bear to hear anything more and, with a heavy heart, crossed the street to his mother's house. Was he about to learn that she too had died?

Late as it was, and although the large house was immersed in darkness, Pascal didn't hesitate to knock on the front door. The old servants had gone, and were replaced by a young couple who in turn stared at him wide-eyed. The woman even went so far as to make a vague sign of the cross as if she were confronted with a scorpion or a wild animal.

"I'd like to see my mother, Madame Fatima," Pascal declared.

After a moment's hesitation the couple told him that his mother was in the mother country. Ever since the inexplicable disappearance of her son, she had gone to live over there and had seldom visited the island since. Though she was often to be seen on television. As it was persistently rumored that Pascal had been involved in the attack that had claimed the life of Norbert Pacheco, she had hired the services of one of the best lawyers in Paris who had sworn he would solve the case. With an aching heart, Pascal went home. There was little else to do but go to bed early and fall asleep.

When he woke, the sun was already high in the sky and powdering the trees, houses, and roads with gold. Pascal opened wide the window and filled his lungs with that invigorating smell specific to each region depending on its distance from the sea, the humus of the soil, and the type of vegetation. At Caracalla, he had been the perfect stranger. At Marais Salant, he was home.

The colony of Rastas did not seem at all prepared to lift anchor, as its head had promised. Washing was hanging out to dry on the hedge and children were running and stumbling around. One of them fell flat on his face and on hearing his shrieks, his mother came running. The head of the colony was strolling back and forth, his head stuck in his newspaper, like a priest reading his breviary.

Pascal came down to the kitchen and made himself a cup of coffee. Already ten o'clock! There wouldn't be enough time to do everything he intended. Primarily, to lay hands on Maria, Marthe, and Lazare.

What had appeared to be so easy turned out to be extremely complicated. When he arrived at Beausoleil, where he remembered the trio lived, he found the caretaker's lodge hermetically closed, sealed with the notice: *Closed for vacation in the mother country.* What on earth did that mean? Pascal wondered in annoyance. Besides, what did this term mother country mean anyway? When he entered the building and bumped into a group of adolescents, half-stoned, who were passing around joints in the hall and unable to help him, he became increasingly exasperated.

Remembering that the trio lived on the third floor, he set off up the stairs, since the elevator, of course, was not working. Was it apartment A or apartment B? He pressed the first bell haphazardly. After a while an old woman, muffled up in a heavy flannel dressing gown despite the warm weather, opened the door and, on seeing him, expressed the amazement he was now getting used to.

"No," she explained. "They no longer live here."

"Do you know where I could find them?"

"That I don't know, but perhaps the people at the Arche de la Nouvelle Alliance could help you."

"The Arche de la Nouvelle Alliance?" Pascal repeated mockingly. "What on earth is that?"

The old woman looked surprised. "You've never heard of the Arche! It's the temple, or church if you prefer, they have created where the like-minded gather for their weekly assembly." Thereupon she scribbled an address on a piece of paper and handed it to Pascal. Without further questions he went back down the stairs.

The Arche de la Nouvelle Alliance was located in the quiet historic district in an elegant building along the wharf, wedged between a shop selling salted codfish and another selling rough red wine. A balcony wrapped around the second floor, blossoming with potted plants. The ground floor door was wide open, befitting a place open to the public, and Pascal walked straight in.

Marthe and Maria were seated behind two tiny desks littered with papers and were busy writing. Pascal was irritated by a photo of himself which covered almost an entire wall.

"You?" they both exclaimed in unison, while Marthe slipped down on her knees with a quick sign of the cross.

"Master," Maria murmured. "You've come back."

Furious, Pascal addressed her sharply: "Is it me you're calling Master? Don't you recognize me, the man who shared your bed and gave you all the pleasure you desired?"

Marthe went on to explain. "We thought you had gone back to your father and that's why you disappeared."

"I didn't disappear," Pascal protested, getting even angrier. "I took a leave of absence, perhaps a little too long, admittedly. Long enough for you to make up such nonsense."

"It's not nonsense!" Maria exclaimed.

Getting up, Maria opened a drawer and pulled out a brochure. Pascal snatched it from her hands. It was a booklet with his photo on the cover, and the title *The Life and Teachings of Pascal*. He frenziedly leafed through it: Marcel Marcelin, one of his former disciples, described inside how they had met and the miracles Pascal had accomplished up to the time of his disappearance.

"Marcel Marcelin! Get him to come here immediately!"

"That's what I intended to do," Maria replied, grabbing her mobile phone while Pascal lit up one of his beloved Lucky Strikes in order to calm his nerves.

After a while a car drew up at the gate and Pascal recognized his former disciples: Marcel Marcelin and José Donovo. Instead of embracing him affectionately, the two men remained standing stiffly and, by way of a greeting, joined their palms together against their chests.

"We should make an event out of your unexpected return," Marcel declared. "We must enthrall the entire island."

"Why would you want to make an event out of my return?" Pascal protested. "I learned nothing new, wherever I was. I didn't learn how to root out evil from the hearts of men. But tell me rather, where is Judas Eluthère? I'd like to see him."

Marcel and José squabbled over who should explain to Pascal what had happened during his absence. Judas Eluthère had soon revealed his true face; he had eliminated those who co-managed with him the other Le Bon Kaffé companies, and, even more serious, had carefully hidden his sexual preferences to win the presidency of the Regional Council. It was his turn to become a despot. Swayed by neither strike nor demonstration, and friend of the Minister of the Interior, it was he who gave orders to the police and gendarmes to maintain law and order.

Pascal declared that all of this was quite predictable. Hadn't he tried to warn them?

At that moment Lazare appeared in the room. Pascal barely recognized him. Stronger-looking, dark-skinned, sporting a well-groomed beard, he was no longer the down-and-out individual who had once been "resurrected." Moreover, he no longer lived with his sisters and had been hired by a palliative care hospice in order to convince the patients they had no reason to be scared of death, which is nothing more than a path leading to another life.

Lazare threw himself onto Pascal and hugged him, much to Pascal's delight.

"Where have you been? I heard you were back in Marais Salant; the rumor has already spread around town. So I immediately came to make myself available should your enemy seek to harm you. If you don't know yet, this enemy is Judas Eluthère. You would never think he had once been your friend."

Pascal shrugged his shoulders. "What harm could he do me? After the bomb attack, I was arrested, cleared, and liberated. No charge could be held against me."

Marthe emerged from the room next door, pushing a trolley. She had a knack for preparing delicious light meals:

crab patties and glasses filled with her signature concoction of golden apple juice, rum, and passion fruit.

"I've also made some olive-stuffed pastries," she said, removing the lid on the dish. "You remember what you once told us: 'Every time you eat this, remember me. I shall be with you.'" Pascal helped himself generously to the rum punch.

"I've got an idea," Marcel intervened. "It's your birthday in two weeks' time, as it's Easter Sunday. Let's commemorate the date with a ceremony that will go down in history."

José Donovo and Lazare were not lacking in ideas for the festivities they were planning, yet Pascal protested: "It's ridiculous! What do you expect me to say?"

The noisy, heated discussion continued the entire afternoon.

31

There was one visit Pascal didn't want to miss; he was anxious to see Albertine again. How could he explain his
departure, his absence, and, more than that, such a long
silence? This question he couldn't get out of his mind. He
knew she had rented from Jean Pierre, his adopted father,
the vast place where he had grown up. She lived there with
her six children, who ranged from two to fourteen years
old, as well as her mother, still attractive despite her gray
hair, who was always prepared to supervise the children's
education and help out with the cooking, the housework,
and the garden.

With pounding heart, Pascal crossed the garden and
walked down to the shed where he had been found one
night thirty years ago, lying at the feet of a donkey, like a
picture in the Holy Scriptures. He had never forgotten Eulalie's extravagant description of that moment: "You were
handsome, as handsome as a young king or prince. It was
obvious you were molded from a precious substance unlike
the majority of humans. When I took you up in my arms,
you opened your eyes and looked straight at me. From that
day on I have become your servant."

Recollecting these flattering words, Pascal nevertheless
believed that a mother, rather than being a servant, should,
on the contrary, reprove, teach, punish, scold, and guide
her child to perfection or something similar. It was something he had always blamed Eulalie for: a mixture of adula-
tion and severity for insignificant things. As a result, his
love for her had always been mixed with reproach.

He stopped from time to time to pick and smell a rose
bud, not a Cayenne or Tété Négresse, both varieties of which
could be found in the greenhouses more to the left. On his
reaching the terrace, Albertine came out of the house wear-

ing an original and elegant ensemble that suited her to perfection.

"You!" she cried on seeing him, with a mixture of stupefaction and anger. Pascal dropped to his knees and clung to her legs. "I realize I have behaved terribly," he declared. "I left without an explanation and then didn't write a word. But I'll tell you what happened and you'll understand. Keep a place for me in your heart."

She caressed his hair as she used to do and said softly, "I've no hard feelings. How could I? But before we make the slightest decision, I have to introduce you to someone."

Thereupon she helped Pascal get to his feet and took him inside the house. They walked through several rooms, rudimentarily furnished it must be said, and came to a bedroom, the curtains of which were carefully closed. There, a cradle had been set on the floor and, inside, a pale, delicate baby was fast asleep.

"No, it's not our child," Albertine told Pascal, who was leaning poignantly over the cradle. "After you left, I was so hurt! It was as if my life was over and no longer had any meaning. A man I had known for a long time and whose advances I had always refused took advantage of my distress and seduced me. He's the father of this baby."

Pascal didn't know what to think of this confession. On the one hand, his heart was torn with jealousy upon learning that another man had managed to seduce Albertine and give her a baby, while on the other, he could see that this painful imbroglio was a consequence of the way he had neglected and abandoned her, actions for which he constantly blamed himself. He took her in his arms and whispered tenderly, "Your child is my child. I've come to ask you to forget what happened and to come back home with me."

And that's how Pascal came to live with Albertine, shuttling between her house and the one in Marais Salant. But he soon began to regret his sojourns at Albertine's, since matters rapidly became unbearable. First of all, her children:

always squabbling and screaming when they played football in the garden, or shrieking when they flew their kites. What's more, they were greedy and rude. Pascal had to admit that the worst was the boy born while he was in Caracalla. When he clung to Pascal's chest, slobbering him with wet kisses and calling him Papa, Pascal couldn't refrain from shuddering with disgust. The child was called Igor.

His father was Russian, one of those numerous down-and-out Whites, who had been dragging his loafers around Fonds-Zombi for years with nobody knowing exactly what he did. Some claimed he was a drug trafficker, others that he wrote articles for *Pravda*, although it was common knowledge the paper had stopped printing years ago. Everyone agreed on one thing: he had abandoned Albertine once her belly had begun to swell and the only worldly goods that he left his son were a splendid pair of blue eyes.

Soon it was Albertine herself that Pascal could no longer bear. Unlike the divine Marcel, he would have been incapable of rewriting *Albertine Gone* precisely because she had never left. Where had the love and desire he had once felt for her gone? She was no conversationalist. She was merely content to boast of her children, whom she spoilt outrageously. She even went so far as to consider her Rosa, a teenager with drooping breasts, a paragon of beauty.

Since she was opposed to both air conditioning and fans, nights with Albertine were a nightmare. Through the open window he could see the round eye of the moon and was convinced it was poking fun at him. Why had he so easily accepted her young baby? Shouldn't a man stand firm and refuse certain things? Did Albertine notice the change in Pascal's feelings? In any case, she didn't show it and life continued to trundle on.

Fortunately, when he was at Marais Salant, his inspiration returned, and alone in his office he got a lot of work done. He endeavored to piece together the experience he had lived at Caracalla. He had chosen the autobiography as a genre which allowed him to tell the truth about what really happened in the colony, since the novelist has a serious problem with truth. Who is the person talking about his experiences and his adventures? Is it the novelist himself or an imaginary character or both? Despite these drawbacks, Pascal had found a title for his work: *The Book of the Just*. Sometimes he wondered whether readers would like it. It was true, people loathed and criticized the Mondongues, but it was to be feared that they would not appreciate a book where the Mondongue experiment was depicted purely and simply as a failure.

At Marais Salant, however, the Rastas didn't look as though they were going to settle elsewhere and were becoming increasingly intrusive. The head of the colony began to take liberties. Every time he saw Pascal, he blocked his path and vaunted the attractions of the Rasta religion, which tried Pascal's patience. One day, when Pascal was coming back exhausted from Albertine's, he went too far. He stopped Pascal with a smirk: "Some of us have been obliged to worship a White god, a Jew to be exact. Others an Arab. And lastly, some worship an Indian god who opens the door to Nirvana. It's the first time we Rastas worship a god the same color as us."

"The same color?" Pascal asked, exasperated.

"Yes," the head of the Rasta colony explained. "Haile Selassie was Black like us."

Pascal maintained his self-control and remained silent, until the day the Rasta once again repeated, "I'm telling you, the Rastas are the first to make a Black the Supreme Being."

Pascal replied with a shrug: "And what about the traditional African religions?"

32

There was a constant string of unpleasant matters, in which, rightly or wrongly, he saw the hand of Judas Eluthère. One morning while he was drinking a delicious cup of coffee, there was a knock on the door. It was a young man with a flunkey face, dressed in an elegant navy salt-and-pepper suit.

He introduced himself: "My name is Déodat Lafitte and I'm a lawyer. I need to have a word with you. Could you drop by my office? I'd like to discuss the bomb attack and the consequences it had on your life."

"Why do you want to discuss an attack that happened such a long time ago?" Pascal exclaimed, irked. "I have nothing more to say on the matter. I was arrested, then released, since no charge could be held against me."

"No charge?" the lawyer said. "Precisely. There's the rub, as the saying goes. The police at the time wrongly transcribed the identity of the homeless man who testified in your favor. And despite a massive manhunt, there's no trace of him."

"He's homeless," Pascal joked lightheartedly. "That means he doesn't have a fixed address. It's only normal that after all these years you can't find him."

Seeing the lawyer's serious expression, Pascal's face darkened and he promised to drop by his office. The troubles were starting up again.

A few days later, Pascal dropped by lawyer Lafitte's office as requested. He merely repeated what he had said earlier. The lawyer asked him the same questions he had heard during his interrogation at Marais Salant: "You don't recall which Hitchcock film you saw? Was it *Marnie* or *The Birds*?"

Pascal couldn't remember and apologized. "I believe both films feature the same star: for me all blondes are alike."

He walked out of the lawyer's office and his heart gripped with a dark foreboding.

The second unpleasant matter occurred several days later when he received the visit of a group of police officers who informed him he was not authorized to leave the island.

At the same moment, Marcel Marcelin and José Donovo were arrested and thrown into prison for disturbing the peace at night. Disturbing the peace? What was that about? Pascal learned that every evening since his return Marcel Marcelin and José Donovo had invited the neighbors over into their garden in order to talk about the preparations for the ceremony of Easter, which was to be celebrated with great pomp at the Arche de la Nouvelle Alliance. It was also intended to highlight Pascal's return among them. In order to make it a grand occasion, one evening they invited over an African orchestra that was performing at Félix Eboué Stadium. It was a hullabaloo of balafons and koras, alternating with screams and yells. The neighbors complained and in the middle of the night two prison vans drew up at the gate to the garden. A swarm of police officers climbed out and shoved Marcel and José inside.

On hearing the news, Pascal dashed to the prison and was told that given the enormity of their crime Marcel Marcelin and José Donovo were not authorized to have visits. A few notes of music ... Is that what they call the enormity of their crime? Give me a break!

But matters did not stop there. A few days later a fire broke out at the Arche de la Nouvelle Alliance and if it hadn't been for the night-owl neighbors who had alerted the firefighters, the fire would have spread to the upper floors. For the firemen took their time to arrive and let the flames gaily devour *The Life of Pascal* pamphlets as well as the huge photograph of Pascal on one of the walls.

As a result of all these events, Pascal decided to get in touch with Judas Eluthère, something he hadn't dared do up till now. He had no idea such an appointment was so difficult to obtain. The secretary, still the same and still just as disagreeable, replied that Judas Eluthère was in the mother country, then announced he was up north where some cousins of his were getting married, before finally telling Pascal he was down with dengue fever, an epidemic from Cuba that was making scores of people sick, and consequently was not seeing anyone. Pascal didn't give up, and after four weeks he finally secured an appointment. The secretary, however, arranged for the meeting to be held at the company's office instead of the Regional Council, a move which made Pascal think twice. Did Judas Eluthère want the interview to be more convivial and intimate?

One Tuesday, then, Pascal set off for Sagalin. During the drive, he recollected all those hours spent at the company, trusting in the future and convinced it would be easy to change the world. The town of Sagalin hadn't changed one bit: still just as filthy and still just as rough and grim, strewn with monkey droppings and stray dogs.

At the company's headquarters, Judas Eluthère's office now occupied an entire floor. Pascal sat down in the waiting room, lulled by some elevator music. For over an hour he stared at the faces of world leaders such as Mahatma Gandhi, Nelson Mandela, Barack Obama, and Kwame Nkrumah smiling back at him from the walls. He was about to leave when finally a secretary came to fetch him.

Judas Eluthère had lost none of his good looks nor his elegance. As usual, his handmade patent leather shoes were soft and polished. But he appeared worn out. His voice came out husky and uneven between his lips, which were a little too red. Pascal remembered the ambiguous feelings they had felt for each other, but dared not confess. Now, all that was long gone.

On seeing him Judas Eluthère jumped up, walked round his desk, and planted an affectionate yet hypocritical kiss on both of Pascal's cheeks. The kiss of Judas, in other words! Then he motioned at an armchair to Pascal.

"I hear you've come back to Marais Salant," he said with an obsequious smile. "To my surprise you didn't try to look me up."

Ignoring this unwarranted reproach, Pascal too gave a smile. "On the contrary. Ever since I came back, I've been trying to make an appointment with you, but your secretary constantly invents excuses. What are you blaming me for? You don't think for one moment that I had something to do with the bomb attack! I didn't like Monsieur Pacheco, but you didn't either, if I remember correctly."

Judas Eluthère, who had sat down behind his desk again, got up and offered Pascal a cigarette.

"I know Lucky Strikes are your favorite and you don't smoke any other brand. I have never believed you had something to do with the attack, but it's only normal you are under interrogation since everyone knows you hated Norbert."

"Why did you arrest Marcel Marcelin and José Donovo? Why is it you have to paint such a dark picture? It's you who's behind all this, isn't it?" Pascal asked curtly.

Judas Eluthère shook his head and became lost in denial. Knowing he wouldn't get anything further out of him, Pascal continued: "When I went to the prison to see them, I was stupefied to be told that they were not entitled to visits. Do you call that justice? There was talk about a crime when it's nothing more than a peccadillo."

Judas Eluthère made a wave of the hand. "Since I'm telling you I had nothing to do with this affair, why are you making such a fuss about it? Why are you wasting your time with these men? Have you read the pamphlet they published about you? It's perfectly useless and claims to imitate one of the Gospels of Our Lord Jesus Christ, Saint Mark's I believe! I'm telling you they've got nothing in their heads and will only cause you trouble."

Pascal drew on his cigarette and Judas continued: "I've already told you, there are two types of men, winners and losers, those whose life is chaos and those who manage to put their house in order."

"You look tired," Pascal repeated. "Is it because you're now in politics? I've got a very effective herb tea made with passiflorine. It's a plant my parents grew at The Garden of Eden which they said worked very well."

Judas Eluthère thanked him with a vague gesture and Pascal continued, unrelenting. "You are now President of the Regional Council. Have you forgotten how we always said the only true path led to independence?"

"Independence?" Judas Eluthère exclaimed. "It's a word which no longer has any meaning. You have to go with the times. Nowadays, no country is independent. China depends on the US, along with Saudi Arabia and other Gulf states. I can only repeat what Norbert Pacheco said: 'Every man needs to be assured of a good wage, adequate housing, and the best education for his children.' He was perfectly right but we didn't listen."

"Man doesn't live by bread alone," Pascal grumbled, not knowing what else to say.

"Since you mention food," Judas said, "I'll take you to the isle of Bédier, where I discovered a small restaurant, Au Bec Fin, managed by Indonesians. You know, you can find anything you want on our island. Last week, a ship unloaded a hundred or so Japanese who were not interested in the restaurant business but rather in computer science. Au Bec Fin has the best nasi goreng in the world."

Pascal hesitated. He could no longer put up with Judas Eluthère's arrogance and his complacency. Yet at the same time, he thought it essential to keep up good relations. Consequently, he accepted the proposition and the two men left Le Bon Kaffé together. Judas Eluthère now owned a brand-new navy-blue convertible. They climbed in while Judas waved to the old guardian whom Pascal remembered from former times.

33

In order to get to the isle of Bédier, you have to drive ten kilometers along a winding road until you reach the harbor of Sagalin. There, sailors disguised as Venetian gondoliers wait in two launches to take you to the restaurant Au Bec Fin. Usually you have to wait a good hour before setting off, but as Judas Eluthère was a celebrity he was given priority. Once they were aboard, Pascal left Judas to wallow in one of the red leather armchairs in the smoking room, and climbed up to the bridge to gaze around.

The sea doesn't look like a graveyard; it's lively, joyous, and sparkling. It changes its finery in order to please the sky, soaring above. Sometimes it dresses in blue, sometimes in green, and sometimes in gray. It only dresses in black when the winds blow up from the lands to the south where the climate is too hot. Its waves then swell and heave, revealing their teeth of foam. Despite its peaceful appearance, the sea is a graveyard, a tombstone. From time immemorial, it has seen countless shipwrecks sink to the ocean floor: slave ships loaded with their cargos of black gold, Spanish galleons with their treasures of precious stones and diamonds, motor launches carrying their lucrative lots of drugs from Latin America, and cruise ships harboring in their flanks the jewels of wealthy tourists. It is said that the ocean depths are blue and always cold; it is said that they are home to shapes difficult to identify. What sort of creatures could be down there? And how did they get there? Whatever the case, they would appear to be happy, playing and dancing freely in the deep silence of the ocean bed. The sea's favorites are the great white shark and the moonstone shark. Contrary to common belief, they avoid humans, as they like neither the smell nor the taste of blood. They chase after each other like harmless, innocent children. Second favorites are the squid and the octopus waving their long slender arms. The sea also likes delicate-shaped little fish such as the catfish, the sunfish, and above all the flying fish who, in a flash of light, leap out of the water. At the very bottom are the shellfish, similar to ornamental caskets, whose golden reflections shimmer in the darkness. The sea is rich with treasures that the human eye cannot see.

After this visit to Sagalin, Pascal and Judas Eluthère resumed contact, though episodically and superficially. Nothing was the same. Pascal sometimes even wondered whether Judas hadn't resumed their relationship in order to keep a closer eye on him and put an end to the plans he toyed with. For example: as the weeks went by, he felt lost in the house at Marais Salant with its ten rooms and its huge garden, especially since the colony of Rastas had finally left. He decided to turn it into a refuge for migrants, those men and women he had always admired who entrusted their life's savings to smugglers and risked their lives on the high seas and whom he had never endeavored to help. By way of a response to his permit request, he received a note from a subordinate at the Regional Council stating that any such request is refused since the migrants are all dangerous terrorists. Second example: he decided to turn the house into a sports center; since Albertine's sons had nothing better to do, he wouldn't need instructors. Once again, his request was rejected.

Disappointed, Pascal immersed himself in his writing again. He sent Judas a copy of his book *The Book of the Just*, which had recently been published at the author's expense by a small Parisian press, and a packet of passiflorine, which he had totally forgotten to send over earlier. A few days later, the secretary, now perfectly agreeable, invited him to a debate at the Regional Council by two visiting and well-known philosophers who were here to discuss his book. He was weak-willed enough to feel flattered. When he announced the news to Albertine, she looked doubtful.

She had had a dream where, according to her, nothing good could come out of such a meeting. On the contrary, it was likely a prelude to even greater dangers. Pascal refused to listen to her. Albertine, like Maria, were members of that depressing clan of people who analyze their dreams ad nauseam. When they first fell in love, they would wake up so late that Albertine didn't have time to interpret her dreams. But her endless confabs with her mother had resumed during the past few weeks. "You dreamed of blood?" Albertine would ask him. "That means an affront. Be careful whom you meet today." Utter nonsense, Pascal thought, determined to do as he pleased. With his mind made up, he set off for Porte Océane.

The Regional Council edifice was the jewel of Porte Océane. It had been rebuilt after the terrible hurricane of 1928 in compliance with the plans of a Swedish architect who had come to spend his vacation on the island and fallen in love with the place. It was a very elegant building adorned with two flights of steps where tourists liked to have their photo taken.

The room where the discussion was to take place was crammed full with the type of people who have nothing better to do with their afternoons. The debate got underway in a very lively fashion and lasted almost two hours. Unfortunately, it was obvious to Pascal that the two philosophers, despite their polite airs, had nothing good to say about his book and were doing their best to attract the audience to their own work. Disappointed, Pascal left before the reception.

Barely had he got home to Marais Salant when the television reported that the President of the Regional Council had been involved in a serious car accident while driving back from Port Océane. He had miraculously survived but his convertible had been totally wrecked against a tree. The journalist explained that Judas Eluthère had probably fallen asleep at the wheel.

Gripped with a gloomy foreboding, Pascal couldn't sleep a wink the entire night. The following morning, he received a call from lawyer Lafitte asking why he had given Judas Eluthère a packet of passiflorine. "I gave him some passiflorine," Pascal answered, "because my parents considered it a powerful tonic."

"Perhaps that's why he fell asleep at the wheel ... don't you think?" the lawyer joked insistently. Pascal swore that such an idea was nonsense.

Nevertheless, however unbelievable it may seem, the rumor that he had given the President of the Regional Council a sleeping pill blew up out of all proportion. It was talked about on the verandas, in the living rooms, in the dining rooms, in the kitchens, and above all in the bedrooms. Tongues wagged triumphantly: Rumor had it that he was involved in the attack that caused the death of Norbert Pacheco, remember? And now he was perhaps guilty of having tried to murder the President of the Regional Council as well.

Pascal felt obliged to consult with a Monsieur Joyau, a French man who had written a book on local medicinal plants. He arrived at lunchtime, dressed in a T-shirt and a pair of shorts, a look that foreigners are all too often fond of wearing in our climes. Pascal explained that there was no risk of falling asleep from passiflorine and that he had drunk liters and liters of it when he was a child.

"Liters and liters?" the visitor repeated. "Why did your parents give it to you to drink?"

"They gave it to me whenever I felt tired," Pascal replied.

Thereupon the Renouxs, his neighbors to the right, who had just built an infinity pool around which they invited their friends to lunch, gave him the cold shoulder. But it's true they had already snubbed Albertine when she turned up in the neighborhood. Gradually Pascal became a pariah again. He only needed to stop by the neighborhood bar for half the customers to leave, while the other half cast furious glances. The atmosphere surrounding Pascal became unbearable.

What tormented him even more was Judas Eluthère's absence. His secretary, now extremely frosty, informed Pascal that Judas Eluthère had been invited by the President of the Republic in person for his advice on the problem of multiculturalism which was causing havoc in the nation.

34

In the midst of all these troubles, Pascal saw on the sidewalk a man who looked familiar. Wasn't it Espíritu? Yes, it was indeed Espíritu, smoking a small Brazilian cigar. Espíritu rushed over and hugged Pascal affectionately. Pascal did not appreciate such a gesture and asked him curtly "What are you doing here?" because Pascal was now convinced that by claiming to come to his rescue and sending him to the Mondongues, Espíritu had made fun of him and knowingly thrown him into the lion's den.

Apparently indifferent to such an idea, Espíritu dragged him inside the house. Once they had settled down with two cups of coffee, Espíritu declared, "I've come to announce an important piece of news. Your father is about to leave. I think you should come and see him before he does, otherwise you'll spend the rest of your life repeating that he abandoned you and wondering why."

"Where's he going?" Pascal asked.

Espíritu made a vague gesture. "Wherever he's called. Wherever he's needed. You must come and take over."

"Take over?" Pascal exclaimed. "What do you mean? Nobody has ever told me what I'm expected to do."

"But," Espíritu declared, "we told you your mission was to change the world, to make it more tolerant and more at peace."

"Make it more tolerant and more at peace!" Pascal shouted. "But how can I manage to do that all on my own?"

Pascal was torn between contradictory feelings. He couldn't ask for anything better than to leave Marais Salant, and therefore leave Albertine. It would be a neat way to bid her farewell. "We'll discuss all that another time. I'm not asking you for an immediate answer," Espíritu continued in a conciliatory tone. "I'm merely asking you to give it consideration."

Pascal suddenly slapped his forehead. It had completely slipped his memory: "But I can't leave. I promised the police I wouldn't leave the island. Besides, they have confiscated my passport."

Espíritu didn't seem moved by the news and burst out laughing. "But you don't need a passport. Let me remind you what I've already told you, I've got a private jet and can go wherever I want, whenever I want. That's how I traveled with your father and visited the countries where we believed evil was at work: South Africa with apartheid; India with the untouchables and the general status of women; Iraq and Iran. I know all the air traffic controllers, and beware anyone who asks me for my ID."

Such an idea was increasingly tempting. Pascal had never given up on the idea of meeting his father and knowing exactly where he came from—although this search for where we come from is common to most mortals.

In order to make things easier, Espíritu moved in with Albertine, whose children adored him like a father. It was a never-ending round of teasing, jokes, and games. Such agitation soon began to annoy Pascal, for Albertine's children, except for Igor, had never treated him like that; on the contrary, they had always given him the cold shoulder. Albertine's mother also seemed attracted to the newcomer's charms. She would cook him special little dishes and serve him glasses of 55-degree rum which she kept in her larder. Espíritu was not to be outdone. He carried her baskets when she went to market and sometimes even accompanied her to see her friends. As for Albertine, she too seemed under the spell of this uncle who had appeared out of the blue.

Matters dragged on for days, weeks, since Pascal was incapable of making up his mind. Until Espíritu, taking him by the arm as he was fond of doing, suggested, "Wouldn't you like to at least come and see the private jet that will take us to Brazil?"

It was two in the afternoon and the heat was stifling. On the deserted streets, the shadows shrunk under the feet of the few passersby. Having just emerged from a copious lunch at Albertine's, it would have been undoubtedly much more agreeable to sleep it off in an air-conditioned room, but curiosity won the day and both men set out.

At the start of the century, Valmondon Airport was the scene of aerial exploits by the sons of wealthy landowners and merchants. One of them, Philippe de Laville-Tremblay, even has his feats mentioned in the numerous tourist guides. Today the airport is known instead for its famous sporting events: ping-pong contests, bicycle races, and boxing matches. It is shaped like a vast isosceles triangle edged on one side by the blue of the sea and on the other by the majestic trunks of sandbox, mahogany, and mapou trees.

The Gulfstream G650ER jet owned by Espíritu was parked in a vast hangar. Pascal inspected it with stupefied admiration. The cabin could accommodate ten passengers judging by the number of seats arranged around elegant low tables. A soft-looking red carpet covered the floor and a flat-screen TV filled one of the walls. Pascal, who was used to the basic features of coach class, couldn't get over it.

"We'll fly to Miami and New York before heading down to Brazil," Espíritu declared.

"New York?" Pascal exclaimed in amazement. "But that's not the way to Brazil. Brazil is much farther south, if I'm right."

Espíritu nodded. "Yes, of course, but these are cities I believe you should get to know. You haven't traveled enough. How many times have you left the island? You haven't rubbed and sharpened your brain enough against those of others."

"We're going to New York?" Pascal insisted.

"I promise!" Espíritu said.

That day, Pascal made up his mind. The two men entered the airport bar and sealed their agreement with a rum punch.

The following days went by very quickly. Filled with a deep sense of liberation, Pascal informed Albertine that he had to accompany his uncle to Brazil. She wept and pulled out all the stops, but Pascal was convinced that deep down she didn't mind. There was nothing between them any longer.

When he really thought about it, there was nothing to keep him here on the island. He had been struck by the lack of logic of his entourage; above all, he had never got over his problems with Judas Eluthère. To think there was a time when he thought they were one and the same. He recalled the times when Judas sang in his pretty, high-pitched voice: "I dream of a world where the earth will be round ..."

A few days before he was due to leave, Pascal decided to pay Maria and Marthe a visit. Ever since the fire that had destroyed the Arche de la Nouvelle Alliance, they had taken refuge in a densely populated housing estate, the Cité des Merveilles, and earned their living from dyeing meters of fabric with blue indigo according to a technique from Africa. As for the Frenchman who for a time had bedded down with Maria, he had vanished and had probably gone back to the mother country. Pascal could never look at Maria without a pang of conscience. To think they had been so much in love. To think he believed he had found in her the woman who embodied all he could wish for. He was now convinced that love is a rebellious bird, as the well-known opera says, a capricious god who does exactly as it pleases.

He therefore went to tell Maria and Marthe his mind was made up. Marcel Marcelin and José Donovo had been so sickened by their arbitrary arrest and their stay in prison that they had gone back to the mother country to look for work.

"You're off again!" Maria reproached him. "You know what the proverb says: A rolling stone gathers no moss. Be patient, one day your suffering will be over and you will flood the world with your light."

"What light?" Pascal asked, annoyed.

Maria did not answer and instead continued excitedly, "We have a lot of followers of the Arche de la Nouvelle Alliance among the French-speaking community in New York. We'll let them know you're coming. They'll be overjoyed to meet you and will welcome you with the honors you deserve."

Pascal didn't like that declaration either. But he kept this to himself and did justice to the drinks Marthe had prepared.

35

Exhausted by his long hours of piloting, Espíritu soon fell asleep, mouth wide open on his carnassial teeth, as he sat in the back of the taxi that had been waiting for them in New York. What an oddball Espíritu was, with his big eyes sparkling with irony and his words whose meaning was often incomprehensible. Pascal continued to ask himself whether he had, after all, been right to follow him once again.

Pascal was seated beside the driver. Little did he know that in America people are very talkative and have no scruples bombarding visitors with indiscreet questions. The driver was a Haitian, his skin weathered like old leather and his face lined with a flowery moustache. He'd been knocking around America for so long he could practically only speak English; mispronounced and halting, his French sounded like a foreign language.

"What!" the driver exclaimed. "You've never been to Port-au-Prince? You don't know New York? And you've never visited Paris either?" Pascal felt obliged to answer his silly questions instead of gazing at the city.

Whereas he had thought Miami a metropolis devoid of interest, embellished mainly by the presence of the sea and the bite of the sun, New York promised to be something rare, precious, and priceless: the yellow cabs, the many-colored, gaily dressed people crowding the intersecting streets, and the skyscrapers, ah the skyscrapers, especially for Pascal who had never been higher than a third floor. What was it like to be way up there? It was said they grew genuine vegetable gardens on the roofs: lettuce, vegetables, and fruit, food from the roots of heaven. They drove diagonally from one end of New York to the other as dusk gradually fell. When they arrived at Brooklyn Bridge it was already dark. Each side of the river was lit up by street lamps glittering like balloons.

The five-star Belo Horizonte Hotel where they had booked two rooms was a favorite with businessmen from Brazil since it offered all kinds of entertainment. For carnival, for example, the staff dressed up and danced the samba. Espíritu seemed to know the area like the back of his hand and took Pascal for dinner at a Mexican restaurant, La Rosita, close by. It was obvious that the waitresses, who were so lovely and so elegant, were not there merely to change the plates and fill the glasses. It seemed highly likely they also escorted customers to more private rooms. Pascal and Espíritu ordered a dish that Pascal had never tasted before: a pork stew smothered with chocolate and downed with numerous tequilas.

Leaving Espíritu, who said he was tired, to return to the hotel on his own, Pascal set out to conquer the city. He walked along streets and avenues, quite oblivious as to where he was. Sometimes he was flooded with light from places above his head one moment and then swallowed in darkness. He walked through splashes of light and the black of night. His feverish brain led him blindly here and there. At one point he found himself on a river bank. A ship blazing with light descended slowly, probably to the mouth of the river. Pascal would have loved to be aboard and raise a glass to friendship and goodwill.

He followed a small crowd of people into a nightclub, The Blue Cockatoo. A Black woman dressed in white was hollering out all the despair and desperation of Southern slavery, segregation, and lynching—when strange fruit hung from the branches of the trees. At the same time, her voice was filled with hope, rich with a vibrato embodying faith and courage. Perhaps she symbolized Black America, how a profound determination was able to overcome tribulation and keep the dream intact. When the couples in the club started to embrace, Pascal withdrew and returned to the hotel. It was around two in the morning.

To his surprise a ray of light shone under Espíritu's bedroom door. Pascal thought he heard two voices, one higher-pitched and crystal clear. Was Espíritu with a woman? Pascal had never wanted to offend Albertine, but he was never under any illusion about the nature of the relationship between her mother and Espíritu. One afternoon he had practically caught them in each other's arms; he was still laughing at the memory when he fell into the watery bed of sleep.

And he was still laughing the following morning when Espíritu came to wake him up. The two men tucked into a copious breakfast in the hotel dining room then climbed into a cab waiting in the nearby parking lot. Very rapidly, Pascal's euphoria on discovering New York the day before changed into a stupefied disillusionment. Where had the wealth and beauty he had caught sight of the day before gone? The morning was gray and dirty. The streets were crowded with people dressed in ugly clothes, all wearing plain, heavy woolen bonnets and unsightly caps, running to catch a bus or dashing down the steps to the subway. After almost an hour, the taxi stopped in front of a small, temple-like, colonnaded building in the center of a shabby-looking garden.

When they walked in, they saw fifty or so people were waiting for them: men, women, and even children. On seeing them, everyone stood up and made the humble greeting that Pascal loathed: head lowered and hands joined together against their breast. A pastor dressed in a blue alb going by the name of Pastor Edison embraced them familiarly and began his sermon.

Pascal had studied English at school but had never remembered much and ranked it with those subjects that were best forgotten. But that morning, to his amazement, he perfectly understood the pastor and all the others who spoke English. Even more surprising was the fact that he himself could speak English: "You don't know who I am, because I don't know myself. It would be presumptuous of me to believe you and I have different origins. What have I done to deserve your attention? My entire life has been one long apprenticeship. Most of the questions I've asked myself have remained without an answer."

Some raised their hands and intervened in Spanish, a language Pascal had never studied but immediately understood. This convivial and friendly conversation lasted almost two hours, ending in a hymn that sounded familiar. Then Pastor Edison asked them for a final favor: to sign autographs, kiss the children, and write their thoughts down in the visitors' book.

It was then that a woman of a certain age approached them with outstretched hands and invited them to lunch. "I live a few steps from here," she smiled. "I would be so pleased if you accepted." On receiving an affirmative reply, she motioned to a pretty young girl, who was her spitting image, to come over, and then turned to Pastor Edison: "If you accept the invitation as well, Reverend, I would be truly blessed."

The woman was called Denim and came from Tennessee. Her daughter went by the name of Norma. Denim was very proud of Norma; having raised her on her own without a husband or her parents' help, she had managed to make her into an elementary school teacher who taught at one of the best schools in Brooklyn. Furthermore, Norma played the recorder to perfection and was a member of an ensemble that was beginning to make a name for itself. "Can you imagine, they've just won a contract with Motown," her mother crowed.

When the small group left the temple, the sight of this narrow street, lined with rundown tenement buildings zigzagged by rusty fire escapes, made Pascal's heart bleed. They entered one of the grim-looking buildings and, since there was no elevator, climbed up the staircase with its threadbare carpet. On the third floor, a door opened surprisingly onto a cramped but pleasant living room. It was flooded with light through the windows. On a low table there were photos of Martin Luther King and his wife Coretta and on the wall a huge portrait of Malcolm X.

"What do you think of your morning?" Espíritu whispered, knowing full well what Pascal thought. So as not to engage in an argument, Pascal merely shrugged his shoulders. The lunch was excellent and consisted of beans, pork chops seasoned with an unfamiliar spice, and oddly flavorful root vegetables.

"After New York, where are you going?" Denim asked.

"To Recife," Espíritu replied, to the amazement of Pascal, who had been convinced they were going to Asunción.

"So we're not going to Asunción?" Pascal whispered.

"Not directly," Espíritu retorted.

"Where exactly is my father?" Pascal asked, boiling with anger.

"Haven't I already told you?" Espíritu said.

It was not the place to start a quarrel, so Pascal decided to keep quiet and concentrate on the cigarette he was smoking.

Pascal was afraid he was being led on a wild goose chase. Wouldn't he have been wiser not to have trusted Espíritu? Where had his father gone? Was he dead? He couldn't stop wondering. After a delicious cup of coffee, Denim asked Norma to play her flute in order to enchant her visitors. She willingly obeyed, and it was a moment of perfect harmony.

When they left Denim's apartment, dusk had fallen; it mercifully masked the city's open wounds and returned the beauty that the day had taken away.

36

Pascal thoroughly enjoyed his stay in New York. While Espíritu constantly conversed with mysterious visitors, Pascal set out to discover the city. He would return in the evening so exhausted and worn out, he could hardly touch his dinner. He deserved a gold medal for visiting all the places on the list of the perfect tourist: Ellis Island, the Empire State Building, the Audubon Ballroom, the Black Star Line Museum, and the Dakota Building. His reason for visiting all these places, however, was not because they were tourist must-sees, but because each and every one of them conjured up for Pascal personal memories.

Take Ellis Island for example. When he was a child, he discovered in one of Eulalie's drawers a photograph of a group of young women from Guadeloupe in traditional costume being interrogated by immigration officers. A few words on the back indicated that the photo was taken on April 6, 1911. Why had these young women decided to settle in America? All Eulalie knew was that one of them was a friend of her grandmother's and had lived in Panama. Pascal was amazed by the courage and determination of these young women from a tiny island sailing so far from home without a husband or a man to accompany them.

The Audubon Ballroom: that's where Malcolm X was assassinated right in front of his family. He could have been a close relative of Eulalie with his high yellow color and reddish hair.

As for the Black Star Line, it was the first of its kind to achieve Marcus Garvey's dream and take Black Americans to freedom.

It was in front of the Dakota Building that John Lennon was shot. John Lennon had become Pascal's idol. In the beginning, he had disliked the piano lessons Eulalie forced him to take with Monsieur Démon. He thought them a boring assignment, part of a well-bred child's education according to his adoptive mother's petit-bourgeois standards. Then the power of music had taken hold of him and, despite everything, he had become a music lover. He made no distinction between classical and pop music, unlike the way he had been taught, and adored all types of melodies.

One evening while he was back at the hotel, Pastor Edison called: Could he bring a visitor who had traveled a long way simply to meet him? The two men made an appointment for the following day. Upon his arrival in the hotel lobby Pascal found them waiting for him. They were complete opposites. Whereas the pastor was short and chubby, dressed in his same old blue alb, the skinny, rawboned newcomer was encased in a heavy camel-hair overcoat, although it was only early September, and his face was draped in a thick white scarf.

Pastor Edison introduced the stranger. "Here's my friend Dr. Saul. I told you he's come a very long way to meet you. He's come from Damascus."

"From Damascus?" Pascal asked in surprise.

"Yes, I've come from Damascus where I'm the director of the Nouvelle Alliance."

"You too have a Nouvelle Alliance?" Pascal asked in amazement.

"It's a long story, which I'm sure will interest you. I belong to a very wealthy Catholic family. I was barely four years old when my parents told me of everlasting life and the ways to prepare for it. Perhaps that's why I came to detest the notion as I grew up and began to dream of a world without God. To worship a divinity, I thought, revealed the weakness of the human heart. I dreamed of a world where, guided by reason alone, every one of us would make sure not to harm our neighbor. I created an association of atheists and freethinkers, always prepared to criticize and run down the believers. Then one day on the road to Damascus a loud voice called out to me and made me fall from my horse: 'Saul, why do you persecute me?' my ears heard."

"This story reminds me of something," Pascal chuckled. "I've already heard it somewhere."

"I'm not surprised," Saul answered. "It's very well known. Have you seen the painting by Caravaggio, *The Conversion of Saint Paul?*"

Pascal confessed he knew nothing about painting.

"If you like, I can take you to MOMA. New York has some of the finest museums in the world."

Then he continued: "From that day on, my life completely changed. Back in Damascus I married the woman I had been living with for years. As soon as they were old enough, our children attended a religious school. I was eager to found the Arche de la Nouvelle Alliance, where we now have numerous followers. And that brings me to you. We would be overjoyed if you could come and visit us. Alas, Pastor Edison tells me you will be unable to accompany me."

Pascal was overwhelmed with questions. How come he had heard of the Arche de la Nouvelle Alliance, which had been created on an obscure, anonymous island? What did he know about Corazón Tejara? He was filled with a strange sense of propriety and he let the visitor continue with his series of anecdotes.

"One day I was called to the bedside of a woman who had just had a terrible car accident (for I was a doctor) minutes before the priest was to come and administer the last rites. But hardly had I laid my hands on her breast and uttered aloud 'Pascal, Pascal' (that's your name, isn't it?) than she got up and trotted around like a young damsel."

Or one more: "One morning, some parents in despair had me come to the bedside of their only son. He had swallowed some lychee seeds and suffocated. I laid my hands on his throat and he sat up, healed, and began to speak with a voice that was crystal clear."

At the conclusion of their visit, not knowing whether he had lived up to expectations, Pascal accompanied Pastor Edison and Saul to the subway. As they were about to perform the traditional salutation Pascal stopped them and said, "What are you doing? I'm your brother, not your master, nor your Messiah—simply your brother."

Once he had exhausted all the sights, Pascal let himself be swayed by the rhythm of the city that never sleeps, its heart beating inordinately. Past midnight, he found himself lost amid milling crowds and deafened by the clamor of vehicles. The day before he left, he found The Blue Cockatoo again, the nightclub he had looked for in vain on previous nights. It was still packed, but the singer had been replaced by an older, buxom woman. The melodies she sang, however, were the same, a blend of despair and unwavering belief. Pascal had never been so moved, listening to her sing "Sometimes I Feel Like a Motherless Child" while he sipped his Glenfiddich whisky.

When he decided to leave, he bumped into an old Black man on the sidewalk who was not begging but whose face was sad and miserable. Taking his wallet out of his pocket, Pascal drew out a wad of dollars and handed it to the stupefied old man. For once he's in luck, Pascal said to himself on his way back to the hotel.

37

When they arrived at Recife around eleven in the evening, the airport was still humming with activity and brilliantly lit. During the final leg of the flight, Espíritu had switched to automatic pilot and the cabin was soon filled with the sound of him snoring while he slept on a sofa. Pascal's heart was gripped with a growing anxiety at the thought that they could get lost at any moment in the darkness, and reach that one shore where nobody wants to arrive before their time.

Suddenly, just before their arrival, Espíritu woke up and landed them safely. Pascal felt strangely sad at having to leave this private jet that had transported them so faithfully and to hand it over to a crew of apparently sturdy and competent mechanics. He was gradually entering an invisible world, beyond his control.

The night was already pitch-black and with a nip in the air. The customs and police officers greeted Espíritu with a respectful familiarity and words of welcome as if the prodigal son had returned home after a long absence. On the other hand, the passengers stared at him in amazement. The children especially had no scruples laughing outright in his face. Pascal had never managed to come to terms with Espíritu's strange appearance: it wasn't just his getup—the outmoded pinstripe suit buttoned up to the neck and his turned-down patent leather boots—more than that, it was his bearing, with that hump hidden behind his back. As for Espíritu, he seemed totally oblivious to the impression he made and strode along holding his suitcase as if nothing were wrong. A line of taxis was waiting in front of the airport terminal and the two men dived into a Mercedes.

The Tejaras lived in Mangistu, an elegant, residential suburb. They had occupied the same house since the seventeenth century, ever since a Tejara had made a name for himself as champion of the poor. The villa consisted of a series of spacious rooms decorated with masterpieces. Two servants welcomed Pascal and embraced Espíritu familiarly. They spoke fluent French and turning to Pascal asked, "Did you have a good trip?"

Espíritu introduced them: "She's Margarita; he's Hermenius."

Despite the relatively late hour, they proposed serving dinner, but Pascal and Espíritu declined and climbed up to the first floor arm in arm.

He had barely opened the door to a comfortable bedroom with its sofa bed covered by a thick orange counterpane, than Pascal felt a strange presence. Turning to Espíritu, he asked, "My father used to live here, didn't he?"

"Yes," replied Espíritu. "It was his bedroom up to the age of seventeen or eighteen. Then one of our aunts lived here. But tomorrow is another day. We'll start the serious business tomorrow."

Left on his own, Pascal walked out onto the small balcony that overlooked the garden. The moon was hidden behind the scudding ink-colored clouds. The wind had freshened up and Pascal had the feeling that this trip would not turn out as he had imagined. And yet this chill in the air and the darkness had a soothing effect. The day before he left, he recalled, the neighbors had once again dumped the contents of their garbage cans on his flower beds. After having smoked a number of Lucky Strikes, he reluctantly went back to bed.

On the bedside table there was a photo of a very handsome teenager with a mass of curly hair and almond-shaped eyes sparkling with intelligence. His clothes were of the latest fashion and it was difficult to say exactly when the photo had been taken. Who was he? Was this Corazón Tejara? Pascal thought he somewhat resembled this stranger. He had never seen a portrait of his father, though he had often imagined him; sometimes good-looking, sometimes ugly and rigged out with a ridiculous moustache, as Sarojini had suggested. While he was putting away his clothes in the wardrobe he discovered four photo albums. Opening them in anticipation, he found he had all the Corazón Tejaras he wanted: from a dandy to a punk, with an attractive girl in tow, from an intellectual squeezed into a Mao suit with four pockets carrying a heavy briefcase to a magus wrapped in a flowing toga. They were all there.

Pascal fell asleep delighted, for he had the impression of having finally got to know the man who had fathered him. That night he had a dream that Albertine would have loved. He found himself facing a high mountain covered in thick vegetation and the question of how to climb it. To climb a mountain, Albertine's mother would have solemnly said, means coming up against an insurmountable obstacle.

Around ten in the morning, Espíritu came to interrupt — his dreaming and, sitting on the edge of his bed with one of his same old cigars stuck in the corner of his mouth, he said, "Make an effort to try and understand me. Your father left weeks ago and gave you the freedom to succeed him and do as you please."

"You mean I won't see him during my stay?" Pascal asked, endeavoring to keep calm, for he had been expecting so much from this meeting. Since he didn't get a reply, he insisted, "I'm asking you to explain what you mean by 'Your father left weeks ago.' What does it mean exactly? Has he simply left Recife? Is he dead?"

"I could reply in the affirmative," Espíritu said. "Would that mean anything? I've already told you that it all depends on the meaning we give to the word 'death.' For some people, it's merely a temporary separation, but for others, it's a door to something else. A poet wrote that the dead are not dead. An African, I think, by the name of Birago Diop. You've heard of him, haven't you?"

"Stop dodging the question," Pascal exclaimed roughly. "Answer yes or no."

"Yes or no, I'm telling you it doesn't mean a thing," Espíritu insisted. "But if you prefer, I can answer yes."

Pascal got up, endeavoring to keep cool and avoid beating Espíritu black and blue, and went out onto the balcony. What was he going to do now? What was to become of him? Here he was stranded in a foreign country whose language and customs he was not familiar with. Who could he turn to? Who could help him? He decided to go back inside.

Espíritu hadn't moved and, sprawling on the bed, greeted him with one of his secretive smiles. "We'd do best," he declared, "to go down and have breakfast. You'll see, Brazilian food is delectable. For our good fortune, Marietta has been treating us to delicious meals for years now. Mark you, she was once your father's mistress and feels quite at home here."

Without answering, Pascal accompanied him downstairs.

The dining room was also elegant and decorated with bouquets of purplish flowers the like of which Pascal had never seen before. They sat down at a white-and-green wickerwork table. Throughout breakfast Espíritu didn't stop chattering in an accumulation of hollow, superficial words, which were aimed at filling the silence and preventing Pascal from expressing his anger and disappointment. "You see," Espíritu said, "this is mango jam. You need to pick the fruit when it's just right for eating, and not too ripe, otherwise it becomes an inedible mess."

It was close to noon when Pascal ventured out to discover the city. Recife is not lacking in charm, its main attraction being the finery of its trees with their thick shiny leaves straight out of a painting by Françoise Semiramoth. But Pascal remained insensitive to the sight. He wondered whether he wouldn't do better to return home. But something told him that his adventure was not over. There remained other dramas to undergo and finally reach journey's end.

An island is oddly located at the center of Recife, linked by a series of bridges. Pascal walked out onto one of them and, standing at the parapet, gazed at the bubbling water below, then set off wandering aimlessly. After a while he reached a neighborhood that amazed him with its ugliness. He guessed it was a favela, the only word he knew in Brazilian. He stared dumbfounded at the stunted trees along the sidewalks and the rundown buildings patched up with mismatched materials where wood rubbed shoulders with iron, cement blocks, and pieces of plastic. The narrow, ill-paved streets seethed with a ragged humanity where women lined up at the water faucets, as they did in underdeveloped countries, and children played football in the hope of one day becoming a future Pelé. The sun in its indifference smothered this misery with its rays as it is used to doing in tropical countries and the heat felt like the inside of an oven.

The following morning, Pascal and Espíritu set off for Asunción.

38

Pascal had retained dismal memories of the ashram The Hidden God. As he remembered, it was an ugly rectilinear building with a flat roof that housed both the guest rooms as well as the auditoriums for concerts, colloquiums, and lectures.

In the space of a few years, it had been entirely remodeled thanks to a generous gift from an American in Nevada, he as well eager to change the world. Now a series of charming one- and two-room cottages had been built under the manicured trees, surrounded by multicolored flower beds. The star attraction of the restoration was a fountain carved out of thick blue glass whose iridescent water splashed into a basin shaped like a shell.

Espíritu accompanied Pascal to the cottage where he was to be housed, an elegant little building that opened onto the garden through a wide bay window and was decorated with the inevitable portraits of Nelson Mandela, Mahatma Gandhi, Pope John Paul ii, and other dreamers who had all hoped for a better world.

They then walked to the reception to meet the new director, by the name of Sergio Stefanini, who, despite his Italian-sounding name, was a native of Asunción. He had an athletic build, which was hardly surprising since during his spare time he coached a swimming team of teenagers, both girls and boys, called The Penguins, who had made an excellent name for themselves throughout Brazil. He too spoke fluent French, which made Pascal feel terribly inferior since he didn't speak a word of Portuguese.

Stefanini whispered to him obsequiously, "Apparently you're the son of our late boss. I can't wait to hear your message." Late? Pascal wondered. Was this proof that Corazón Tejara was truly dead? What message was he talking about? Up till now he hadn't achieved anything.

At that moment, as if to prove Sergio right, a group of men and women, obviously Indians, swept into the lobby. After some whispering and sidelong looks, they greeted Pascal with that traditional gesture that Pascal loathed. Fortunately, they rapidly left the reception and entered one of the conference rooms.

As usual, Espíritu was in a hurry to return to Recife. Left on their own, Pascal and Sergio crossed the garden to the restaurant-bar The Narrow Gate, which was a welcome innovation. Here Scandinavians with straight shoulder-length hair congregated with swarthy, stocky Latin Americans and every type of mixed blood imaginable. This gaily colored company even included Africans dressed in long Muslim djellabas and wearing soft leather babouches. Pascal and Sergio sat down at a table away from the others.

"Do you like swimming?" Sergio asked straight off. "If you do, then come with me to my team's training session."

"Where do they train? At The Blue Lagoon?"

"The Blue Lagoon!" Sergio exclaimed in amusement. "Do you know the place? That's where I'm going to take you."

On his way to The Blue Lagoon Pascal remembered fondly the hours he used to spend on this very same road with Sarojini. He saw the same old man again pedaling along his cart selling barley sugar–flavored snowballs. He remembered that this was where a beekeeper lived who boasted of his honey on a gigantic poster. The Blue Lagoon hadn't lost its charm: three pools of blue water lined up along the seashore, one of them reserved for synchronized swimming, in which a group of young girls were performing graciously.

Pascal and Sergio entered the locker rooms where a small group of teenagers was waiting for them. "These are my children," Sergio pointed out. The captain of The Penguins introduced himself with a nerve that Pascal disliked: "My name is Jorge," he said. "Like the writer Jorge Amado. My mother worshiped him and we've read all his books and seen every film the Americans have made about him. I hope you've read him, otherwise I advise you to visit the nearest bookstore." Pascal didn't appreciate his sense of humor, but kept his cool regardless.

He followed the team, who headed towards one of the pools, and sat down with Sergio under a tree, which shaded them from the day's heat. The two men stayed so long at The Blue Lagoon that night had fallen when they decided to leave. This was the moment Pascal preferred, when the evening softly laid its fingers on his forehead and the ocean breeze began to sing in his ears.

Henceforth his life unfolded along a regular routine. He woke up late and had breakfast, which also made do as lunch. He became a regular customer at The Narrow Gate, where they served an excellent feijoada on Fridays. And in the afternoons his lectures drew such a crowd of students that latecomers had to sit on the ground.

What did he lecture on? After much cogitation, he decided to lecture once again on his experience at Caracalla. He endeavored to explain why he had fled. Was it because he was afraid that he would be tried and sentenced? Had the thought of his death terrified him? Why had the Mondongues gone to so much trouble to build a better world and yet achieved no tangible result? Perhaps they didn't know how. Was that all it required, to build a world without alcohol, without cigarettes, without private ownership, and without adultery, in which every man would be equal in the face of death? Hadn't they forgotten something essential? But what did the essential consist of? That was the question he was unable to answer.

The interrogations by the students were numerous and passionate. They couldn't understand either the reasons Pascal had fled Caracalla or why he had not sought to disclose the name of Amanda's murderer. They believed he had proved to be a coward and had been incapable of defending himself and the more time passed, the more he blamed himself. Perhaps the students were right. He should have defended Amanda and revealed those who were behind these tragic events.

After his lectures, he attended concerts that reminded him of the evenings he spent with Joseph at Caracalla, when they would listen to rock music, operas, or groups performing zouk, kompa, highlife, and reggae.

While he was in Castera, he thought a lot about Sarojini. To think she had never replied to any of his letters! He recollected her dazzling beauty and had never managed to forget her voice. He remembered the tragic and comical stories she told. One day, she said, the untouchables went on strike for better wages. As a result, the latrines overflowed, and fecal matter piled up in the chamber pots while a terrible stench floated throughout the town. But then one morning, the inhabitants woke up to discover the gardens and terraces covered with roses whose unexpected radiance had replaced the ambient ugliness. This miracle marked the end of the strike.

Pascal constantly wondered why the ashram hadn't kept alive more enduring memories of Sarojini. All he was told was that she was no longer a mere nurse at the hospital in Jaipur but had been appointed director of an association that defended the rights of women who, it goes without saying, are untouchable the world over. The only right they are entitled to is the right to suffer.

One evening in desperation he wrote her a letter, another one, where he informed her of his presence at the ashram and reminded her of the wonderful moments they had shared together.

Pascal had sensed during their first meeting that Sergio Stefanini would soon become a firm friend. Pascal recounted the story of how he had been unjustly suspected of having organized a bomb attack and how he had been obliged to escape. He had taken refuge in Caracalla where he had been unjustly accused of illicit relations with his young servant girl and had only managed to save his life by sneaking over the border, which again could be seen as a show of cowardice.

He hoped that by confessing in such a way he would come to a better understanding of himself and set his life in order. Sergio listened to him intently but uttered no more than a string of banalities: "It's because you're too preoccupied with other people's opinions. Each and every one of us must do what he thinks is right and not worry about what other people think."

The two men often chatted till nightfall, then crossed the ashram and went to have a last drink at The Narrow Gate, which was crowded with students.

One evening on returning around midnight he found a letter slipped under the cottage door. It was from Maria who often wrote to let him know what was going on at home. He opened it, with no suspicion of the news that was to hit him like a bomb: Judas Eluthère had left the island. He was no longer the company director of Le Bon Kaffé but had been appointed Minister of Social Cohesion by the President of the Republic. Social Cohesion? What did that mean? he asked himself in amazement. Then he remembered the debate against multiculturalism raging in Paris. Multiculturalism was presented as absolute evil, likely to destroy democracy and national unity. Such an argument would be laughable were it not for the fact it was highly dangerous. Consequently, Judas Eluthère was now bestowed with an extraordinary amount of power and could choose any violent act he liked. Maria never stopped blaming their former friend, who now revealed his true face. Pascal tore up the letter. All that no longer concerned him. He had other things to accomplish, although he still didn't know exactly what was expected of him.

39

Soon Pascal was fed up with the respect—the word's an understatement, let's say rather, the devotion—he was shrouded with: boys and girls, young and old, groveled at his feet to greet him as soon as they saw him. One of his students, François, had published a brochure called *The Aphorisms of Pascal.*

Every time he leafed through it, he felt something akin to shame: was that me, he wondered, who produced such platitudes? "You need to be pure of heart like a small child. That's what our Creator likes." Or else: "Don't hold a grudge against he who harms you. On the contrary, open up your arms and hug him." Although he had always refused to comment on them publicly, he had nevertheless been obliged to sign almost a thousand copies.

It was early September, the start of the rainy season, the worst since 1920 according to the weathermen. Days were as dark as night. It never stopped raining and one wondered when the sky would tire of unleashing all this water on the earth.

One morning Pascal received another letter, this time one that rekindled the glow in his heart, not from Maria but from Sarojini's secretary. She asked whether Sarojini could come and give a lecture at the ashram as part of her world tour. She was advocating the cause of a certain fourteen-year-old Barati Mukerjee who had been forced to marry an old man of seventy-five. One night when the old fogey was about to exercise his marital right, she had hacked him to death with a knife. The affair had made headlines and been spread over the first page of every newspaper. She had been the subject of a drawn-out trial. Barati had emerged free as air, cleared by a jury who had acknowledged legitimate defense. Wasn't that a brilliant victory for women's rights, not only for India but for the whole world? Pascal dashed over to Sergio who, rummaging through his papers, informed him he had received the same letter and was about to reply in the affirmative.

So, Sarojini was coming back to Castera, bringing the perspective of delectable days for Pascal. He couldn't get over it and started to behave like a madman. He changed the furniture of his cottage and chose a soft rug instead of the existing carpet; he decorated the walls with Matisse reproductions and covered his bed with a damask eiderdown. Then, unsure of himself, he tackled his physique. Hadn't he grown old since he last saw Sarojini? Hadn't he grown fatter and developed a paunch? Despite Sergio's claims that he remained an attractive man, he went swimming at The Blue Lagoon every day and resumed his daily walks. Finally, he hired a coach, who instructed him in weight lifting and pedal training intended to make him look younger and give him a flat stomach.

In his euphoria Pascal telephoned Espíritu and invited him to come to Asunción so that he could share his happiness. Alas, a few weeks later, amid the preparations, he received another letter from Sarojini's secretary, this time informing him that Barati had disappeared and her body had been found on the edge of a forest, devoured by wild animals. The murderer was still at large. Pascal thought he would die. He tried to get in touch with Sarojini but to no avail. It dawned on him he would likely never see the woman he so longed for again.

Alerted by Sergio, Espíritu landed in Castera. He had managed to switch off the mocking look in his eyes and smother the sarcastic curl of his lips. His mourning was almost perfect. He was flanked by Antonio, the man who had piloted his private jet from Recife. A handsome, very handsome young man with an angelic smile and a well-combed beard that floated down to his chest. He had the look of an archangel, Saint Michael for example. Espíritu made Pascal three propositions: come with him to Recife, or else travel to Rio or São Paulo, both fascinating cities, and favorites with tourists.

Unfortunately, Pascal had no inclination to travel and rejected all three propositions outright. From morning to night, he was sunk in grief and asked himself whether the only way out was to go home and live anonymously. Espíritu then made another offer: "Your father Corazón Tejara owned a house in San Isabel. Some people will tell you it's a strange place. The island belonged to three different governments until it declared its independence in 1910. Nowadays, it has nothing in common with Brazil except that they speak Portuguese. Corazón not only had a house there, it was his domain, his realm. That's where he went whenever he had a problem to solve. You could draw inspiration from him."

To everyone's surprise, Pascal accepted this offer. He had been shaken by too many events: Judas Eluthère's appointment as government minister and now the death of Barati Mukerjee, Sarojini's protégée.

The following morning, accompanied by his uncle Espíritu, he took his seat in the jet piloted by Antonio. The fear that had gripped him during the previous journeys vanished thanks to Antonio. All that remained was the grief into which he had been plunged. He stretched out on a sofa during the five-hour flight and slept soundly. Once they had flown through the storms and the black clouds of rain, the sky turned blue like a freshly washed article of clothing. Gradually, his heart perked up and, this time, Espíritu was the very embodiment of a savior.

The three men arrived at San Isabel as night fell. The setting sun lit up a landscape of loose stones and prickly brush and made the rocks glow purple. It looked as though the sea was lapping the shore from every angle.

The Republic of San Isabel made no mystery of its convictions. Not only was the airport called Corazón Tejara but a huge portrait of the graying, potbellied benefactor draped in his inevitable blue tunic lorded over the waiting room.

The taxi driver who picked them up in the parking lot had an unexpected skin color for the region—jet-black—so different from the brownish and yellowish colors of the Brazilian mixed bloods. Intrigued, Pascal couldn't help asking him, "Where are you from?" Starting up his engine, the driver answered as if it were the most obvious thing in the world: "From Dakar, of course." Somewhat surprised, Pascal could find nothing to say.

Corazón Tejara's villa was located in a picture-postcard setting: it was a long, single-story Californian-style ranch house with large windows opening onto a patio where a man and a woman holding a small child stood waiting for them. All three were also jet-black, which surprised Pascal once again. Were they Senegalese as well? Their smiles lit up their faces like the crescent of a moon on a dark night. They introduced themselves: "I'm Saliou, this is Aminata, and he's Amin, our son. We're from Senegal." Amin was a most adorable little boy. His round head, dented here and there where his mother had smothered him with kisses, his sparkling eyes, his toothy-pegs stuck askew in his mauve gums, were downright attractive.

Espíritu, Pascal, and Antonio did credit to the excellent rice dish that Aminata served. "With the fish they sell here," she said, "I manage to cook a thieboudienne, our national fish and rice dish, almost as good as back home." Pascal asked the question that had been nagging him ever since he arrived: "But how did you land up here?" he asked Saliou.

With a nod of the head from Pascal to go ahead and tell his story, Saliou began: "All was perfect. Our country was run by the greatest president Africa has ever known, a president and an incomparable poet whose poems were taught in every school, even in France:

Naked woman, Black woman. Clothed with your color, which is life, with your form, which is beauty. In your shadow I have grown up. The gentleness of your hands laid over my eyes. And now high up on a sunbaked pass, I come upon you, my Promised Land. And your beauty strikes me to the heart like the flash of an eagle.

"You see, I haven't forgotten. Alas, after he died, everything changed. We fell into extreme poverty. We were forced to survive by any means possible and that's why we had to leave our country. By plane, by boat, and even by pirogue. Some people died during the crossing, others had the good fortune to survive and reach Europe. We heard of an ancient technique in Brazil that made corks out of a variety of cork oak trees. The technique had been abandoned but all it needed was the will to work hard in order to revive it. Consequently, our fellow countrymen rushed to Brazil. Some of them sent for their wives and their children. That explains why we are here, so far from home. It was either emigrate or die of hunger."

40

On the point of losing hope, Pascal found an unexpected opportunity to achieve an old dream, that of building a school. The migrants consisted not only of adults, but also teenagers and forty or so young children who, forced to follow their parents into exile and displacement, found themselves destitute as well. Migration, in fact, is a total dispossession, similar to the one four centuries ago which ravaged the African continent.

In its generosity the municipality of San Isabel had allocated to the migrants a collection of disused hangars with the pompous name of the Gilberto Freyre Education Center. The younger ones were taught differently from the teenagers and initiated into basic Portuguese with the same old videos they knew by heart without understanding a word but ended up liking. Their favorite was *A bela e o monstro*, in which a ravishingly beautiful young girl was pursued by a beast who was transformed into a prince charming; it ended with the two of them exchanging a long tender kiss. What was the story called? None of the children could remember, but nevertheless they clamored for it.

Pascal seized the opportunity to open a kindergarten. He wrote to the authorities for permission to teach French to the youngest of the deprived children, so they might know they had a mother tongue, which was theirs, acquired no matter how, be that through colonization or exile. It would be their tool for dreaming and creating images, sounds, and beauty. His request was approved by a government officer who had no interest in the project but was solely concerned with putting together a dossier according to the rules.

That's how Pascal obtained the authorization he had requested. He called the kindergarten Le Blé en Herbe, not because he liked Colette, whom he had barely read, but because the name conjured up a bright and promising future. He replaced the insipid nursery rhymes with short poems such as "Mignonne, allons voir si la rose." Above all, he set to work on a reader where our small hero travels the world and has us admire the riches of the underprivileged territories.

Pascal wasn't used to the company of children. He'd idealized them and had no idea he would come up against so much unruly behavior and jeering. Nevertheless, his plan was to show them the reality of the world. He had always guessed it was these youngsters that needed to be taught, before their hearts and brains became petrified as they grew up.

In order to help him, he chose a young girl, up till then in charge of changing the chalk in the classrooms and mopping the tiled floor. Her name was Awa and she had just reached twenty, though she didn't look more than fifteen. One day on entering the music room Pascal overheard her humming the poem by Verlaine she had put to music herself: "The sky above the roof is so blue, so calm." She stopped as if she had been caught committing a crime and hastily explained, "It was Madame Noël who taught me to play the piano. At Ziguinchor she was Maman's neighbor. She came from France and taught the little ones."

Henceforth, Pascal and Awa became perfect work companions. She put to music the poems he then taught his pupils. Nevertheless, Pascal openly confessed that he had chosen her as assistant mainly because she resembled the late Amanda, his beloved Amanda whose constant presence was as painful as a splinter thrust into a wound that never heals. She was a little too plump as well, like Amanda, with the gash of a smile that unexpectedly lit up her face. Awa had traveled to San Isabel with two of her older brothers, Hassan and Cheikh, who dreamed of leaving for England and found little consolation being in Brazil.

Every time he heard them talk about their plans, Pascal slapped his forehead in amazement.

"Your brothers are totally crazy. Don't they realize the enormous distance between Brazil and England?"

"It's merely a question of organization," Awa replied, not liking her beloved brothers to be criticized. "All they need do is to find smugglers with a solid boat who will take them safely to their destination."

"What a stupid idea to go to England," Pascal insisted. "It's one of the most racist countries that exists."

"All European countries are racist," Awa shrugged. "That won't stop us. My mother's brother lives in Plymouth. We won't be on our own and he promised he'll find us work."

Pascal dropped the discussion, which was going nowhere.

One day he waited in vain for Awa in the music room, where they had arranged to meet. After an hour, he left in a huff and met her in the playground where she was covered in sweat, her clothes in tatters. "It's the boys who chased me," she explained in tears. "They swore they would tear me to pieces."

Pascal was livid and discovered that the inhabitants of San Isabel hated the migrants and never ceased calling them filthy scum and telling them to go home. His dream of brotherhood didn't exist; what existed instead was the never-ending stain of hatred and contempt.

Henceforth, Pascal became Awa's bodyguard. He accompanied her to the crossroads where she sold roasted chestnuts, then brought her back home. The photos of her family back in Senegal rested on a chest of drawers and Awa would point out in tears, "That's my grandmother who knew better than anyone else how to cook fish and rice. That's my mother, she had six children but you can see she kept the figure of a young girl. That's my father, ever since he fell from a tree, he can no longer work and remains sprawled in a folding chair all day long."

What was destined to happen happened. One night, Pascal and Awa ended up in bed together. Pascal had never had relations with such a young girl; Maria and Albertine were several years older than him. He couldn't help feeling like a schoolteacher imposing his authority on a young mind incapable of defending herself. He wondered whether she wasn't intimidated by an experienced older man. Above all, he had never had an affair with such an ignorant young girl.

It wasn't just that Awa didn't know that our good old earth had lasted twenty-five billion years or that Galileo had been condemned for daring to think it was round, she transformed the universe to her liking, giving it a life force of its own, which surprised and even scared him at times. She believed the night was inhabited by spirits ready to swoop down on humans. She would jump at the slightest noise. "Didn't you hear something strange?" she would whisper.

"It's a car passing by on the road," Pascal would reply. She would read hidden things in Nature. When he called her "my little fairy," she protested: "Fairy? I'm not a fairy. In my country, fairies don't exist; call me 'my little djinn' if you like."

One evening, while emerging from her arms, Pascal felt like talking about himself, explaining why he was in this place so far from home, in a country where he didn't speak the language, and he began to talk about his origins. She listened, eyes tightly closed as if she was hearing a fascinating story. When he finished, she burst out laughing and exclaimed, "So you're the son of God? I'm not surprised, all men say that; they're gods whom we women have to serve."

Offended, Pascal swore he wouldn't broach the issue again with her.

A few days later, she was the one who returned to the subject.

"So it's your father who is responsible for all our misfortune?" she struck back.

Pascal was taken unawares by the attack.

"What are you talking about!?" he exclaimed.

Hands on hips, she confronted him face on.

"When I was ten my father fell from a tree. My mother then had to raise my brothers and me all alone without a husband. The word misery isn't strong enough to portray the situation we found ourselves in. Who was responsible?"

Pascal endeavored to find an answer.

"But it's not my father, for heaven's sake! You could blame him for much more serious crimes, such as colonization, and while you're about it, why not exile, dispossession, and racism?"

But Awa would hear nothing of the sort.

"You're the son of an assassin," she repeated. "An assassin."

Pascal could have considered these words a joke if they hadn't echoed some of his own interrogations. From that day on, his relations with Awa changed in a subtle way. He wondered whether she wasn't more lucid than him and stopped playing the role of schoolmaster with her.

Thanks to his constant presence by her side, nobody could manhandle her. He would bring her home to where her two brothers were busy guzzling beer after beer down the hatch like all good Muslims. Pascal was not fond of either of them and consequently climbed up straightway with Awa to her room under the roof where they made love until morning.

One night, about 2 a.m., someone knocked on his bedroom door at Corazón Tejara's place. It was Saliou. "Something's going on in town," he shouted excitedly. "We don't know what exactly but we heard the sirens. Through the bedroom window we could see a large glow lighting up the sky. Could it be a fire?"

Pascal hurriedly dressed and the two men ran outside. In the garden they bumped into Aminata, muffled up in a Terry Toweling dressing gown and holding little Amin in her arms. Half awake, Amin was sulking and buried his head against his mother's breast. "I think it's a fire," Aminata told them. "I saw the fire engines race by."

Pascal and Saliou dashed off, leaving Aminata and Amin alone in the night. They were later to learn that a fire had started in the Bellavista district where most of the migrants lived. Was it accidental or arson? That was the question.

The police first arrested a gang of youngsters, who were quickly released due to lack of evidence. Then they arrested two individuals from Bahia, also released due to lack of evidence. After initially making headlines, the event ended up as a paragraph on the last page of the papers. The migrants were rehoused in striped canvas tents that reminded Pascal of the Rasta camp in Marais Salant. Soon they were forgotten and life resumed its daily routine.

Strangely, Pascal felt responsible for this dramatic event. One afternoon, coming out of a music class, Awa took him by the hand.

"I've got something to tell you: my two brothers have made a deal with a smuggler. I already told you about our plans, didn't I? We're leaving for Plymouth the day after tomorrow."

"Are you leaving with them?" Pascal asked sheepishly.

"What do you expect me to do?" Awa exclaimed. "Stay here on my own, in a country where I don't know anyone?"

"I can marry you," Pascal proposed impulsively. "That way you'll stay with me."

By way of an answer, she gave him a sagacious look.

"Marry you! You don't really mean it; you're saying it out of pity."

Pascal took Awa back home. The following day, however much he referred back to the subject, he was wasting his time.

That evening he accompanied her to the wharf where the boat *É o meu Salvador* was waiting for her before setting out to sea. It was there he bade her farewell.

41

Awa and her two brothers were not the only ones to leave San Isabel. After the intentional or accidental fire of the migrants' neighborhood—nobody would ever know exactly—the living conditions there became quite unbearable. They were piled onto a patch of waste ground where the tents were uncomfortable and the showers few and far between, as were the toilets, which were always blocked and filthy. It was a genuine exodus. Smugglers rushed in from every corner promising a safe passage to Europe for those who had enough money to pay for the crossing.

The excitement spread to Saliou and Aminata. They didn't dream of England. Saliou wanted to go to Paris and see the Eiffel Tower. Expressions such as "The City of Lights" or else "The Champs Elysées, the most beautiful avenue in the world" kept running through his head. However much Pascal repeated that he would be disappointed by Paris and what did he expect from such a place and wasn't he fine where he was, Saliou shook his head: "No offense, but no man is born to serve another like I serve you, the way I bring you drinks, cook your meals, wash your clothes, and polish your shoes. In Europe, I'll find work worthy of a human being; I'm prepared for anything. What's more, I'll let you in on a secret: I want my son Amin to become a doctor and care for the sick, the poor, and the destitute. He'll make me so happy and I, his father, will forget the nightmare I had to go through."

At San Isabel, the luminosity of the air was so bright it was impossible to sleep late of a morning. Awake at six, dressed in a tight pair of shorts and a cotton T-shirt, Pascal and Saliou would set off for a good hour's run. Avoiding the asphalt paved streets, they preferred to run along the bike trails where the gravel bounced under their feet, shooting up little gray clouds. As a rule, they pushed on as far as the sea, a rough blue canvas that spread to the far corners of the horizon. Once on the beach, they caught their breath and sat down on the sand where they drank liters of water that Saliou always had the good sense to bring along with him.

There were no longer any French classes, since there were virtually no longer any migrant children. Only a small dozen remained in San Isabel, screaming with laughter as they watched the same old cartoon over and over again. Back in his home, Pascal settled down on the terrace and endeavored to reflect on his stay at Caracalla. The more he thought about it, the more it eluded him. It was as if it had all been a bad dream.

Amin sometimes left off playing to come and talk. Since he only spoke Wolof, Pascal didn't understand a word he was saying. Consequently, after a few minutes, the child left disappointed to join his mother, busy cooking Senegalese delights in the kitchen. Some days, Amin spread out his toy trucks and police cars on the terrace, convinced he could catch Pascal's attention. However, as Pascal remained plunged in his papers, the child uttered angry little cries and went on playing alone.

After lunch Pascal went to have coffee in a bar he had discovered with Awa where posters proclaimed that Brazil is the world's number one producer of coffee. That's where Numa came to meet him: Numa, his new friend. A few months earlier a man of about fifty, who was drinking at a neighboring table, had started up a conversation:

"Aren't you one of the Tejaras?" he had asked in fluent French.

"Yes," Pascal replied. "I'm the son of Corazón Tejara."

"You're the son of Corazón Tejara!" the stranger repeated in amazement, collapsing onto the chair facing Pascal, who attempted to qualify his words.

"Well, I'm the son, if you like, but I've never met my father and I've never lived with him."

The man ordered a coffee and went on to explain: "In our country where only money and the color of your skin count, your father was a benefactor always prepared to assist the destitute. He built I don't know how many hospitals, as well as low-cost housing for the needy, and he laid out sports grounds for teenagers. You can't imagine the good he did!"

"That's not what I heard," Pascal replied. "I heard he was a laughingstock and I was even made to believe he was a usurper and a ridiculous impostor."

A few days later Numa came to pick Pascal up in his old Renault Clio, which was used as a taxi. "I hope you have a few hours to spare," he murmured, starting up the engine. "I'd like to show you an aspect of San Isabel that you don't know."

For ten or so kilometers, the car drove alongside the sea, which was dressed in its usual splendor. Some fishing boats were returning to the shore where a crowd of housewives was waiting for them. Finally, a sign indicated Corazón Tejara Foundation.

The Corazón Tejara Foundation comprised a row of low-cost housing built of the dark stone characteristic of the region and set among flower beds and greenery. In addition to a dispensary and a school, there was housing for single mothers and needy couples as well as playgrounds for youngsters to play football. As they were all dark-skinned, Pascal realized he was dealing with the underprivileged. In this country, as in many others worldwide, skin color is a signifier. If it is dark, it means the family is living in poverty.

After having given Pascal a guided visit of the Foundation, Pascal led him to the dispensary and knocked on the consulting-room door. A young doctor in a white coat was examining with a stethoscope the body of a child in the arms of his mother. "This is my son, Augusto," Numa told Pascal. "Without the help of your father he would never have become a doctor. As a small boy, he was mad about football and wanted to be another Pelé." His voice resonated with deep pride.

"I haven't seen you the entire week," Numa reproached his son.

"It's because there's an epidemic of dengue fever," the doctor replied, staring at him with his green eyes. "Believe me, we're snowed under."

From that day on, Numa and Pascal became close friends. Thanks to Numa, Pascal was overjoyed to discover an unknown aspect of his father. He might not be a god, but without a doubt he was a generous individual, a benefactor determined to do good.

On leaving Numa, Pascal returned to the villa where Saliou was waiting for him for a music lesson. Saliou had made himself a series of traditional instruments such as koras and balafons out of leather, wood, and calabashes. "When I was young," he told Pascal, "I was hopeless at math, French, and natural science, every major subject, in fact. The only one I excelled in was music. I played every musical instrument to perfection."

Saliou patiently taught Pascal the traditional sounds of melodies, some of which went way back in time while others took their inspiration from jazz and highlife. He placed Pascal's fingers on the kora while a metronome beat out the rhythm. These music lessons lasted for hours as neither of them ever got tired. Emotions he thought were lost forever surged up in Pascal's heart. He pictured again the women he had loved, and the memory of their beauty gently overwhelmed him.

One day, coming back from lunch with Numa, Pascal found Saliou waiting for him holding Amin in his arms. He seemed very excited, as if he had something special to announce.

"Sunday! Sunday, the Day of Our Lord as you say, we're leaving for Europe. For Italy to be exact. From there, the smugglers assure us it's easier to get to France. I hope the Lord will give us his blessing."

"You must be joking!" Pascal exclaimed.

Saliou set Amin down and caressed the child's head.

"I told you I want this boy to become a doctor. He won't manage to do so if he stays here. We are finally blessed with good fortune."

But, three days later, Pascal couldn't pluck up enough courage to accompany his friends to the dock: Saliou decked out with a hat and tie, the likes of which he had never seen before; Aminata, wrapped in a shawl as if she was already prepared for the rigors of winter; and Amin, adorable little Amin, in his red tracksuit. Pascal felt weak and powerless. He had never managed to get Saliou to change his mind about this mad idea of going to France. What on earth was he going to do over there? Empty garbage cans in Paris, as a popular song says? What an absurd idea to want to see the Eiffel Tower! Pascal had never been to the capital but he felt a strong antipathy for the Eiffel Tower, its heavy, chunky silhouette, sinking its elephantine feet into the gravel of the Champs de Mars.

42

Once Saliou, Aminata, and Amin had left, Pascal found himself alone in a place that was much too big for him. He missed Amin terribly and was amazed that this child with whom he had made little contact occupied such a large place in his heart. As Pascal recalled his gestures and comical expressions while he played in the garden under the sun, he had difficulty holding back his tears. However hard he attempted to write and remember his time at Caracalla, his mind went blank. By way of compensation, he got in the habit of inviting Numa over at mealtimes, for, as Maria said, he didn't know how to boil an egg, whereas Numa managed quite well in the kitchen. His specialty was smoked chicken with corn on the cob.

Numa became invaluable to Pascal not only because of his cooking but also because of his entertaining stories. He could talk forever. Since he left his taxi on Thursdays with a mechanic to make the necessary small repairs, he had lots of spare time. From morning to evening then, he had time to open up his heart to Pascal:

"*Lan mizè pa dou*, as a friend of my mother who was Haitian used to say. Misery worms into your brain and your heart. It turns you into a wild beast and all you can think about is how to fill an empty stomach. I never saw my mother with a man. Admittedly, she was no beauty. I suppose the men were a bit ashamed of her and slipped into her bed once night had fallen. Even so, she had ten children. In order to feed all these mouths, she found a job, far from brilliant, as you can imagine, in the town's street cleaning services. She would sweep the flagstones with a horse-hair broom, and the kids at school nicknamed us *zobalai* (broomsticks). We didn't care, all that mattered to us was filling our empty stomachs, even with water, for there wasn't much to chew on. Nothing for breakfast. Hardly anything for lunch. We stole anything we could lay our hands on. At the age of thirteen, I went to jail for the first time and, in a manner of speaking, only emerged in later years. Theft, drug trafficking, and violence, anything was good for us."

"How did you get to know my father?" Pascal inquired.

"It was later, much later. I was living with Rosy. She was pregnant with our second child but life doesn't tell us the dirty tricks it's planning: I had no idea our second child would never see the light of day and Rosy would die in childbirth from puerperal fever. I found myself all alone with a child, our first, on my hands. A child who soon followed in my footsteps, robbing and dealing drugs when he was not playing football. I'm telling you, it's your father who took charge of him and made him what he is today—a doctor."

"Do you think my father had a divine origin?" Pascal insisted. "Do you believe he was what they say he was?"

Numa looked him straight in the eye and asserted, "Your father was someone out of the ordinary. He wanted the heart of the world to beat to another rhythm."

Pascal would have liked a more clear-cut response.

One morning, when it was not yet seven, Numa burst into Pascal's room, deeply distraught.

"Something terrible has happened," he murmured. "Follow me."

They dashed out onto the street, which was already swarming with people. The more brazen were using their bicycle bells and motorbike horns to force their way through. Where was everyone going? Pascal wondered. He didn't dare ask Numa, who was walking a few steps in front with a serious expression.

They soon reached the beach at Buena Vista. At this time of day, the sea was still misty and there were no bathers. A huge crowd was gazing at a small object lying under the sea almond trees. Pascal's heart filled with a strange foreboding as he elbowed his way to the front. A child, a small boy, was lying on the sand. All he was wearing was a pair of navy-blue shorts. His eyes were closed but his mouth was wide open.

Shaking all over, Pascal recognized Amin, little Amin who had left a few days earlier. In a panic he collapsed on the ground. His eyes brimmed with tears and his chest shook with desperate sobs. What had become of Saliou and Aminata? If they were not lying beside their child, they must have sunk to the bottom of the ocean.

The people around him were getting restless, shoving each other and whispering. The most disconcerting remarks could be heard: a few days ago, the weather had radically changed, a gale had snapped the tree branches and the sea had turned rough. The migrants' boat must have been shipwrecked. But when the San Isabel municipal services dispatched an army of divers and rescuers to locate the wreck, they found nothing. Absolutely nothing.

Pascal never knew who brought him home, probably Numa since he himself had no strength left and his legs felt wobbly.

So, Amin, whom unknowingly Pascal had loved so much, was dead. He who had never had a child, never even wanted one, found himself as inconsolable as a father.

The deaths of Saliou, Aminata, and Amin caused quite a stir. Their shipwreck made headlines in all the European papers, and even in the Americas. Such a tragedy spotlighted the migrants' distress and their terrible fate. Instead of finding work and a decent way of life, they met with death.

One day when Pascal was vacuuming sadly, he came across a small wooden truck under the furniture. It was obviously a toy belonging to Amin. He wept all day long and through part of the night. He was weighed down with a feeling of guilt; he believed he was responsible for the death of this innocent child. He realized that the world was filled with greater misfortunes than his own, he who had never known the kind of poverty and destitution that force you to leave the country where you were born and then totally destroy you. Amin would never be a doctor and would never fill his father's heart with pride and joy.

When he tried to return to his writing, it seemed to have no purpose. What did he want to prove? Evil was in the heart of man. Man had no worse enemy than himself. What was the use of political revolutions? What was the purpose of ideologies? In order to find an answer to his questions, which never stopped tormenting him, he liked to walk along the seashore. The sea had always had a soothing effect on him, giving him the impression of infinity and the feeling of vulnerability.

He called Espíritu and asked him to come and join him for he felt totally lost and had no idea what he was doing in San Isabel. Espíritu, who seemed to have little sympathy for the fate of migrants, asked him to come to Recife. Pascal hesitated a long while. He was so weak that Numa became worried and invited him to dinner at his son Augusto's place.

Augusto lived at the Corazón Tejara Foundation in an untidy, poorly furnished apartment, since he was the father of six rowdy children: six girls. Every time he wished for a boy his wife Lisa dreaded that fate would not favor them. She rejected the predictions of clairvoyants who, according to the shape of her belly, assured her that this time she would give birth to a baby boy. Lisa was from Guinea-Bissau. Augusto had met her in Lisbon where she, too, had been studying medicine.

The meal was enjoyable, Pascal liked Brazilian cuisine. He especially liked peccary, a type of pig whose meat was savory and aromatic. At the end of the meal, having let himself go and downed several glasses of Frontera—the only way he could keep sane under the cruel circumstances he was experiencing—he plucked up courage and looking

Augusto straight in the eye, asked, "We've never talked about it, but you've never told me what you thought of my father. I believe he had a great influence over you."

Augusto laid down the fruit he was peeling. With sparkling eyes, he declared, "For me he was a god. It was he who gave me the desire for another world, more just and more tolerant, where people would not be judged on appearances."

Pascal continued, "And now, today, what do you think? Do you believe he is dead?"

Augusto replied ardently, "He will never die: his words and deeds are engraved in our hearts."

Pascal promised himself one thing: when he stopped off in Recife, he would ask Espíritu for clarification on the mission he was supposed to accomplish and the explanations he had always refused to give him. When Pascal called a second time to take Espíritu up on his offer, Hermenius picked up the phone and told him that Espíritu was absent.

43

On blank sheets of paper where the white stands guardian, that's what Stéphane Mallarmé wrote didn't he? Pascal was sprawled in his armchair in front of his computer, incapable as usual of finding a single thought to write down, when the doorbell rang at the front gate. Who could that be at such an hour? It wasn't Thursday. Numa was working, conveying market women with their heavy loads returning home from all corners of the town.

Reluctantly, Pascal crossed the garden, admiring in spite of himself the beds of multicolored pansies and the hedges beautifully manicured by the gardeners. Behind the gate, a genuine delegation was waiting for him: about twenty men and women of varying ages and attire, from an attractive young girl wearing a tight-fitting, sparkling white tracksuit to an obese grandma leaning on a walking stick.

It was a man with a gray crew cut who began to speak. "We hope we're not disturbing you. We have a major problem to solve and we'd like to tell you about it. My name is Juan Bastos," he concluded with a broad smile. He spoke slowly in an affected French, like people do when they are speaking a foreign language.

Pascal preceded the group back to the house where he went to fetch some chairs in the living room. But he then found that most of the delegation had already sat down on the ground along the terrace.

"We have come in a great number," Juan Bastos continued, "to prove to you that our association is vital. It is named after someone you no doubt know, a world-famous Argentinian musician, Atahualpa Yupanqui."

Pascal didn't dare confess he had never heard of him, and Juan Bastos continued, "Most of us don't speak French." Pascal waved his hand meaning that this had little importance.

"Apparently little Amin's parents worked for you and you treated the child like your own."

Such an affirmation was no exaggeration and Pascal didn't contradict him. "The Atahualpa Yupanqui Association has asked the town to let us have a plot of land in order to erect a stela as a way of engraving Amin's tragic death forever in stone. But the municipality refuses, claiming that the stela would spoil San Isabel's beauty for the tourists."

Somewhat taken aback, Pascal asked him, "Are you on good terms with these people?"

The man made a face. "We haven't been on good terms ever since the new mayor was elected. He's right-wing and does everything he can to put a spanner in the works. Consequently, we have decided to pass round a petition to collect signatures from those in favor of our project. Would you agree to sign? Your name means a great deal and carries considerable weight."

If that is all it requires. Pascal nodded and signed each of the documents they handed him. With that, Pascal went to fetch a bottle of Frontera from the kitchen to celebrate. Unfortunately, most of the visitors didn't drink alcohol and the conversation was soon over.

On taking his leave, Juan Bastos whispered, "Thank you so much for your hospitality. You are the true son of your father." The true son of my father? Pascal wondered, closing the gate. Did he deserve such words of praise?

He told Numa about the morning visit, and he was visibly overjoyed. In fact, Numa couldn't understand why Pascal had decided to leave San Isabel and return home. "You could become the association's honorary president," Numa suggested. "There are so many things to do now that the municipality has changed."

The Atahualpa Yupanqui Association's visit gave Pascal the unexpected courage to return to the place where little Amin's body had been found a few weeks earlier. His grief had thus far prevented him from doing so.

On the afternoon he made up his mind the sky was low and cloudy. The sea, smooth and blue-gray, was as flat as a tombstone. To his surprise, the place had become like an amusement park. Crowds of tourists were forcing their way there, with some snapping pictures like obscene souvenirs surrounded by others who were praying. One woman was kneeling with her arms stretched out in a cross, another was sobbing her heart out with both hands joined while a teenager was pedaling past in his small truck selling barley sugar, mint, and grenadine snowballs.

Pascal could not get over the tragedy: "This tragedy which is unpardonable," as Albert Camus says, "the death of a child." He would feel responsible all his life. Added to his feeling of grief, Pascal now felt a sense of revolt: who was responsible for so much suffering and loss? Certainly not Saliou or Aminata. They had wanted to give their son the life they had dreamed of. No, he who was responsible for such a crime was someone else. It had to be said, this crime came from a higher power, the caprice of a being who moves in mysterious ways. Such thoughts tortured him more and more every day. He recalled Awa's sarcasm: "You're the son of an assassin." He had taken her words as a joke, but increasingly he realized how true they were. With a heavy heart, he slowly returned home.

He was on his third glass of Frontera when Numa burst in, trembling with excitement: Lisa had given birth, this time to a baby boy. Hearing the news, Pascal's heart was filled with disgust and a kind of anger: the Creator was playing a pathetic game, taking away with one hand what He was giving with the other. Little Amin was dead but Augusto and Lisa had a son.

The two men remained inside the house to have the dinner of stewed rabbit and a chestnut purée that Numa had brought. They were seated at table with the television switched on when Pascal, who wasn't really watching, was suddenly struck by the thought of the little red box that

Espíritu had given him. Hadn't Espíritu told him that if he ever needed him all he had to do was press the box and he'd answer immediately? He dashed up to his room and found the longed-for object in a drawer among the erasers, the ballpoint pens, and a compass. He pressed it with all his might.

Unfortunately, a day, two days, three days, an entire week went by and still Espíritu hadn't answered his call. Puzzled by this silence, Pascal began to get worried. He absolutely needed to have a conversation with Espíritu before returning to his native island.

Numa and Pascal were forever quarreling on the subject. "Why don't you want to stay here with us?" Numa shrieked. "I've tried to tell you the new mayor intends to destroy everything we are trying to achieve. He is demanding rent from everyone who lives at the Corazón Tejara Foundation and has increased the rates on all public services."

Pascal turned a deaf ear, but Numa did not admit defeat and was soon to prove it.

One evening, very late at night, Pascal received the visit of a man whom he did not recognize at first: it was Juan Bastos.

"I've good news and bad news," he said. "Which would you like first?"

"Start with the bad news," Pascal smiled.

"The municipality has refused to give us the ground we asked for. That was to be expected."

"And the good news?" Pascal inquired.

"We've appointed you honorary president of our association. Look at all the names on the list of those who wanted you to be our president."

Pascal shook his head and said firmly, "I very much regret to have to tell you that I have decided to join my uncle in Recife at the end of the week and I don't think I'll be coming back to San Isabel."

Disappointed, Juan collapsed onto a chair, but Pascal,

although touched by his chagrin, returned to his personal concerns and asked, "You knew my father, didn't you?"

"Not personally," Juan replied. "He was much older than me. He left the Faculty of Medicine while I was just beginning. But I've read a lot about him. You know, we Latin men, we're not raised to respect women. Corazón Tejara first made a name for himself by the number of his female conquests. Anyone was good for him: proper young girls from wealthy families, prostitutes, chambermaids, young women, old women. Then one day the despicable character of his behavior was revealed to him in a dream, when an angel told him that the next woman he seduced would give him a son who would amaze the world."

"An angel told him?" Pascal chuckled. "You're telling me quite the opposite of the biblical version: an angel brings good tidings to the father and not the frightened virgin. What will we do with all these paintings called *The Annunciation of the Virgin Mary?*"

The two men burst out laughing, banding together in complicity.

There was silence before Pascal continued, "In your opinion, was Corazón Tejara everything he's been made out to be?"

"It all depends on who's speaking," Juan replied. "For some he was a troublemaker whom the government should have thrown into prison, an outcome that actually occurred when he made a brief incursion at the Ministry of Health. For others, he was a benefactor, even a god, I'd say."

Pascal didn't dare probe any further and the two men drank a glass of Frontera before parting. Once Juan had left, Pascal felt uplifted. So, some people considered Corazón Tejara a god. Perhaps they were right and this justified all the turmoil that had so far turned Pascal's life upside down.

44

San Isabel is less than two hours from Recife, yet the flight path between the island and the continent is often subject to violent turbulence and is every pilot's nightmare. Luckily on that day the weather was exceptionally fine. Gazing at the golden sun as it gilded the clouds, Pascal suddenly felt inundated with warmth as if he was coming back to life after a very long absence. He believed that the fiasco of his stay in San Isabel, coming after that of Caracalla, would be the last.

The afternoon was coming to an end when he arrived at the airport in Recife. Unfortunately, Espíritu was nowhere to be seen. And the only signs of welcome were disinterested customs and police officers and passengers in a hurry, dragging their suitcases. He jumped into a taxi and headed for Mengistu.

Here the doors and windows of the handsome house, which had so impressed him on his first visit to Recife, were tight shut. The place appeared deserted. Where was everyone? In despair, he went and knocked on the gardener's small lodging. The beanpole of a man obligingly stepped outside to see him but, not speaking a word of French, was of no use. He was wondering what to do when Espíritu's two servants, Margarita and Hermenius, turned up in the garden.

When he exclaimed that his uncle was not at the airport to meet him, they did not appear surprised and without saying a word picked up his bags and took him into the house. While Hermenius was opening the front door, Pascal mentioned, "I wrote to my uncle to say I was coming. Do you know where he is?"

"No, we don't know a thing. He's been gone over a month and there's been no news of him," Hermenius claimed.

Pascal was convinced the servant was lying and remarked on the side, "People just don't disappear like that. What are the police for in that case? Is he dead, wounded, sick?"

"We know absolutely nothing," Heremenius repeated. "I swear."

Pascal clasped his head between his hands. "The same thing happened with my father. I have never been able to find out what happened to him. My uncle Espíritu made conflicting declarations."

"Do you want us to go to the police?" Hermenius offered.

Pascal shook his head, sensing that he was faced with a mystery even the police would be unable to solve.

At that moment he discovered on the sideboard a small pile of letters, addressed to him. Strangers had written him asking for help with a number of problems: their landlords had evicted them for no longer being able to pay the rent; they were ill but couldn't afford to go to the hospital; their son had been thrown into prison arbitrarily and beaten to death. Leafing through all these letters, Pascal's heart was filled with an unexpected feeling: Yes, the world is not fair but how can we make it better? The letter which caught his attention the most came from Maria, who often sent him news of the Arche de la Nouvelle Alliance.

It was a bulletin in which the journalists extolled the merits of Judas Eluthère, recently appointed Minister of Social Cohesion. Pascal was first struck with amazement, then he realized what the President was playing at: he had sought to pull off a major coup by appointing an important minister to pay tribute to this obscure island. The photo of Judas Eluthère, as handsome as a movie star, was spread across all the pages of the pamphlet.

It was almost nine in the evening when Margarita emerged from the kitchen with a delicious salad she had hastily prepared. All three ate without appetite, each absorbed in his own thoughts. At the end of this modest meal, Hermenius declared, "We live opposite, if you need something don't hesitate to knock on our door." All that remained was for Pascal to climb up to his room, the same one he had occupied during his previous stay.

It was then an event occurred whose exact nature we will never know. Was it a dream, a vision, or something real? Pascal would have been of no help since he was incapable of distinguishing its true nature. It was very different from his disappearance a few years earlier, which had left a blank in his memory. On the contrary, he remembered every little detail of this strange conversation.

Night had fallen, pitch-black and formidable as a dungeon. He had walked out onto the balcony for the simple reason that it was too hot inside. Sweat streamed down his chest and soaked into the collar of his pajamas.

Suddenly he heard the sound of an engine, then Espíritu appeared, emerging out of the darkness, his perpetual smile curling over his well-defined lips, while the protuberance behind his back (was it a hump?) had vanished. He seemed younger and refreshed, his hair carefully combed and a neatly trimmed beard clipped over his chin.

"About time!" Pascal exclaimed, exasperated. "Where were you and why didn't you answer my call when I urgently needed you?"

Espíritu dismissed this reproach with a wave of his hand. "Are you still talking about these migrants? You're old enough to manage without me. And don't forget I have to satisfy your father's every command, first and foremost. I travel wherever he wants me, wherever he needs me. I disappear and reappear at his command. In spite of that, you should never doubt my affection."

"Can you explain to me," Pascal insisted, "where my father asks you to be and what he orders you to do?"

"No, I can't. It all depends on the moment. I've already told you on several occasions what I think: the greatest gift given to man is his freedom. The freedom to act, to dream, and interpret his own truth."

"You know about little Amin's death?" Pascal asked in all seriousness.

"You know what I told you about death," Espíritu replied. "It's a word that has a different meaning for everyone. Everybody has his own version of the facts, that's all!" Then Espíritu added sadly, "I told you that now you're old enough to do without me."

"Does that mean I can no longer count on your help?" Pascal groaned.

Thereupon Espíritu embraced him affectionately and disappeared as suddenly as he had appeared. This was followed by the sound of an engine.

Pascal was shattered. Once again, he hadn't understood a word of what Espíritu had said. He didn't sleep a wink the entire night and in the morning his mouth tasted of ashes.

Around noon, Pascal went out and, without thinking, headed straight for the center of town. It's not easy to have a clear idea of a town since it is composed of so many different neighborhoods with no common identity. A town is a bit like a human being; it all depends on the mood and frame of mind of the person who approaches it. Some people remember the residential districts, the Beaux Quartiers as Aragon says, with their opulent buildings and wide, well-paved sidewalks. Others prefer the so-called picturesque neighborhoods dating from the time it was a hamlet or fishing village and where nothing could foretell the shape of things to come nor the town's future splendor. Yet others prefer the business districts, austere and rectilinear like certain areas of Paris redesigned by Haussmann.

Pascal once again headed towards the favelas. *Favela* was the first word he had learned in Portuguese. How could a city as lovely and arrogant as Recife have allowed such a canker to grow and spread in its bosom? The trading posts of Fonds-Zombi and Porte Océane, made for selling slaves and hogsheads of sugar, and which he had frequented from an early age, had never allowed such a disgrace. Furthermore, Nature's beauty had always softened any possible ugliness.

Since Jean Pierre and Eulalie were only intent on earning money and never went on vacation, Pascal had always hung out with boys at a loose end like himself. Always in search of a mean trick to play on someone, they filled the streets with their dangerous idleness. But however much they roamed through the town, they never came across anything truly ugly. In fact, all it took was to gaze at the sea to be dazzled.

One year he went and spent his holidays with his friend Marcel, whose family couldn't have been poorer and lived in a fishing village. The sea was a constant presence. As soon as he opened his eyes in the morning it was there, covered in white foam and slipping on the day's first garments of soft blue. As the hours went by it became more colorful. Sometimes waves loomed up from the horizon spinning and whirling any fishing boats that had ventured out. How could you forget the smell of brine and the open sea, which spoke of the call of faraway lands? Pascal hadn't realized how in love he was with his native land, its radiance and changing moods.

45

After having wandered through the favela, Pascal sat down on a bench in a small square under some magnificent ficus trees to catch his breath. A group of boys nearby were playing marbles. When he was little, he loved playing marbles. Nowadays, this type of game belongs to the past: the computer reigns supreme and the world is divided into those who know how to use the internet and those who do not.

He suddenly realized he was very hungry. It was almost three in the afternoon. He got up and went to look for a restaurant. He found a small café nearby called Tem Boa Carne that wasn't much to look at. Unfortunately, it was also full. Men and women were crowded in front of a TV screen while a bunch of hotheads were pulsating to the sound of some wild music from a jukebox. On the wall, a portrait of some unknown woman, signed by a certain Waldomiro de Deus, was giving a broad, welcoming smile.

He was about to leave when a waiter took him familiarly by the arm: "Come with me, I'll help you find a seat." He led Pascal to a table where a young girl was painting her lips with red lipstick while looking into a pocket mirror. "Are you about to leave, Soledad?" he asked.

"I won't be a minute," she smiled.

Good Lord, how pretty she was with her tropical-fruit complexion, her eyes as black as agates, and her lovely curly hair. Pascal felt aroused as never before. Well, almost never. And yet the first sight of this woman made him forget all the other women he had previously held in his arms; her charm worked on him like a magnet. He watched her with an odd feeling of nostalgia as she got up to leave and walked through the restaurant with a delicate yet resolute step. He sat down and forlornly ordered a feijoada and a glass of beer.

Once he had finished eating, he left and walked around the neighborhood, which was incredibly crowded and, like the café, not much to look at. He caught sight of a cinema where they were playing an old film he had once adored. The theater was empty except for a few teenagers who were kissing and making out. The romantic film gave him the same pleasure he had felt when he was younger. He had always loved the movies. When he was a boy, he used to spend hours at the movie theater while skipping math classes. Of an evening, he would be so lost in his daydreaming he had nothing to say to Jean Pierre or Eulalie.

When he left after the show, dusk was falling and the street lamps were being switched on. A squalid populace was chatting along the sidewalks. No use looking for a taxi in such a place. Pascal decided to take a bus. Walking back along the sidewalk he bumped into a young woman who looked familiar. It was Soledad, yes Soledad. He ran to meet her exclaiming, "We're destined to meet again!" The young woman stared, at first not recognizing him, then her face lit up. "You!" she cried. "I live just opposite. Would you like to come in and have a coffee?"

Soledad lived in a walk-up on the fifth floor of a nondescript building in a small, plain, rudimentary apartment where a few chairs were set around a wickerwork coffee table. Pascal, who had the impression he was dreaming, took off his coat. "I thought I heard you were called Soledad." He thought to himself that no name could be so inappropriate, since it conjured up solitude and loneliness whereas such a graceful and attractive young woman was probably the object of many men's desires.

"Yes, my name's Soledad Thébia. I'm from French Guyana. That's why I speak fluent French."

"The name Soledad doesn't suit you at all," Pascal said gallantly.

"It's because life plays such dirty tricks," she explained. "A few months before I was born, my father was knifed and killed by a man he thought was a brother. My mother had to bring us up all on her own, me, and my brother and sisters. I'm the youngest, that's why she called me Soledad."

Pascal had heard similar tales but never from such a charming voice. Soledad revealed she was a singer, a thankless profession as in today's world the arts don't pay and instead financial backing has to be sought from people in high places.

We have to be honest and confess that on this particular point Soledad was lying. Poverty had forced her to leave her family in Guyana for Brazil, a place where she had no option but to sell her body. Fortunately, her beauty attracted numerous clients and this generous network allowed her to live an honorable lifestyle.

Of course, Pascal did not doubt what Soledad was telling him. When they had finished drinking their coffee, they fell into each other's arms. Neither of them could explain what led them to embrace and make love given that they barely knew each other. It was a sequence of unconscious moves and a succession of unintentional words. They suddenly found themselves in a tight clasp, Pascal breathing in Soledad's perfume and whispering words which made little sense.

Night had fallen when they finally parted. Soledad looked at Pascal in disbelief, used as she was to making love for a price. What had drawn her to this man who was no more handsome or attractive than another? Just a pleasant face, square shoulders, curly hair, or rather, frizzy hair, and a dark complexion.

With a laugh, she slipped out of bed. Pascal watched her as she crossed the room entirely naked, gazing at her high-lift butt, her never-ending legs, and the black nipples of her breasts, and convinced himself he was dreaming. Wasn't he being given the best present of his life at this moment? Why complicate his existence with questions he was incapable of answering: How to build a more harmonious world? How to root out the evil in men's hearts? He would never manage on his own.

Soledad brought out two glasses and a carafe of an amber-colored liquid: "It's a liqueur my mother makes," she explained, "from ginger and alcohol."

Pascal emptied his glass with the altogether new impression of being in seventh heaven, of being all-powerful. "I have to leave on Thursday," he murmured apologetically. "The trip was planned a long time ago and I can't postpone it, although I'd very much like to, now I've met you. Will you come and see me? Some people think my country is not really a country; it only makes news when there's a hurricane or a natural disaster. Hurricane Hugo totally destroyed it but Katrina and Maria spared it, miraculously. But I love it nevertheless. Like a child who refuses to question her mother. Is she ugly? Is she too fat? Is her skin too wrinkled?"

"Yes," Soledad agreed. "I'll come and see you if you like, but I don't have much money, so try and get me a job as a singer or something similar."

Pascal promised her anything she wanted, but couldn't help feeling he did not deserve the gift fate had finally given him.

Pascal spent the following days holed up in Soledad's plain, rudimentary little apartment. She introduced him to one of her sisters who, like him, was a fan of John Lennon, and sang "Imagine there's no countries." She introduced him to one of her brothers and to her mother who sold root vegetables at the market and moved around in a wheelchair. When he looked at her mother's old wrinkled face, Pascal's heart was inundated with a wave of tenderness. He caressed her deformed and swollen legs and softly ordered her to get up and walk. Thereupon the old woman stood up and hobbled across the square. Some people say it was the only real miracle Pascal performed, claiming the others were questionable.

After such an occurrence, Pascal felt obliged to tell Soledad about the rumors concerning his origin. She listened to him in earnest. "I've heard a lot about the Tejaras," she said. "They've given their name to hospitals, daycare centers, and schools. They're philanthropists. But going so far as to say they're divine is a bit exaggerated!" Thereupon she burst out laughing.

"Mind you, you're handsome enough to be a god!"

No need to say how the conversation ended. A few hours later, Soledad returned to the subject: "Nobody can manage to change the world. Instead of brooding over all these thoughts in your head be content with loving me, for it's the Good Lord who has brought us together."

She was probably right.

46

The private airport of Sangue Grande took its name from one of the bloodiest slave revolts, which had transpired on this very spot. In a single night, dozens of guards were massacred, and there was no counting the number of slaves who died. In order to put an end to the mutiny, the plantation owners had to call on the French, who ran the neighboring territory of French Guyana with an iron hand. Some historians claim that the violent nature of the rebellion was one of the reasons why slavery was abolished in Brazil a few months later.

Pascal had made an appointment with the young pilot, Antonio, who had been kind enough to fly him home, despite his heart aching at having to leave Soledad. She had promised to come and visit him. But could he trust her words? With a heavy heart he entered the airport bar and the souvenir shop that was selling objects from places as unexpected as China, Hong Kong, and South Africa. A fat woman was even selling "moonstones" from Ethiopia, which, according to her, allowed you to see into the past.

Pascal, insensitive to all this extravagance, could only regret having to leave Soledad and wondered whether he would ever get to relive that intense moment of love they had spent together. He got the impression that no woman besides Soledad had ever made him feel so mistaken about the meaning of life. As he was about to return home, he realized he had not made the right decisions. Was he going to keep turning over and over in his head the same experiences, in particular the episode in Caracalla? For a while he thought he had wanted to be anonymous again; now he had arrived at the conclusion that this was not enough.

He had difficulty recognizing Antonio in his elegant navy-blue uniform with wide gilded epaulettes and a cap with a mica-tinted visor. The two men shook hands and Pascal asked, "Have you any news of my uncle? Do you know where he is at the moment?"

Antonio shook his head. "No, I have no idea. Espíritu, as you know, travels the world, and anyone who wants to find him will quickly lose track."

Piqued, Pascal followed Antonio outside and pointed to the darkening sky above their heads. "The weather looks threatening, doesn't it?" he commented, for ever since morning the sky had been black and streaked with lightning and a violent wind was shaking the tree branches.

"It's nothing," Antonio replied casually. "It's a squall; it will soon blow over."

Pascal hadn't forgotten the comfort and luxury of Espíritu's private jet. He clambered joyfully up the gangway but became very angry when Antonio drew out of his briefcase three large photos representing Corazón Tejara, Espíritu, and Pascal himself with the caption: the Father, the Son and the Holy Spirit. "You're crazy! Get rid of this crap!" Pascal shouted angrily. But Antonio refused to obey, growling, "Let me do what I want!" and went and locked himself in the cockpit.

They took off shortly before noon. "Make yourself comfortable," Antonio proposed. "We shall be flying over French Guyana where we'll start our descent to your island, eventually landing near Fonds-Zombi. The trip will take about seven hours."

Pascal rolled himself into a ball on one of the sofas and wrapped himself in a blanket. After a few minutes the hum of the engines helped him fall asleep.

It was then he had a dream, a very strange dream. He found himself in thick darkness, as thick as the first day of creation. In the sky, Zabulon and Zapata were squabbling, causing sparks to fly and flames to flicker. In a cave an ox and a donkey were grazing on the hay piled in front of them. Between the donkey's hooves lay a newborn baby fast asleep, whose head the donkey was gently licking with its rough tongue. The baby was strikingly beautiful: a brown complexion, straight hair as black as an Asian's, and a round, pulpy mouth like a cherry. One might wonder to what race he belonged. Let's just say that he had an incalculable number of mixed bloods.

Close by, a young woman, no doubt the mother who had just given birth, was washing herself as best she could in the reddened water of a calabash. She had brought some talcum and a powder puff to apply over the baby's body, but her thoughts, riddled with pain and chagrin, were elsewhere. She didn't stop sobbing. A soft, celestial music, perhaps Mozart, could be heard from somewhere being played on a hidden instrument. There was a mysterious note to these melodious yet plaintive sounds. Suddenly the dream was interrupted.

What made Pascal wake up? The heat. It was stifling hot. The pillow under his head was soaked and streams of sweat trickled down his chest. He threw off the blanket, jumped up, and anxiously ran to the cockpit. "What's going on?" he asked Antonio. "Why all this heat?"

"It's nothing to worry about," Antonio reassured him, perfectly calm. "I had to switch off the air conditioning. Go back to sleep, there's nothing to be afraid of."

When did they realize they were in serious danger? We shall never know, since there were so many different points of view and reports of the event. What we do know is that the plane dived into the darkness and crashed at Saint-Sauveur. It was three in the morning. Pascal was thirty-three years old, the same age as Jesus.

Saint-Sauveur covers a large territory of ten thousand inhabitants and has never made headlines. We don't know exactly where it got its name from. The surrounding sea is full of fish and all you need do is row out a few miles to catch all the tuna, bonito, and bill fish you want. On the hills, they grow patches of sweet potatoes, yams, and okra, plus the inevitable bananas, which grow just about anywhere. Saint-Sauveur consists of a school complex, a mosque, and a church, but no hospital or doctor's surgery. Ever since Dr. Cassubie retired, the young doctor who replaced him drives the fifteen kilometers between Fonds-Zombi and Saint-Sauveur three times a week.

When the plane crashed, alerted by the glow of the flames licking at the silk cotton trees of a neighboring wood, the four French firemen who lived in the barracks with their wives and children jumped out of bed, dashed outside, and climbed into their fire engine, and within a few hours, managed to extinguish the fire with their hoses. But, strangely enough, there were no human remains among the ashes. All they found were three large photos intact, their edges slightly burned, representing three men with the caption: the Father, the Son and the Holy Spirit.

Back in his office the head fireman reported these strange events to his superior at Fonds-Zombi. Matters would have remained there if the superior had not, by an extraordinary coincidence, been a member of the Nouvelle Alliance. He immediately informed Maria of the night's events, who in turn, in a rage of frenzy, informed Pascal's former disciples Marcel Marcelin and José Donovo, once again unemployed having returned from the mother country unable to find work.

The disciples rushed to Saint-Sauveur and this was the first of the annual pilgrimages that then went on to have such an impact. Soon they had a chapel built on the site of the accident and bought two tuna boats on credit, each holding fifty followers.

Several months later Fatima returned home with a major announcement. She had fought hard and, thanks to the lawyer she had hired, she had managed to have Pascal's responsibility for the death of Norbert Pacheco dismissed. Pascal's name had been cleared and, more than that, completely whitewashed.

But the most remarkable day was unquestionably that day when Judas Eluthère came to attend a ceremony at the chapel. The minister, Judas Eluthère, still just as handsome, still dressed to the nines, no longer lived on the island of course but in a six-room apartment on the avenue Mozart in Paris. He was often to be seen on television, giving polished, well-phrased speeches on Muslim separatism. The members of the Nouvelle Alliance present that day could hold back neither their applause nor their tears when he paid a magnificent tribute to the late Pascal. He declared that Pascal had been a great soul, much like Mahatma Gandhi. He even dared to suggest that the rumors about him were true: that he was the son of a divinity—though that divinity he nevertheless refused to name.

Henceforth, Easter Sunday marked the date of a major pilgrimage that assembled followers from all over the world. Saint-Sauveur, which up till then had never made headlines, became one of the island's Meccas.

EPILOGUE

However, if people had used their common sense and taken a closer look, they wouldn't have failed to notice a couple by the name of Gribaldi. When had they arrived at Saint-Sauveur? Nobody could remember. Where had they come from? From a land on the other side of the sea, from Brazil perhaps. Yet neither the husband nor the wife had the slightest trace of a foreign accent and both spoke perfect French.

The couple lived in one of Saint-Sauveur's most magnificent mansions, called The Garden of Eden. You entered via a wide sandy path that became narrower and narrower until it ended up in the sea, into which Monsieur Gribaldi would dive headfirst, come rain or shine, night or day. For the occasion he was dressed in a strange swimsuit, a sort of chemisette that reached up to his chest, because he was trying to hide a nasty scar on his right side. The skin was discolored, pinkish, and inflamed, oozing a strange liquid.

The couple seemed not to have any friends. A servant did the cooking and a gardener took care of the vast expanse of land where Cayenne and Tété Négresse roses grew and which Madame Gribaldi arranged in large bouquets in vases in the living room and dining room. Both types of flowers are rare and cost a fortune but at the Gribaldis they grew in abundance.

Both Monsieur and Madame Gribaldi were very handsome, and of mixed race, though nobody could say exactly the degree. The wife had the complexion of a tropical fruit, soft silky skin, and sparkling white teeth. Her person diffused a somewhat questionable charm, just a little bit too tantalizing, which suggested she had lived a tumultuous past. The husband, too, was handsome with his sad velvety eyes and quizzical expression.

Madame Gribaldi sang. As for Monsieur Gribaldi, he was

bone idle. He collected his thoughts. Okay, we know everyone thinks, ever since Descartes established his famous *ergo sum*, I think therefore I am. Monsieur Gribaldi, however, poured out his thoughts in the shape of pamphlets, which were on sale at Les Heures Studieuses bookshop but which nobody ever bought: these were titled *My Experiences*, Volumes 1, 2, and 3—well, "volume" is perhaps exaggerated since each pamphlet was no more than a hundred pages.

Every year on July 14 they opened wide the doors of their house, for although this date commemorates an important event in the mother country, it was also Madame Gribaldi's birthday. They would then invite everyone from the poorer neighborhoods and Madame Gribaldi would have them listen to songs by Edith Piaf, such as "Hymne à l'Amour": "I will dye my hair blonde, if you ask me to. They can laugh at me, but I will do anything if you ask me to."

And Madame Gribaldi, while singing, would be gazing fondly at her husband's handsome face.

Then one day in May, the Gribaldis disappeared. Where had they gone? When asked, the servants replied they had gone to Italy to adopt a child from among the numerous little migrants. After two months they returned home holding by the hand a small boy of two or three years old. "He's my son," Madame Gribaldi proudly declared.

The child was handsome, as handsome as his parents. It wasn't his beauty, however, that caught everyone's attention but his color. Being of Eritrean origin, he was black, jet-black. Intrigued, people crowded into the reception organized by Monsieur and Madame Gribaldi to introduce him. "We've baptized him 'Alfa,'" Monsieur Gribaldi declared. "Because we want him to be first in everything." Alfa? He was probably referring to the preeminence of this letter in the Greek alphabet. Unfortunately, the inhabitants of Saint-Sauveur are uneducated and did not understand the allusion. People pouted in disgust: "Alfa? Wasn't that a

Muslim name? Wasn't it the sign of this separatism condemned in higher places?"

Soon the disgruntled had other reasons to be concerned. Monsieur and Madame Gribaldi refused outright to send their child to school. Every morning, holding his father's hand, the little boy walked to the pavilion at the bottom of the garden, furnished with a large bureau and a school desk. Mind you, Monsieur Gribaldi put all his heart into it. He bought maps and globes from Les Heures Studieuses bookshop so as to teach his son the geography of oceans and continents. He had him recite numerous poems. For example, "A stag belling in the moonlight, Eyes full of tears blurring its eyesight." Or else, "The drawn-out sobs of Autumn's violins wound my heart with a monotonous languor."

But the thing that scandalized people the most and was openly disapproved of was when little Alfa was deprived of his catechism and thus his first communion. Father Rousseau slipped on his best cassock and made his way to The Garden of Eden. When he had finished speaking, Monsieur Gribaldi shook his head: "It's precisely what my wife and I want to avoid: we don't want his head to be stuffed with extravagant stories, we don't want him to read books with conflicting facts, and we don't want him to believe he has a special ancestry. We want to respect his freedom and for him not to entertain dangerous illusions."

"What do you mean?" Father Rousseau protested.

Monsieur Gribaldi looked him straight in the eye and simply said, "I'm going to ask you a question: In your opinion, isn't God the Father of all men? Not just me, but also Nestor the postman, Hugo the farmer. Every one of us."

If there was someone who could untangle this imbroglio and reveal the truth, it was a homeless man lying on the ground in the garden whose clubfoot Monsieur Gribaldi, unlike Charles Bovary, had healed by a simple laying on of his hands. He was the one who could have explained the facts, which everyone found incomprehensible: "A few years ago, a migrant child whom Monsieur Gribaldi adored died in mysterious circumstances. Monsieur Gribaldi never recovered from this tragedy. Shortly afterwards, he met by chance the woman who today is Madame Gribaldi. They fell in love with each other. They adore each other, I'm telling you. They have understood that thanks to the love between two individuals, thanks to their hearts beating in unison, an individual can put up with suffering, disillusionment, and humiliation of all sorts and that only this love can transfigure the world and make peace on earth."

RICHARD PHILCOX is Maryse Condé's husband and translator. He has also published new translations of Frantz Fanon's *The Wretched of the Earth* and *Black Skin, White Masks*. He has taught translation on various American college campuses and won grants from the National Endowment for the Humanities and the National Endowment for the Arts for the translation of Condé's works. Philcox's translation of Condé's *Waiting for the Waters to Rise*, published by World Editions, was longlisted for the 2021 National Book Award for Translated Literature in the US, and his translation of her *Crossing the Mangrove* is now a Penguin Classic. Condé's *The Wondrous and Tragic Life of Ivan and Ivana* is also published by World Editions.

Book Club Discussion Guides are available on our website

On the Design

As book design is an integral part of the reading experience, we would like to acknowledge the work of those who shaped the form in which the story is housed.

Tessa van der Waals (Netherlands) is responsible for the cover design, cover typography, and art direction of all World Editions books. She works in the internationally renowned tradition of Dutch Design. Her bright and powerful visual aesthetic maintains a harmony between image and typography, and captures the unique atmosphere of each book. She works closely with internationally celebrated photographers, artists, and letter designers. Her work has frequently been awarded prizes for Best Dutch Book Design.

The cover design fits in perfectly with World Editions's two other Condé publications, *Waiting for the Waters to Rise* and *The Wondrous and Tragic Life of Ivan and Ivana*. Here, the S-shape separating the yellow and purple parts is based on the Blakely Light font by Mark Simonson. The rounded letters of the title complement this dynamic shape. They are in Sugo Display by Zetafonts.

The cover has been edited by lithographer Bert van der Horst of BFC Graphics (Netherlands).

Euan Monaghan (United Kingdom) is responsible for the typography and careful interior book design.

The text on the inside covers and the press quotes are set in Circular, designed by Laurenz Brunner (Switzerland) and published by Swiss type foundry Lineto.

All World Editions books are set in the typeface Dolly, specifically designed for book typography. Dolly creates a warm page image perfect for an enjoyable reading experience. This typeface is designed by Underware, a European collective formed by Bas Jacobs (Netherlands), Akiem Helmling (Germany), and Sami Kortemäki (Finland). Underware are also the creators of the World Editions logo, which meets the design requirement that "a strong shape can always be drawn with a toe in the sand."